Being the sniper's sight... opens more than her eyes.

CUCKOO

Kindred Book Three

SCARLETT FINN

Also by Scarlett Finn

NOTHING TO...
NOTHING TO HIDE
NOTHING TO LOSE
NOTHING IN BETWEEN: ONE
NOTHING TO DECLARE
NOTHING TO US
NOTHING IN BETWEEN: TWO
NOTHING TO SAY
NOTHING TO GAIN
NOTHING IN BETWEEN: THREE
NOTHING TO YOU
NOTHING TO THIS PREQUEL: ONE WILD NIGHT
NOTHING TO THIS
NOTHING IN BETWEEN: FOUR
NOTHING TO DO
NOTHING TO FEAR
NOTHING IN BETWEEN: FIVE
NOTHING TO DENY

GO NOVELS
GO WITH IT
GO IT ALONE
GO ALL OUT
GO ALL IN
GO FULL CIRCLE

KINDRED SERIES
RAVEN
SWALLOW
CUCKOO
SWIFT
FALCON
FINCH

EXILE
HIDE & SEEK
KISS CHASE

THE EXPLICIT SERIES
EXPLICIT INSTRUCTION
EXPLICIT DETAIL
EXPLICIT MEMORY

THE FORBIDDEN NOVELS
FORBIDDEN DESIRE
FORBIDDEN WANT
FORBIDDEN WISH
FORBIDDEN NEED
FORBIDDEN BOND

WRECK & RUIN
RUIN ME
RUIN HIM

MISTAKE DUET
MISTAKE ME NOT
SLEIGHT MISTAKE

THE BRANDED SERIES
BRANDED
SCARRED
MARKED

TO DIE FOR...
TO DIE FOR TRUTH
TO DIE FOR HONOR
TO DIE FOR VIRTUE
TO DIE FOR DUTY
TO DIE FOR LOVE

RISQUÉ & HARROW INTERTWINED
TAKE A RISK
FIGHTING FATE
RISK IT ALL
FIGHTING BACK
GAME OF RISK

FORBIDDEN PREQUEL DUET
ALL. ONLY.
ONLY YOURS

LOVE AGAINST THE ODDS STANDALONE COLLECTION
SWEET SEAS
HEIR'S AFFAIR
RESCUED
MAESTRO'S MUSE
GETTING TRICKY
THIRTEEN
REMEMBER WHEN...
RELUCTANT SUSPICION
XY FACTOR

LOST & FOUND
LOST
FOUND

ONE

"THANK YOU FOR MEETING WITH ME."

Zara lowered into the seat that Julian Scanlon held out for her. His invitation to join him for a drink in Purdy's had been unexpected. But once he made it clear the offer wasn't social, she couldn't refuse. Raising her eyes, she scanned the space that had once been so familiar to her. She hadn't been here since the raid where she'd killed a man.

Purdy's was bustling again, alive with the upper tiers of management from the surrounding business district as if the night they'd all been attacked here didn't happen. The robbery hadn't deterred patrons. Its location had always been convenient for the major businesses that occupied the blocks around it. The fact that there was some danger attached to the establishment probably helped reinvigorate trade. The rich and gorgeous could walk on the wild side without venturing out of their preferred zip code.

Elvis had blasted holes in the ceiling with his automatic weapon. But the scars of the night that changed her had been patched. All new furniture had been brought in since that fateful night. The owners obviously took the trauma and used it as an excuse to remodel.

Despite all of the changes, the room still felt familiar. In the countless times she'd sat here, reminding herself of how far she'd come since walking out of her father's house against his wishes, she would never have been able to project who she'd become.

Taking in a breath while Julian seated himself opposite her, Zara adjusted her focus to look past the CI lawyer to the bar. A major reason for her comfort and familiarity was there on a stool, hunched over a beer. As soon as she told Brodie that she was meeting Julian here, he began to make plans as though this was a full-on Kindred op. She had to remind her love that she'd only been on one date with Julian in the past and it had been a bust, so he didn't need to wage war.

He'd still grumbled his displeasure and refused to let her come alone. So he was observing from not too far away. Given what had happened the last time she was here, Zara wasn't averse to having backup on hand. She wouldn't want to take action without her chief's direction like she had to the last time.

Brodie had been in a bleak place when she'd pulled the trigger and taken her first life. By choosing to be with her tonight, she guessed he was trying to make up for not being around to execute Elvis for her.

Julian cleared his throat and the tension in his body intrigued her, though not enough to ask what was bugging him. That much became apparent when he spoke in a slow, deep tone. "First of all, I'd like to extend my condolences. Losing Mr. McCormack, it was a… a shock to us all."

He didn't have the slightest idea how they'd lost Grant. Only those present in Sutcliffe's kitchen when the lethal shot was delivered knew the truth. "Yes," she said, examining the grain of the wood beneath her glass.

It had shocked her to find out just how easy it was to obtain a death certificate, even without a genuine body. But when your boyfriend was an assassin, he knew how to handle these things. Brodie's initial concern hadn't been explaining where his older brother was. The Kindred were deep in their own project of trying to decipher who Benedict Leatt was connected to. But questions were being asked, mostly of her, so she had to become vocal to the point of nagging when highlighting to her colleagues that when rich CEOs went missing, people noticed.

So, when one of Grant McCormack's cars was found burned out after a tragic road accident and the dental records of the single corpse in the car were found to match the CEO, a death certificate was issued.

Brodie had covered their bases, the Kindred knew how to conceal death and misdirect, even if they didn't usually work on the scale of someone as well-known as Grant McCormack. Zara had never questioned Brodie about the people he'd assassinated, meaning she couldn't be sure about how far the Kindred had gone to protect themselves or cover their tracks.

The pity in Julian's countenance was disconcerting. She wasn't Grant's widow, but as far as anyone in CI knew, she was closer to Grant than anyone else. "His lawyers are tracing his relatives," he said. "Cormack Industries is at an impasse. Grant held the controlling stock of the company and that will be passed to his next of kin. Until we know who that is and what they plan to do with the firm, decision making is difficult."

Grant's death had just been announced at the start of the week, though it had been three weeks since he took the bullet that killed him. She hadn't been back to CI because she and the Kindred were still basing themselves in New York. Zara knew enough of the process and the people to understand that CI would be in disarray while the lawyers tried to fish their heads from their asses.

Brodie shunned every mention of CI, but he wouldn't be able to avoid it forever. He was the last of the McCormack line. Grant had no wife and no kids, their parents were long gone. Brodie was going to inherit his father's company, whether he wanted to or not. That would mean talking to lawyers and learning how to handle business—fast.

"Yes," she said, peering at him. While everything he was saying was true, she wasn't sure what she was expected to do about it. No one knew about her personal relationship with the younger McCormack brother, who no one in the business or the media had seen or heard from in decades. "But I don't understand what that has to do with—"

"The board asked me to approach you because we had a personal relationship," he said with a furrowed brow.

A personal relationship that lasted as long as it took her to make her excuses and leave him on a street corner not too far from here. "Approach me about what?"

"You know Grant's office better than anyone. No one can even get into the room."

Her and Grant's fingerprints were the only two that were authorized to open his office door, though IT could probably find a way to override that. Tuck, Kindred's hacker, would be able to do it. It had to be a show of respect that they hadn't gone snooping yet.

But his statement brought this meeting into focus. CI wasn't expecting her to trace Brodie, they were expecting her to hold down the fort, which given its current state of uncertainty would be a hefty task for anyone to achieve alone. She was experienced in running Grant's office, but she wasn't superhuman.

"Are you asking me to come back?"

As far as Julian and the others there were concerned, she had never left her job at CI. Except without Grant, she had no role there, no reason to return. After Art's death, she had resumed her duties as Premium Personnel Coordinator as a way to monitor Grant. Now that he'd been eliminated as a threat, she had no further mission at CI.

Although, if Brodie ended up in Grant's position, she would have to guide him through dealing with day-to-day life as a CEO. Somehow, she couldn't picture her love in the grand executive chair in Grant's immaculate office that had once been his father's.

Brodie wouldn't like not being able to take Maverick into meetings, and he had zero interest in platitudes. His talent for small talk and polite civilities was nil. Being that he didn't like people, he would struggle to deal with them every day without the constant risk of a potential body count hovering over them.

It was obvious that Julian was uncomfortable tonight. His expression shifted from a frown to something more solemn and then it became sterner. Any speculation there had been about her relationship with Grant must have intensified in recent days. She and he were both away from CI at the same time, and the nature of their relationship had slid into a gray area since Brodie had come into her life.

The introduction of Brodie led to her and Grant broaching more sensitive personal topics and their conversations were often fraught and emotional. It wouldn't surprise Zara if the volatile nature of their encounters hadn't been noticed by staff.

"Yes," Julian said. "Once the lawyers locate the beneficiaries of Grant's will, there could be a shakeup. I don't know what will happen. But we will need a strong hand to steer the ship. All of Grant's staff are used to reporting to you. I know they would appreciate it if you were around to lead them again."

Managing the CI giant from behind a PA's desk wouldn't be possible. But having been with the company for more than five years, she knew its quirks, knew some of Grant's secrets about how to keep the business running without a hitch. Turning off her loyalty to the place wasn't simple, and she had wondered about the corporation's prospects without Grant at its helm.

Adjusting her focus, Julian blurred when she peered beyond him and made eye contact with Brodie, who was managing to watch their table without watching. The patrons in this bar were too enamored with themselves to notice that she wasn't paying attention to the man at her table.

The brute at the bar wearing worn Levi's and a leather jacket didn't fit in the picture of eloquence that surrounded him. The stark difference between him and his environment made her speculate about how much he'd stick out if he marched into a CI board meeting. His appearance would be jarring enough, but his words and attitude would probably lead to the requirement for smelling salts.

Sighing, she sipped her wine. Julian was uncomfortable enough that he was happy to stare into his glass, giving her time to think. Brodie would hate being stuck in an office. He knew nothing about business and would have no inclination to learn. Thus far, he'd avoided discussing the future of CI. It had taken her long enough to spur an explanation for Grant's sudden disappearance. Next, she would have to coax him into talking about the family firm.

"Let me think about it," she said. "I don't know how I'll feel about being there, working there, without Grant right next door, you know?"

And that was the truth, so it didn't take much effort to sell it. Grant had been her boss for more than five years. She'd gone through the full spectrum of experience with him, from simple boss and employee to friend to enemy. Processing his death took its toll on her because she wasn't sure if she was happy or sad that he was gone. She didn't want anyone around who might be a threat to her, Brodie, and the Kindred. But in the end, Grant was a sad, misguided man, full of rage and regret. She pitied him as much as she hated him.

"Of course," Julian said and was surprised when she stood up. "Would you like another drink?"

More than half of her wine was still in the glass on the table. She shook her head and picked up her jacket from where she'd laid it over the back of the chair. "No, thank you. Being here"—she lifted her chin to scan the space—"It's bringing back too many memories."

They said goodnight and that included a kiss on the cheek, which she'd have to soothe Brodie about when they got home. But she slipped out of Purdy's and began to walk down the block. She didn't have to turn around to know that Brodie would have departed Purdy's after her. They had a rendezvous point a couple of blocks over; he'd be following behind probably at a considerable distance.

Knowing that her love was stalking her made her smile as she swept her jacket around her shoulders and zipped it up. The fitted leather number hugged her waist and laced at the lower back and it was just perfect for tearing around on Brodie's bike with him. She couldn't turn, that would make their association obvious, but she was prickling all over. Emphasizing the sway of her hips, she expected that Brodie would be watching her ass—literally.

Having her own personal bodyguard and guardian angel relaxed her about walking on this street. She'd been attacked at CI, which wasn't far away, and she was just about to reach the corner where Tim Sutcliffe had died. She'd come so far since that night when she'd cowered in an alley fearing for her life. Brodie had been the one to take the shot, and she knew now that she'd never been in danger, but that didn't soften the memory of her visceral distress.

It had been real at the time, and its draining power was the reason she'd had no fight left when she came home to find Brodie in her bedroom. Thinking back to their dramatic roots, she knew she'd live every minute of her terror over again if she had to, because in the process of it all she'd managed to capture Brodie's love, making every emotional experience worth it.

Cutting across one street, she got into the alley where Brodie's bike was secreted and hurried to traverse the length of it. The heels of her boots clicked as she walked, echoing through the narrow space. But she didn't hear Brodie. He had to be there and his footwear was heavier than hers, yet he moved in stealth mode.

A prickling chill zipped up her spine and she shivered. They were alone here, in this private space, and a dangerous predator was on her tail. She didn't feel his approach, but a heavy hand clamped over her mouth. She was dragged sideways and spun around to be thrust against the wall.

"You let him kiss you," Brodie hissed, wiping her cheek with the back of his hand. "That slimy, good for nothing—"

"He wants me to go back to CI," she said, flattening her hands on the cool leather over his chest.

Brodie pushed his body into hers. "I know. I heard."

Another concession she'd had to make was giving him an earpiece so he could listen in to what was going on at the table. Putting on Brodie's mother's pendant, which now had a Kindred camera hidden in it, was becoming part of her normal dressing routine.

"I think I'll have to do it," she said.

There was no space for her hands on his torso when he compelled more of his weight onto her. The coarse, freezing concrete at her back cooled her neck and caught her hair. But she'd learned to like it rough.

"We'll talk about it later," he said, crouching to kiss the side of her neck.

Talking about it later was Brodie's go-to place when it came to anything family or CI related. She'd heard that from him a lot when she was trying to get him to talk about Grant. But if she tried to push a conversation onto him that he was done with, he'd force her to forget it in his own lustful way.

"Can we go home?" she asked, scratching her fingers through his hair. "It's cold."

He took her hand and pulled her away from the wall and over to his bike. He helped her on, got the engine started, and then they were on the road to McCormack Manor.

TWO

"IF THERE'S ANYTHING you need, pack it up, and—"

Persuading Brodie on the necessity of this trip back home had been a feat. She hadn't lied when she said it was necessary to deal with Julian's request for a meeting and with the future of CI. But she had to admit to herself that the excuse to leave Sutcliffe's former compound, now Rigor's new digs, was welcomed.

Brodie had only relented when she promised the trip would be short, except Zara wasn't so eager to get to the place of negative memories. In that kitchen she got flashes, not only of Grant's lifeless body lying on the floor, but of the terror that overwhelmed her when she'd thought she was going to lose Brodie.

The Manor was safe and it wasn't until they returned here that she realized how alluring that security was and she didn't want to give it up. She couldn't tell Brodie that Rigor's compound made her feel weak and emotional, she didn't want him to think that she couldn't handle what the Kindred had to face. Convincing him to let her be a part of missions was tough enough sometimes, without throwing in the chance that she might suffer effects of PTSD after each one.

In front of Brodie, she had to be strong. "No," she said, lowering to sit on their bed before she flopped onto her back. "This bed feels so good." Bringing her feet up to the mattress, she pushed herself toward the middle and opened her arms. "Look how big it is."

Brodie returned from the walk-in where he'd been headed and stood between her feet that overshot the edge. Running her big toes up his outer thighs, she smiled and stretched her arms over her head. She was lying horizontal to the headboard, reveling in the space afforded to her here as opposed to the full-size they'd been sharing in New York.

It wasn't that she minded having to sleep on top of Brodie in cramped quarters, it was that they had little room for acrobatics or fighting over dominance during playtime, which was why they'd taken to having sex on the floor more often than they did on the mattress. Of course, that gave the guys still awake in the room underneath them plenty to guffaw about over breakfast.

After racing away from Grant's death, they'd regrouped in one of Rigor's safe houses. The man might have come off as a sleaze initially, but he'd lost a lot of men in Sutcliffe's compound that day, so she understood Brodie and Tuck's desire to stay and help him with his revenge.

It was their revenge too. Brodie broke into Benedict Leatt's apartment and his physical therapy practice, but nothing pointed to who he was working for. While her love was doing direct investigation, Rigor and Tuck were observing the compound. The option of storming the place had been discussed, but if they killed Leatt, they would never know who the power behind him was.

Almost as soon as their vehicle exited the gate of Sutcliffe's compound on the night Grant died, a stream of black vehicles coming from the opposite direction drove into the property. She and her allies had gotten out just in time. The men who had rushed in after their quick departure stood guard around the perimeter and made direct confrontation or observation impossible. All they could do was watch from a distance.

Late on the third night, a black helicopter came down

into the grounds and after a brief spell, it took off into the night. On that same night, vans and trucks poured out of the estate, proving that the land was now vacant, and Rigor wanted in before anyone else could think to claim it.

Taking advantage of access to the house was more viable than chasing Leatt down in a helicopter because they had their own investigations to do. Rigor had been promised the estate as payment, so the Kindred moved in with Rigor and what was left of his men. After that, they conducted a thorough search of the house and the surrounding land.

Leatt had been on the inside with Sutcliffe for months, meaning he would've known where to look for what he wanted. The Kindred still didn't know what that was. What the Kindred wanted was confirmation that Sutcliffe had no backup cache that could suggest his mission wasn't over. So far, they'd found no indication of one, so attention turned to finding out what they could about Leatt.

"You know, if you love this place so much," Brodie drawled, shrugging his jacket from his shoulders to let it fall onto the floor before he pulled his tee shirt up over his head. Sucking her bottom lip in around her teeth, she bit into it as her fingers and toes curled. He had a body made for exercise. Seeing the hard grooves of muscle in his torso always made her salivate. "You shouldn't have ripped your place off the market." He hooked his thumbs into his jeans and widened his stance. "I'm not getting my jeans off 'til you're naked."

His raised brow made her grin and she scrambled up to stand on the bed and strip, tossing her clothes past him left and right until she was as bare as he requested.

"That's better," he said, lunging forward to grab her thighs to tug them and send her onto her ass in the center of their bed.

She laughed just before his mouth claimed hers and when she coiled her limbs around him, she was peeved to feel his jeans still covering his legs. "You cheated," she murmured as he moved his jaw to scrape his stubble on her chin.

"I haven't heard you laugh for weeks."

There hadn't been much to laugh about. Under his present probing scrutiny, she lost the impulse. "Can we leave the mission at the door?" she asked and lifted to kiss him. Taking his face in both hands, she scratched her thumbnails under his jaw. "I don't want to think. I just want to exist with you for a while."

His mouth descended until his tongue plunged against hers, offering the sweet oblivion that she needed. In recent weeks, it had been hard to discuss anything personal with Brodie when there were ears everywhere. They still referred to each other by code names and held important talks outside or off the compound because despite regular bug sweeps, they were paranoid enough about Leatt and his superior to play their cards close to their chest.

"You just need a little loving, don't you, pretty baby?" he breathed into her ear as his hands roamed her body. "You've missed the mighty fuck sessions we used to have in here."

They'd had them in other places too, but she wasn't going to deny her desire to connect with him. After spearing her nails into his flesh until his expression got hard and dark, she smiled. "You've missed fucking me hard and putting me in my place."

"I sure have, plaything," he said and sat up to flip her onto her front. With a scream, she tried to push onto her hands, but his body landed on hers and with his weight holding her down, she was immobilized. He rubbed his face into her hair. "You need a guy strong enough to keep you in check." His teeth tangled in her hair when he opened his mouth, but the painful sting made her breasts swell as her nipples hardened. "You like it rough. You need it hard."

Pressing his hand to her ass, he forced it between her legs to push two broad fingers into her. She hissed and managed to turn her head sideways while he kissed and nibbled on the back of her neck. "I need you to fuck me."

"You need what I fucking give you," he said, dragging his teeth along the curve of her neck to her shoulder. "You're horny. You want cock, baby? You want me to slide my dick home and use you to get off."

His getting off in her was a powerful experience. This man controlled life. He took it. He had seen horror and pain.

Yet, it was her who gave him satisfaction. "Fuck me, Brodie," she panted, trying to move with his fingers that were pumping into her.

Brodie kneeled up, and she tried to twist to look at him over her shoulder, but with one heavy hand on her ass, he spanked her. "You move when I fucking tell you to move."

Burying her face in the bed, she tried to quell a smile, but excitement was making her wriggle. She heard him cast off his jeans, and the rough hairs on his legs abraded the softness of her inner thighs when he pulled her ass up, pushing himself into her just an inch. When she tried again to use her hands for support, he let her hips go and grabbed her wrists to pull them to her lower back.

With her face in the mattress and her pelvis in his lap, she had little control and any she did have was taken from her when something soft and strong was bound around her wrists, leaving her helpless.

Brodie picked up her hips again and pulled her back to push himself into her again. In all the times they'd had sex, she'd become accustomed to his size and as he pumped her hips up and down, she knew he was only treating her to the bulb of his thick cockhead.

Groaning, she tried to pull her knees under herself, but he yanked her legs straight then shunted her forward to toss her onto her back again. "You're not in control, baby," he sneered, dragging his eyes over her body. Her weight was balanced on her shoulders and her balled hands, which were still bound at her lower spine. In spite of her attempts to free her hands from the fabric he'd used to tie her, they stayed locked together.

"Just do it," she said, opening her legs and lifting her knees to present herself to him.

Instead of accepting what she offered, he shoved her legs aside and came up the bed to kneel beside her head. With a handful of her hair, he pushed the moist head of his dick against her mouth, but she clamped her lips together and shook her head. She didn't mind sucking his cock. She enjoyed the power it gave her to torment him when he allowed her to administer his ecstasy. But putting up a fight was half the fun of their foreplay.

"Cute," he growled and squeezed her nose to block her airway.

She couldn't keep her mouth closed for more than another few seconds. When she opened to gasp in for air, he waited half a beat before he shoved his dick between her lips. He waited half a beat because he wanted to give her time to use their safe word. They'd been together for months and she had never used it. But when things got rough, he was wild and never took her consent for granted.

The taste of his mass made her body move. Her hips came up as he plunged toward her throat. Then her pelvis lowered, allowing her to squeeze her thighs together, when he retreated. Smearing her lips with the juices seeping from him, he pushed his head into her cheek until it was stretched to its limit.

"Say no to me again and your diet will consist of nothing but spunk for a month, hear me?"

His threat might have been meant to intimidate, but it infuriated her hormones further. Whispering his name, she turned her head and began to suck for her life. Stirring her yearning provoked her into wanting to spur him on, to get him into the same state of frenzy that kept her from having a complete thought.

He let her slurp and lick, pulling him into her mouth with each forceful suck. He stroked her hair from her face until he had enough to gather it inside his fist. The grip gave him the ability to direct her gaze to his so they could maintain eye contact. He loved to watch her do this, and she liked to see the heat between them glaze over his eyes. With one hard shove, he blocked her throat then pulled her back to take himself from her.

Her breasts begged for attention and when he dove onto his side and examined her body, he slipped a hand between her thighs. Arching, Zara tried to compel his touch to her breasts. But he half-smiled and winked at her before sliding down the bed. Keeping her on her back, he lifted one of her legs over his shoulder and rolled onto his front to insinuate his mouth between her thighs.

Licking his way to her clit, he kissed and sucked, returning the favor she'd bestowed on him with every flick of his tongue. Her balled hands were digging into her lower back causing bruising pain on her spine. But the position meant her pelvis angled to better receive his mouth. She couldn't keep quiet, couldn't keep still, and when his tongue drove into her and he reached up to fondle one breast, she screamed and bucked up.

She was still panting, trying to catch her breath, when his hips rose and he matched their bodies, docking himself inside her in one hard shove. Still sensitive from her last crescendo, she winced and whispered his name, trying again to pull her hands free, but it was futile.

He stilled inside her. Through narrow eyes covered with hair and clouded by heat, she smiled at him. "Tell me you haven't missed this," she teased, huffing in each breath as she tried to calm her heart.

His palm landed on her forehead, and he pushed her damp hair out of her eyes. "My dick's only happy when he's right here," he said, shunting himself into her and pulling her hips up to rub her clit with his groin. She hissed again, and he lowered to kiss her. "Your sweet little pussy, hugging him so tight."

Pushing up to slide her tongue into his mouth, she could only show her affection through her kiss because she had no hands to caress him. But he broke away to look at her eyes as he lifted up and pushed in. Each thrust made her gasp, she wheezed in a breath and bit her lip, trying to restrain the pressure boiling in her belly.

He ducked to bite her lip away from her and let it drag out as he pulled back. "That belongs to me. I want to hear those breathy little gasps you can't keep in when my dick pumps the air out of you."

His pace was even, in deep, slide back, shove, retreat, fast in, easy out. "Brodie," she whimpered. "Give me my hands, beau."

"Not a chance," he said, kissing her nose then her chin. "This is my rodeo."

Grabbing her knees, he pushed them up into her

torso, giving himself leverage to rise higher and pump faster. Watching their bodies connect and part, he got faster and started to grunt when she squeezed tighter, clenching herself around him, trying to keep them locked together.

Stuttering, it took her a few tries to get his name out. But when orgasm hit her, the sole word left in her vocabulary was his name. She must have said it ten times before he tightened his grip on her legs and hit her hard with one final dive of his dick into her.

Her heart was working so hard that her other organs had to be suffering, but she made herself open her eyes to look at him. Their eyes locked for a few seconds, then with a loud exhale, he dropped onto his back on his own side of the bed. His hands landed on his chest. Ten seconds of silence passed before he rolled over to shove her onto her side so he could free her arms.

Her spine hurt and her arms ached. Brodie tossed aside the ripped, crumpled mess he'd used to restrain her, which turned out to be the panties she'd discarded for their tryst. Trying to stimulate feeling, she circled her wrists and extended her fingers. He took her hand and yanked her body over so her chest was pressed into his arm, and he began to massage her palm.

"We should get out of here," he said, pressing his thumbs into her palm then working them up, squeezing her fingers in a stretch. "There's a flight in an hour and—"

"I'm going to stay here," she said, relaxing her neck so her head flopped onto his chest.

"You don't have to do anything," he said, with amusement in his voice betraying that he had misconstrued her statement as a declaration of exhaustion. "I'll carry you to the shower and soap that sexy body… maybe we'll aim to hit the flight that leaves in two hours."

Wearing a smile, she freed her hands and rolled on top of him to kiss him then press her cheek down on his beating heart that shook his ribs. "No, I'm not tired from the sex." She was, but that wasn't the reason she planned to stay at the manor. "I meant I'm going to stay here for a few days."

His voice became firm. He was no longer her pliable,

relaxed lover. He was asserting his authority. "Swift needs us," Brodie said, leaving no wiggle room. "Rigor's been stand up so far, but he's not Kindred and I don't trust him to have Swift's back all the way."

Requesting to stay behind wasn't something she'd done in the past, so he had to be curious about her reticence. She kept her reasons to herself because she knew he'd never understand them. She struggled to understand herself.

Rigor's place shouldn't be scary now that all of the threats had been flushed out. Zara felt uneasy there. Brodie and Swift handled being there like pros. But she didn't like facing the paranoia that lurked when she moved through the halls or the traumatic memories that speared her without warning.

Following Art's death, it had been her job to stay strong, and she had. Zara was proud of the way she slipped into the Kindred ranks and she didn't want to lose her confidence. Rigor's place would always be Sutcliffe's compound to her and she didn't want to spend any more nights there than she had to because it was having an effect on her conviction that she belonged in the Kindred. After all, how could she be equal to Raven or Swift when she couldn't look at the spot Saint had fallen in without getting nauseous?

But Brodie was right, they couldn't abandon Swift there, the Kindred had chosen Rigor's as their base and so that was where Brodie needed to be. If she could keep him here and lose herself in him then she would, but it would be selfish to ask him to stay just because Rigor's place made her feel vulnerable. Swift needed backup and it made her sick that she didn't feel secure in being able to provide that support.

"You should go," she said, opening her hand on his heart as she rose to meet his eye.

His brow furrowed. "You want to stay, but you want me to go," he said. He wasn't often confused, but she heard it in his tone now. "This from the woman who was begging to be allowed to come on the last trip."

Learning that it wasn't easy to evade the truth with him peering at her, she traced her fingertips up and down his sternum. "I have to check in at CI. I have to see what's going on. Julian's right, it will do the others good to see me there."

Her closest colleague at CI had always been Grant. She wasn't concerned with synergy because those left working there would have to learn to get along without her soon enough. But it seemed like a reason he might buy. "They'll have questions," he said, wearing a scowl. "Do you want to deal with that alone?"

No, she didn't, but she was better at skirting awkward questions since going through her breakneck Kindred education. "What's the alternative?" she asked. "Are you going to come in and field those questions for me?"

His scowl deepened. There wasn't a chance in hell he would consider that an option. "I don't want us to be separated. We've got a lot of enemies out there, baby."

More with every mission. "You left Swift alone," she said, dragging a fingernail over his pec as she rested her head on him again.

"Swift's been doing this a lot longer than you have. And he doesn't suck my dick."

Which was his way of saying that he was worried about her as a boyfriend instead of a colleague. Turning her head to kiss his chest, she acknowledged his concern. "That's good to know. Yeah, I guess if I got kidnapped or murdered, your dick would be neglected."

"Yep," he said.

The grump in his voice made her look at him again, this time with a smile. "That's not why you're worried about me."

"No, it's not," he said and when he tried to look away again, she caught his face and climbed on top of him to tease. "You worry 'cause you love me."

Though he considered it for a second, his sullen expression didn't relax. "Yeah, so fuck, how am I supposed to keep an eye on you here if I'm there watching Tuck's back?"

"This house is a fortress. I carry GPS wherever I go. CI is one of the most secure buildings in the city. Besides—"she cast a look over her shoulder—"You have eyes on me everywhere."

She still hadn't established where the cameras were,

but Brodie had disclosed that he watched her, even in their private space. Instead of being shocked or feeling violated, she found his variety of attentiveness to be arousing.

At any time or in any place, he could be watching her. Since learning this secret, she'd done her best to tantalize him through her actions, especially if he was too far away to touch. She hoped it might entice him to come home to her.

Brodie wasn't easily persuaded after he'd made his mind up about something, but she wasn't finished trying. Staying here at base and working at CI was safer than hanging around with Rigor and his men. Using these facts and some intimate persuasion, she was confident he'd leave her here and go to New York alone.

She was a distraction to him there and being the solitary female in the house, she got more than her share of leers and suggestive comments. If she stayed here, Brodie would be less likely to put his fist through one of the men they were supposed to be working with.

Being the lone woman in the Kindred was something she was getting used to but sitting in Rigor's new home surrounded by skilled men who could be counted upon to protect the sanctity and secrets of their kin was highlighting to her just how confused her role in the world had become.

"If we're separated, I can't help you if you get into trouble," he said.

Slanting her lips, she pressed them into his body and slid her hands up to squeeze his shoulders, which allowed her to lever up enough that her breasts hung close to his mouth. "You've taught me how to look after myself and I'm always armed. Think of how much fun it will be if I call you up and tell you to kick someone's ass for upsetting me. You'll have an excuse for some sport. If I'm at CI, I'm out of the way of Rigor's handsy men."

Grabbing her body, he pulled her down. "Someone touched you?"

"No," she said. "But we both know they've thought about it."

And that was probably the decider because he didn't even try to argue. "Forty-eight hours," he said, coiling his hand in a fist around the locks at the nape of her neck to force her cheek onto his chest. "Go to sleep. I won't be here when you wake up."

Complying, she nestled close to him and closed her eyes. "Brodie," she sighed.

"What?" he asked, loosening his fingers to comb them down her back.

Being away from base meant following Kindred rules and adhering to them was often frustrating, so she wanted to exploit this rare moment that they weren't constrained. "Nothing. I just like being able to say your name." His hand moved to her neck and squeezed.

"My girl," he said, stroking her until she drifted off to sleep.

THREE

INVIGORATED BY BRODIE'S agreement, they'd enjoyed each other again in the dark. Before he stroked her back to sleep, he added some provisos. She was to stay at the manor every night and had to report in several times a day. Once she was satisfied that CI wasn't going to burn to the ground without her and Grant there to hold it up—which Brodie assumed would take no more than two days—she was to join him and Tuck at Rigor's place.

Her task was to return to her old life, sans Grant. Brodie wasn't the only one who needed to be free of distractions to get the job done. Keeping her eye on the company would be easier without him noticing and questioning every nuance of her actions.

Brodie departed the manor before she was out of her morning shower. He advised her that he'd leave a car for her in a concealed parking space outside the perimeter of McCormack land. Having a car to get to and from work would be easier than having a cab drop her off each night.

She still had her parking spot at CI and the codes hadn't changed, so getting inside was just like old times. For a while she fooled herself that going through the motions would be enough. That was until she reached the executive floor. The staff there stopped to greet her and express condolences, but when they were all gone, she was left staring at the interior glass wall of Grant's office. The blinds were closed on the other side concealing her view. Not that she needed to see to know what was there.

Returning to her place of employment was supposed to be a comfort that would chase off the demons that had plagued her. It was supposed to bring her peace and restore her to contentment. Except as she stood staring at the shielded window she felt like a detached stranger, irrelevant to the company that had given her purpose for so long, and all of her insecurities came rushing back.

The appeal of the job came in her importance, in her value to the corporation through the CEO. Without this job and with the man gone, the last part of Zara Bandini, corporate lackey, had died too. She'd been struggling with the loss of that part of her identity.

"Zara!"

Whirling around, she cast off her thoughts of Grant and the uncertainty of her future to smile at Julian who was striding toward her. "Hello," she said when he came to a stop in front of her and laid a hand on her shoulder.

"I'm so glad to have you back," he said, giving her a pat then turning her body toward her office and walking at her side to accompany her inside. "I'm sure I don't need to tell you that things are piling up."

He didn't. She knew how the backlog mounted if she chose to go home early one night of the week. That she hadn't been here for a month left her with no illusions. "I'll delegate as much as I can. The team works efficiently so long as there's someone driving them."

"And there's no one better at that than you," he said. "If you need anything signed at an executive level, bring it to me. I'll act as liaison with the board. It's not that they don't trust you—"

"Just that I'm beneath them," Zara said, nodding and turning to her desk, which was just as she'd left it. With events at Sutcliffe's compound and Grant's vicious duplicity, she couldn't remember the last time she'd sat at that workstation with nothing but CI business on her mind.

"They want to check everything out before we make any executive decisions. We don't want anything too drastic to change before the new owner comes in."

That piqued a different kind of interest, but she tried to subdue her vehemence in the face of Julian's ignorance. "Have you found him? The new… owner?"

"No," he said. "Mr. McCormack had a brother but pinning down his location is proving impossible. He had cousins too. I hadn't realized he had so many living family members, he never talked about any of them."

Julian was obviously parroting what someone else had said because he had no close relationship with Grant that would afford him the chance to make such an observation. But Grant was known as a private man who kept his personal life away from work. That there were lawyers probing into his history and his family tree would mortify him, as it would Brodie. Picking up on the similarity between the brothers when she so often noticed their differences didn't help to assuage her turmoil over Grant's death.

"You never know, it could be that he finds you," she said and noted that she should talk to Brodie about asserting his authority over CI before any of the lawyers or board members delved too deep into what he and his family had been doing for the last twenty years.

He smiled. "That would certainly save a lot of time and money," Julian said, squeezing her shoulder. "Do you need anything? If it's too difficult being here, we can find you somewhere else to work."

Again, she felt categorized as the grieving widow when that couldn't be further from the truth. When she'd heard Grant's body hit the floor, she'd feared it was Brodie and when she turned to see that it wasn't, her prevailing emotion was relief. Horrified by such a hideous response to the death of a man she'd been close to for half a decade, she struggled with the nature of her own character and how it had developed since the night she met Timothy Sutcliffe. That was the night her life changed.

"This place is home to me," she said, glancing toward Grant's office. "There's work that has to be done and there's nowhere else I'd rather do it."

Getting stuck in a broom closet with a laptop wouldn't ease her confusion about where she fit in without her corporate identity. She had to sit down and wade into the mounds of work that would have been growing since she and Grant last walked out of here.

If she kept her focus, the structure of CI would help her settle again, she was sure of it.

***

SHE WAS WRONG. Every day for a week, she'd gone into CI hoping to rediscover the sensation of fluency. Each day she failed. Struggling to find her identity again in such a familiar place thrust her further into the uncertainty of her future that raised questions about who she was.

Her internal conflict spilled from business to personal when one night she drove the Kindred car she'd been using back to her apartment instead of the manor. That she did it on autopilot betrayed how deep into her subconscious this battle had gone.

Zara hadn't even considered staying at her apartment. She'd just driven away from CI, parked, and turned off the engine. Then when she got out and looked up, she found herself in front of her apartment instead of at the manor.

Because of Leatt and their mission in New York, she'd called to cancel the listing of her residence using the excuse of not being around to pack up and hand over keys etc. Now she wondered if she'd been entirely honest with herself and the others about her need to retain her apartment.

As she'd ended up there anyway, she went upstairs to look around the space she'd fallen in love with at the first viewing and decided to stay that night. While going through old routines, she considered that it might be easier to "find herself" in the place that had once been her private sanctuary. One night in the apartment turned into two, then three, and then four. Without making a conscious decision, she'd found herself living in her own pad again.

It was dark out and the CI building had been pretty much empty when she left, but she was getting through the work, though that was little consolation. Having parked out back, she ascended the stairs and let herself into her apartment. Closing and locking the door, Zara stopped trying to figure out what she should do next.

She hadn't been eating much, as food hadn't been high on her priority list. Indecisiveness was a new personality trait for her to grapple with too. Sort of tempted to work out, because she'd picked up the habit as Brodie's girl, Zara's feeble treadmill didn't inspire her. It was nothing on the fully kitted-out functional gym at the manor. So much in her life had changed quickly. She'd suffered losses but gained so much. Sometimes when looking in the mirror, she didn't recognize who was looking back.

Sloping toward her bedroom, she figured she'd take a shower and make a decision while soaping herself. It had become another habit to check the chair in the corner of her bedroom every time she entered. Usually she dismissed the piece and went on with her business. Today, she stopped short and dropped her purse at the sight of her man filling the seat.

Contending with her own issues had left her with little mental leeway to think about Brodie's and the Kindred's. Though if she had, she'd have concluded that it was only a matter of time before Brodie appeared to chastise her for ducking calls and avoiding the manor.

Maybe some subconscious part of herself wanted this, needed him to show up and shake her because she wasn't having much luck in doing it herself. She always did feel more grounded when he was around. Even if she was still hesitant to share her vulnerabilities with him, at least he was proving that he wasn't going anywhere.

"Did you think I wouldn't notice?" he asked, putting on the lamp next to the chair.

"I don't know," Zara said in response, and the even tone of his deep voice, which ordinarily soothed her, agitated her insides. Maybe it was arousal, maybe she was wary that he'd take one look at her and know she was having the wobble she'd bypassed after losing Art, or maybe she was scared that he'd look through her and see a fraud who didn't belong with the Kindred after all.

Slipping off her shoes, she kicked them under the bed. "With you, Rigor, and Tuck spending so much time drinking and playing cards, I wasn't sure you'd notice that I wasn't there." Lifting her foot from the floor to put it on the bed, she began to unroll her stocking.

"Leave them on."

She paused. Good humor hadn't joined her this week and that wasn't his fault, she just hated feeling so hollow all the time. "Is that supposed to be funny?"

He remained expressionless. "Worked the first time I said it."

She slid her foot to the floor. Worked was a matter of opinion, taking a long-term view, yeah, the mysterious stranger act had worked. But his memory wasn't that sharp if he thought the night he'd first said those words to her had had a happy ending. "We didn't have sex the night you said that."

Inhaling, he rose from the chair to cross to her. "Didn't take you long to surrender your panties to me."

"Why are you here?" she sighed when he took her neck in one hand and her face in the other, holding her in place with his entitled grip.

"That's what I came to ask you," he said, drumming his heavy fingers on her cheekbone. "You should be with us."

Nothing made sense to her anymore. Fraught by the conflict within herself, she couldn't handle conflict with him too. Which was why she hadn't coveted talking to him this week. She'd never gone as far as to ignore his calls, though she did have a missed "Unknown" call after her morning shower a couple of days ago that she had never tried to return.

"Us?" she asked, wondering if he was here for the Kindred or for himself. "You don't need me out there anymore. I understood staying in the neighborhood to monitor the compound. I understood going in after Benedict choppered out. Investigating the building satisfied your curiosity. But Sutcliffe is dead and his plan went with him. He's no threat anymore. Rigor has moved in and turned the place into his own private drinking den." Rigor got pissed when he talked about Leatt, but he and his men didn't have the drive of the Kindred. Another question had plagued her this week, in the nights she was missing her love's attention. "Why are you still there? How can you hang out and laugh a few feet from where your brother fell?"

Now he became incredulous. "You ditched me because of Saint?"

"No," she sighed and tried to remove his hands from her, but he wouldn't let her go.

She tried to stay relaxed so as not to further arouse his suspicions. If she put up too much of a fight, then he'd begin to think she was hiding something from him or she was in some sort of trouble.

"Then why?" he asked, strengthening his hold.

She hadn't ditched him, she'd just been trying to find something that didn't want to be found. His entitled touch marked her. He had to feel her skin to restore his connection to her. It was his way of reassuring himself that she was safe and within reach. Having such a physical show of his feelings for her typically encouraged her, too, but the half-truth she had to tell him poisoned her tongue.

"I had to be at CI," she said. "Someone has to keep up appearances."

CI was supposed to remind her of who she was because she'd always been assured there, it hadn't. Warring with her feelings about Grant's death had made being there a struggle too. She shouldn't be pleased that he was dead, but part of her was because he'd threatened her love. In her mind, he'd become two men. She mourned the first with the weight of devastating grief, the man who had been her friend and employer. The second, was the conniving, back-stabber who'd wanted power and to destroy Brodie.

It was this second guy that made her question the essence of herself. Before the Kindred she would never have imagined herself pleased that someone had lost their life. Being relieved after watching someone be murdered made her question her own moral center. Was she as evil as Sutcliffe and the others because she was willing to go to any lengths to protect what she held most dear, Brodie and the Kindred.

He drew his index finger around the curve of her jaw, it came to a stop on her chin. "I've made a call. Soon, you won't have to worry about CI."

FOUR

AS PROUD AS he sounded of himself, she was suspicious. That statement could mean any number of things. Could he be planning to abandon the company? Or was he thinking about ruining it, planting a mole who could dismantle generations of work? Whatever he meant, she planned to find out.

Brodie didn't make external phone calls, as far as she'd seen. So, did he set the plan into motion? "You made a call or Wren did?" she asked because if the doctor had signed off on the plan…

"No, this is a phone call I had to make myself," he said, running his finger down her throat and into her cleavage.

"I've never seen you make a phone call," she said. Never having seen it with her own eyes, she knew he did make them because he'd called her. Except she liked to think she was in a unique position being his girlfriend. "Did Wren refuse?"

She trusted that if Thad was against making the call, he didn't support whatever Brodie had done. Brodie scoffed. "Wren does what he's told."

Which suggested Brodie hadn't told him to do it and

had elected to act on his own. "You chose to do it yourself?"

"I had to. She wouldn't have come otherwise."

All the elements of her internal war came to a deafening halt. "She?"

"Like you said to me so many times, the CEO goes missing, someone notices. I called on an old friend who knows everything there is to know about running a multinational."

Zara might not have the qualifications but she'd been doing fine at CI and had needed the distraction. Although she'd avoided going into Grant's office so far. But Brodie had called someone who was going to take everything away from her?

"You called another woman?"

"To take the weight off your shoulders, yeah," he said, dipping to slant his mouth on hers. "You're Kindred, not a corporate flunky. I need you beside me."

Answers were more important than amour. "She's not Kindred?" Zara asked, ducking back from his next attempt at a kiss.

"Never made the final cut," he said. That implied to Zara that there had been a time it was considered.

He tried to kiss her and she leaned away on a gasp as she recalled a conversation she'd once had with Art. "What is this woman's name?"

"Mischa Corvi."

"Cuckoo," she exhaled the word. Instant heartache and jealousy didn't last long, disappointment became anger, and she smacked his chest. "You called your ex-girlfriend?"

Examining her, he reeked of skepticism. "How the hell do you know about Meesh?"

Brodie didn't hang onto her, Zara read surprise and anger in his expression before he let her go and retreated. He might doubt what she knew about the woman he'd called or maybe he was worried that she knew too much. Art or Tuck were the only ones who could've given her any details, it wasn't like Brodie kept a secret diary she could've snooped in.

But dealing with his dubiousness was secondary to making her own point. "If I called my ex-boyfriend and invited him to stay with me while he bailed me out—"

"She won't be staying with me," he said. "You know the rules of the manor."

Setting her weight on one leg, she folded her arms. Doubting his intentions, she found it a stretch that he could have a personal relationship with the woman and call her up in his time of need, but not secure her a place to sleep. "So you'll stick your dick into her, but you won't invite her over for dinner?"

Snide was a much more comfortable reaction for him. "Thanks for the offer, but I don't think I will be sticking my dick in her this time."

"You don't think?" she said. The rumble of irrational anger let her express some of the emotion she hadn't been able to vent in the last month. "If you've already figured everything out then why did you bother to come here? Is the spunk in your balls weighing you down? You need me to empty them?"

Without waiting for his retort, she spun to storm away from him, but he lunged forward to grab her upper arm and haul her back. "What the fuck is wrong with you?"

A torrent of rage made her breathe in deep. But before she screamed out at him, her desire for an argument vanished and she sagged. It wasn't his fault that she felt like shit every minute of the day. It wasn't his fault that she didn't know who she was anymore. Punishing him because her complicated thoughts were muddling her would drive him away. If he abandoned her now, she would have nothing left to live for.

"My mind is all over the place," she said, touching her temple with the heel of her hand. "And my feelings… I don't know what I feel." Swinging wildly one way then the other, she couldn't get a handle on thinking straight.

"You don't know what you feel?" he asked. Yanking her to him to grab her other arm, he forced her body against his. "I'll tell you what you fucking feel. You're my girl. You love me and I'm not letting you go fucking anywhere, hear?"

"B—"

"Don't you fucking turn your back," he growled.

"Don't you even think about it for a second. If you dare try to walk away, I'll hunt you down and make sure it won't happen a second time. I won't let it."

The ferocity of his anger was fueled by his love. She knew what it was to fear losing the object of love. Opening her hands on the chest he pinned her to, she moistened her lips but lost her breath when he whipped her around and tossed her down to the bed where she bounced.

"I'm gonna remind you where we started and where we're going, and it's damn well not separate ways."

Moving in to the side of the bed, he widened his stance and folded his arms, glaring down at her as he waited for her to comply.

The strange thing was, Brodie's commands gave her direction. She didn't need to think or make decisions. All she had to do was focus on him. Without sitting up, she unbuttoned her shirt and opened it out, then spread her arms.

"Expose them," he said, nodding at her chest.

Arching up, she finagled herself out of her shirt, then unclipped her bra. Brodie leaned over to snatch up her clothes. When he had them, he threw them in the direction of the door.

"Close your eyes," he said and she let her eyelids grow heavy and slide together. "Don't open them, stay quiet, stay still, and don't move an inch."

Not being able to see him was arousing, her own breathing sped up, but she tried to keep each breath shallow so she could attempt to decipher where he was and what he was doing.

Tensing, she struggled to relax, and curled her hands until she had fistfuls of the comforter beneath her body. The bed moved and his hot palm stroked its way from one breast to the other. The horizontal rubbing grew more insistent until he was squeezing and pinching each soft mound in turn.

Sucking her lips in over her teeth, she fought the urge to moan or move into his caress. Being still allowed her to feel the texture of his rough palm and the weight of his hand while not being able to see him, was almost like he was violating her in her sleep. But the idea that he might be overcome by the urge to fondle her when her body was naked beside him heightened the sensations of his entitlement.

Belonging to this man, loving him, of that she had no doubt. Telling him that she didn't know what she felt wasn't an indicator that she had doubts about their relationship as he had taken it to mean. It meant she didn't know how she felt about Cuckoo coming into their lives to take over at CI. Instinctive emotion made her want to oust the woman who'd once been intimate with her man. But Zara didn't want the burden of carrying CI alone. Brodie would never adopt Grant's position and without a steering hand, the company would flounder.

The hand caressing her chest was joined by its partner, doubling his ability to tease her breasts. With no other contact between their bodies, she could only focus on this act while being unaware of where Brodie was or what he had planned for her next. If she had to guess, she'd say he was kneeling beside her. But what he was doing felt so good that location didn't matter.

When he stopped groping, he skimmed his calloused palm down her belly and she rose into that caress, hoping to encourage him and to highlight her delight, but he used his strength to force her down and hold her still for at least half a minute.

After releasing his pressure on her abdomen, he unzipped her skirt and moved from the bed to pull it off with her underwear. He picked up each of her legs to separate them, then he parted her folds with two damp fingertips and began to rub her clit.

Damming a whimper in her throat, her toes pointed and her legs tensed because glittering arousal was sending her muscles into spasm. He hummed when he slid one long finger into her and her mouth opened to gasp in the oxygen she'd been denying herself.

"You just can't do it," he murmured and his address gave her implicit permission to release the moan that was lodged in her chest. Another escaped in reaction to the second finger he probed her with.

"I love it when you touch me," she whispered. "I feel

amazing. You know what I need."

His being left hers, and she relaxed her eyelids enough to get a slit-high view of him grabbing his tee shirt behind his neck and pulling it off.

"Tonight, you need to feel, not think," he said and dropped onto his knees. Lifting her knees to his shoulders, he leaned in to kiss the button between her thighs that he'd heated up. Writhing under his tongue, she stroked her body, experiencing the ticklish flesh beneath the upright hairs stimulated by Brodie's attention.

Just before the rush of adrenaline that hailed the onset of orgasm, she gasped and rubbed her hands over his soft, short hair. It wasn't yet long enough for her to take handfuls of it, but that didn't stop her from trying when the gush of climax clenched each inch of her inside and out.

With strong hands on each of her inner thighs, he forced her legs wide. As he stood to unbuckle his jeans, she scrambled back to give him room to get on the bed with her.

He climbed aboard, pulling one leg his way so he could get between them. Focused on linking their bodies, he glanced up at the last second and reading his intent expression made the slippery slide of his shaft plundering her all the more potent.

"You won't be going anywhere after this," he said, grinding out the words as he pumped faster.

It felt like months since she'd smiled, but she did it as she propelled her fingernails into his pecs and marked their route up to his shoulders. "I love you, beau," she said, cupping his face and scratching his shoulders to his upper arms until he growled at her. "I'm not going anywhere."

"It's cute that you think you have a choice," he said with a half-smile that widened hers.

Tightening the grip of her legs around his hips, she panted out the words, which were punctuated by his plunges.

"Yes! More! Harder!" Variations on each of these got louder and his grunts got closer together. Another shower of pleasure stretched her bones and tightened her muscles until none of her nerves or limbs seemed to connect.

Pushing so hard into her that her pelvis was crushed

by his, Brodie swore once, then twice and kept on going until every drop of his gift was soaking into her cervix. Products of their agitated pulses and overworked sweat glands, their hot, sharp breaths mingled, but he stayed with her, on top of her.

"How do you feel now?" he asked, proud of his ability to claim her.

Leaving him would never have occurred to her, Brodie gave her reason. "My feelings for you were never in doubt," she said, stroking his stubble. "I was never going anywhere."

As her hand drifted from his face, he rolled off her to lie beside her. "You're grieving, that's why you feel so screwed up inside."

Grieving, like Brodie had done after losing Art. She had grieved for the mentor, too, but the label reminded her of losing her mother and that was a memory she liked to ignore as much as she could. Without classifying the cause, she recognized that some of the difficulty she faced at CI was because she knew the truth of what had happened to Grant. People there asked about him every day, but she couldn't tell the truth and had to keep smiling. Grant was gone and she still had questions. But that wasn't the whole truth.

Her vision blurred and her chin fell toward her chest in time with the balls of moisture that rolled off her lashes. She didn't want Brodie to see her crying, but it was too late. Brodie was with her, pulling her forward until she was in the grasp of his solid arms.

Brodie had lost his parents. His guardian. And now his brother. Since she'd come into his life, he'd lost person after person and yet he wasn't the one falling apart. She was the one sobbing into his chest, clawing at him, clambering for the reassuring chill of oxygen in her lungs. But her breaths were so short they got only as far as her throat.

"I got you, baby," he whispered, tightening his hold.

She hadn't cried for Grant, no one had, and that in itself was sad. This wasn't the first time she'd lost grip of her emotions in front of Brodie and despite his aversion to being too emotional himself, he always managed to comfort her in the cocoon of his arms. All she needed was his embrace. It could protect her from all kinds of pain, even the imaginary kind.

With reddened eyes and damp cheeks, she pushed back and blinked up at him. "You make everything better," she murmured, brushing her thumbs over his lips when she squeezed her arms up between them.

"I don't know how," he said and his grimace made her smile. "When you're upset, I want to shoot the shit out of something."

"That's how," she said, rising to rub her cheek on his and kiss his lips. "You feel what I feel… in your own way."

He searched her face and was as confused as she was certain, but that only made her kiss him again before yielding his hold and putting some distance between them. There were things she had to say and if she stayed in his arms, they'd either relax into sleep or divert their energy into more sex.

She shifted onto her side and stuffed a pillow under her head to support it. "I had to stay away," she said, trying to explain why she hadn't returned to her allies this week.

"You didn't. Who told you to—"

"I'm of no use to you anymore, no use to the Kindred." Her love for Brodie hadn't been in question, but her place in his ranks was because she felt like a fraud. She'd done her piece and didn't see how she could be of use to such a clan anymore. "Yes, you're right. I probably am grieving Grant, and there's some part of me that wonders why you're not more affected by it. We didn't get to say goodbye to him or to Art. There was no ceremony, you took him away, and put him straight into the ground." She kept on going before he could respond to what he'd consider an insult. "But I've been worried about my place in the Kindred. I don't have special skills like the rest of you do. Sutcliffe's gone. Grant's gone. Game Time is under our control, and now you're bringing people in to take CI out from under me too."

He was on his back with his hands resting on his abs. He just laid there scowling at the ceiling, and she hoped that he wasn't going to ignore her insecurities.

"Do you want CI?" he asked, turning his head, his expression loosening. "If you want it, it's yours. It didn't occur to me that you might want to take over running things. You'd have to stay at the manor and if the Kindred are working overseas we'd be apart—"

"This isn't about CI," she said, covering the back of one of his hands with her palm. Physical contact anchored them both, the feel of his skin grounded her, and she regretted putting a wedge between them this week.

Brodie needed a reason, he needed to understand and with her offering no answers, he was forced to speculate. "It's about us? Do you think I'm replacing you?"

If only it were that easy. "No," she said, rubbing his hand. "This is about me figuring out who I am in this setup. Before we lost Grant, I could gather intel for the Kindred, I always had a purpose. I'm just feeling a bit useless and that's not your fault. I just have to figure out how to adapt."

Obviously, he still wasn't satisfied. It was tough for her to explain what she didn't fully understand herself. "Did you think I wanted you out of the way at CI?" he asked. "Or are you determined to be there because it makes you feel closer to Grant?"

She'd often stopped and stared at the CI walls wondering why she was there. Sad as it was, she knew the reason. "It's comforting."

"Comforting?"

Taking a deep breath, she explained what she knew. "When I feel lost or confused, I can lose myself in work. Having strict policies and procedures gives me structure that saves me from having to make decisions on my own when my head is screwed up like it is now."

Brodie wasn't panicked. He never panicked. Reassuring her was something he was getting better at and that he made the effort meant something to her. His patience endured longer with her than anyone else. "There will always be a place for you in the Kindred," he said.

Except what he didn't know was that her insecurities lay there and they seeped back in as sought reassurance. "As more than just your whore?" she murmured, arching a brow. She didn't mind that role, but it wouldn't help on missions. It wasn't his view that she questioned, it was her own. If she was useless to the group in any practical capacity then all she could be was Brodie's mate. Leaving him wasn't even close to an option, but she wasn't sure if she could adapt to being homemaker rather than active participant in the Kindred. "I appreciate that you want me around and I promise I'm not even thinking about leaving you. I just have to figure things out."

"Meesh will need your support for the transition to new management. You're still vital to CI."

Something she liked to be. He turned his hand to curl his fingers in hers and took her knuckles to his lips. Brodie didn't have the same affinity for the McCormack family firm that she did. In fact, she'd guess he was a bit affronted that she got her solace there rather than with the Kindred. For her, it wasn't about choosing sides. Kindred missions meant patience, long periods of waiting, especially in the case of Leatt when they had no solid leads thus no solid plans.

CI was a distraction. It wasn't one that would last. She'd do what was needed to ensure the place didn't go to ruin, but she couldn't see herself buddying up to Brodie's ex, Cuckoo and working under her in the same way Zara had worked under Grant.

One point needed to be asserted without equivocation though. "You should always consult me before calling an ex, just for future reference," she said.

He put up no argument and picked up her hand to kiss each of her fingertips. "Noted and understood. Now, are you gonna tell me how you know about Mischa?"

Zara told the truth. "Art told me that you worked with her father," she said. Amusement contorted his lips causing her to peer closer and scoot toward him some more. "You didn't?"

Kissing her fingers, he was calm as he admitted, "I didn't work for him, I worked him over."

With a shallow shake of her head, she frowned. "I don't—"

"I killed him."

Inhaling through her nose, she wilted some. She should be used to those abrupt words by now, but they still blindsided her every time. "Why?"

"Meesh paid me to," he said, letting go of her hand to shift onto his side. "She'd spent months sleeping her way around the criminal element in Italy's major cities looking for a hitman."

Zara couldn't see what the trouble would be for her. Mischa was dynamic and cosmopolitan according to what Art had said, even those who weren't killers by trade would probably offer to do the job if it got her between their sheets. "She's beautiful, isn't she? I would think men would be falling over themselves for her."

"She didn't want men. She wanted the best."

"Which is you."

"Right," he said, lifting a strand of hair from her cheek to tuck it into place with her other locks. "My name came up again and again when she made it clear what she wanted, no mess, no repercussions. But getting a referral is tough, even those who know me are scared to piss me off by connecting me with a client... Especially one that could be volatile."

"But she found you eventually?"

"I found her," he said, skimming a hand over her hip to squeeze her ass. It didn't surprise her that he had taken control when he found out Cuckoo wanted him; Brodie liked to be the one who made the first move. "A couple of guys told me about her, Art and I checked her out, then I made the approach and we made the deal."

"Sex in exchange for?"

He stopped enjoying her body to meet her eye. "I don't take payment in sex, never have," he said. "Mischa had the capital and plenty of it. We fixed a price and she told me to make it look like an accident."

As simple as that, Mischa wanted her father dead, and Raven did the job. "What kind of accident?"

His hand returned to its expedition across her exposed body. "I talked her out of that, it's a rookie mistake. When billionaire's die accidentally, there's a heap of paperwork and a long wait for the beneficiaries. I have some experience with this." From when his parents died. Though he seemed to forget all of those details after Grant died. Or maybe he didn't want to face how big a deal his brother had become in the business world. "We settled on suicide."

"You set it up to look like suicide?" she said, horrified and impressed, yet curious about how someone went about doing that.

"No," he said. "It was suicide."

She was lost again and she would guess the descent of her brows betrayed her confusion. Brodie curled his index finger under her chin and pressed the pad of his thumb to the front of it so he could tilt her head back and grip her at the same time.

Trying to think it through, she knew it would be quicker just to ask. "How do you make someone commit suicide?"

The faint smile on his lips was that of a learned man passing on his wisdom. "Easy. Do your research. It's as simple as that." He kissed her plumped lower lip. "A man will do almost anything if you threaten the thing he loves most."

The tingling in her shoulders and awareness in her belly were making her itchy in an amorous sort of way. But that awareness wasn't enough to distract her from the sadness of the truth Brodie had just revealed.

"You got him to kill himself by threatening his daughter? The one who wanted him dead in the first place?" He'd thought he was protecting his child when all along it was the child who had instigated the plot.

But Brodie wasn't tormented by her assumption. "His daughter wasn't what he loved most," he said. "His company and his money were the catalyst. Destitution is what the super-rich fear most."

That was even sadder and decreased her pity for Mischa's father. Whatever the Corvi family politics were, it was none of her business. Brodie, on the other hand, was. "How did you end up with her?"

"You don't need to know the details," he said and took a section of hair in his hand, but when she drew back to focus her expectation, he sighed. "It was just lust, baby. Went to tell her the job was done, and she was grateful."

Zara could imagine just how grateful, especially with what Art had said about Mischa enjoying the kill. Raven would have turned Cuckoo on in a flash with that brooding stare and his aloof manner. Zara and her father were not close. She'd gone out of her way to avoid him since leaving his home against his wishes when she was a teen. Yet, she didn't think that upon hearing of his death the first thing she would think about was sex with the man who'd killed him.

Mischa had paid to have her father killed and when the job was complete there was no remorse, sorrow, or guilt. No, she'd jumped the assassin.

Rolling onto her back, her hands spread on her ribs as she absorbed his tale. "And now this beautiful, intelligent woman who you couldn't keep your hands off is coming to run the family firm." She couldn't even hide her sarcasm. "Great."

"You have nothing to worry about with Meesh and me," he said, rubbing her abdomen.

Stretching, she returned to his side and welcomed his arm when it curled around her. "I know."

"You just like freaking out?"

She didn't like freaking out and wouldn't say that she had. Pressing one fingernail into his ribs made him move his leg in a quick motion to scoop both of hers under his that were still jeans clad and that made her sigh.

"Forgot about that, didn't you?" he teased. "Maybe next time you'll remember how much you hate me screwing you with my jeans on and stay at base like you're supposed to."

"I didn't know you were going to visit here," she said.

"You were told forty-eight hours. You ignored that rule and the one about staying where I left you. You knew I was coming for you, baby. Whether you admit it or not, you fucking knew."

Her subconscious had a lot to answer for today, and she had to wonder if that reasoning had contributed to her decision to stay here at the apartment. In retrospect, Brodie had always come to her here in her bedroom. Misbehaving, flouting his orders, was a surefire way to bring him to her.

Her issues weren't resolved, but lying here, pressed into Brodie's body, she found some peace. Being with Brodie made sense and she'd meant what she'd said about him making everything better. What she needed was closure on her former life before she could move into her new Kindred one at Brodie's side, and she wasn't sure where to start in achieving that.

FIVE

BRODIE WAS STILL there when she went to sleep, and she'd expected him to be gone before first light. But he was still holding her and wearing his jeans when she woke up. They had breakfast together, and he was vague in answering questions about his plans, cryptic was his specialty. With a smack on her ass, he sent her out of the apartment and on her way to work, closing the door, and staying behind himself. Though he'd insisted she return to the manor after work, he hadn't confirmed or denied whether he was going back to join Tuck.

Entering the CI building through the executive parking lot, she got off on the floor below hers to make her way through the law bullpen to the offices beyond where she knew she'd find…

"Julian," she said, taping her knuckle on his open door causing him to look up from the pile of papers on the desk. His desk was a mess and the cluttered cabinet to the right suggested he wasn't as much of a neat freak as his meticulous appearance suggested.

"Hello, good morning," he said, rising from his seat. "I'm sorry for the mess. I'm changing the office and we just lost an associate yesterday."

Panic made her take a stride forward. "Lost him?" she asked, hooking her thumb over the purse she had across her body.

"Yes," he said, coming around his desk. "He was poached by a Manhattan firm… I can't lie, people are twitchy around here since, you know."

He got that odd look of solemnity again, so she smiled to try to put him at ease. "I came to reassure you about that," she said. "I know the board isn't meeting until next week but stability will be returning to Cormack Industries."

Concerned with his work and consumed by his own thoughts, he spoke as though he may not have heard her. "I'm glad you came because I was going to call your office. A client got in touch, an important client who CI has done a lot of business with."

That narrowed it down to about a million. CI didn't have unimportant clients. Reminding herself to stay cool and patient, she did her best to pace her words. "That's good. Things are getting back to normal. Who is heading up the—"

Julian's smile was joined by a shake of his head. "Oh, I'm sorry, I meant, he's looking for you. Specifically you. He stated that you are the sole person he will deal with."

Her thoughts stalled. She was an assistant, she didn't head negotiations, she got doughnuts and Danishes… at least, she sent one of the girls to do it while she lined up the presentations and set out contracts. While all of their assistants knew her by her first name, few of the clients knew her as anything more than a voice at the end of the phone or a name on an email. No client would request to talk to her on the phone, let alone have a private meeting with her.

Naivety was a liability, so she greeted this development with suspicion. "Who is he?" she asked. "What does he want?"

"He didn't leave his name, just said that you'd met before and that you knew what it would be about," he said. "He requested to have the meeting in Grant's office. Will that be suitable for you?"

If the client had asked for it, she had no choice, she

knew that much about being professional—personal issues didn't matter a damn if someone was going to spend a shitload of cash with the company.

Given her association with the Kindred, and the possible outcomes of this peculiar request, she didn't probe Julian for any more information or let her true curiosity show. If she played down her confusion, Julian shouldn't follow up with questions when they next saw each other after the meeting. If it turned out to be Kindred related, she wouldn't be able to be honest with the ignorant lawyer. The less he knew, the safer he would be.

It could be that the appeal for an audience with her was benign. One of CI's longer standing clients might just want to snoop now that Grant's obituary had been printed. In their eyes, she would be the most likely candidate to have salacious details, and they'd probably guess she was weak and stupid enough to share them. Though if that were the case, there would be no reason to specify a meeting location or to be so guarded about who they were.

"Yes," she muttered, taking her attention to the sunshine beyond the window. "I'll go upstairs and set it up."

"What did you want to tell me?" Julian asked and she looked at him again.

Her forehead was still tense, but she didn't have time to speculate about who the stranger might be. So she did what she'd come here to do. "I wanted to let you know that there is a woman coming in to take over Grant's position, subject to board approval."

Julian didn't flinch. "Yes, Mischa Corvi."

His knowledge was unexpected. "You knew?" she asked. Brodie didn't make phone calls, didn't like to talk to people, yet he'd apparently called ahead. "How did you—"

"Her people called last night. The rest of us were notified this morning," Julian's face lit. "She's an incredible woman. She triumphed after her father's unexpected suicide. She took over the family firm and has helped several others return from the brink of bankruptcy. She has a knack for business."

Wasn't it just wonderful that everyone worshiped this

woman who Brodie used to fuck? Zara did her best to smile. "CI is not near bankruptcy," she said, trying to remain upbeat while being visited by an immature pang of jealousy.

"No," Julian concurred. "And I didn't know she was affiliated with the McCormack family. Grant was so private about that sort of thing."

Grant didn't know Mischa Corvi personally, at least as far as Zara knew. But it turned out there was plenty she didn't know about the man and the company she thought she knew so well.

"What do you know?" Zara asked, finding it difficult to maintain the façade.

Julian was too distracted by his own eagerness to notice her discomfort. "She knows the family, was sent by them according to her people, hand-picked. I'm looking forward to meeting her."

She never would've guessed. "I can tell. We're all in for a treat."

"I think we are."

Observing the clutter of the office, she took a deep breath. "Well, I should let you get back to tidying up. We want everything in order for Ms. Corvi's arrival, don't we?"

"Yes," he said and his glee dissipated to concern. "Yes. Yes, you're right."

Having notified the man of something he already knew, Zara left him to his work and began to think about her own. A day of preparing for the arrival of Cuckoo to the company was bumped down the priority list too. A mysterious client wanted a meeting with her.

Leaving the law floor, she went up to her own and set Grant's office in her sights. Zara wanted time to walk around the CEO's office that she'd so far avoided before she was expected to take a meeting in it. On several occasions in the past, she had been party to Grant's discussions with important clients. But she sat in a corner, out of their eye line and took notes or offered facts as they were requested.

Grazing her finger over the fingerprint receptor on Grant's office door, she was disconcerted to feel tears burning in her ducts. Grant had screwed her over and wanted her to suffer for falling in love with Brodie. But he was a damaged man, desperate and alone. There wasn't anyone on the planet who knew him through and through.

She wondered if there was anything more she could have done to bring him closer to Brodie. She didn't have to turn her back on him in the Atlas warehouse as she had. So many 'what ifs' and 'could've maybes' presented themselves to her now that she had the full picture. Retrospect gave her the unwelcome chance to make excuses. The Kindred didn't tell her that they were going to be at that warehouse or that they planned to intercept the deal.

But she could pinpoint the moment that her relationship with Grant had been broken. It was that second she tossed the van keys to Brodie instead of him. Zara already had a sense of responsibility for what happened with Art. Guilt over her decision still often kept her awake at night. If she'd tossed the keys to Grant maybe Sutcliffe would've made it out of there with the device, but Art would be alive, wouldn't he?

Maybe Grant would never have found out about her relationship with Brodie. Sure, Brodie would've been pissed at her and it would've taken some explaining, but… She'd had to make a split second decision, and the crux of it was that she trusted Brodie to be compelled by the Kindred's motives that were more virtuous. When she'd made that instinctive choice, none of them knew that Sutcliffe was packing a weapon or that any of them were in immediate danger of death.

Replaying the past over in her mind wouldn't change their circumstances. She was here now, outside the CI CEO's office, and no matter how she justified it, she had to go inside. With one long hard breath that shook her shoulders, she straightened her spine and pushed her thumb against the security plate. It flashed in acceptance, so she strode inside.

Her concern should've been what was coming, who this strange client would be, and why he wanted to meet with her. It was disconcerting that he knew her well enough to want to talk to her while she had no idea who he was. That left her at an instant disadvantage.

Less than five paces into the room, she paused, her

vision snagged on the black leather chair that hadn't been used since Grant was last here. Grant. The room still smelled like him. Rolling her lips around her teeth, she squeezed hard but couldn't stop her chin from wobbling. Maybe that was why this was so difficult. Grant was gone. He had nurtured CI, it was his legacy, his passion, and now like a lost child, it stood as an ominous reminder of what was missing. This building was a glass and steel headstone bearing the name of the man she had once idolized and who would never again visit its hallways.

It would be easy to attribute her emotional reaction to thoughts of Grant McCormack to the five years they worked together when there were good times. But it wasn't so much the man himself, or the happy times they shared, that she grieved. Her regret came from the way things ended, so abruptly that no one got the chance to say goodbye.

And guilt. The weight of it kept her awake. It was ironic that she could see strangers die and hear of Brodie's work without blinking an eye, yet the demise of one man who had become their enemy plagued her. That fact was the root of her guilt.

He had become their enemy. But why was that? Because of her. Maybe the foundation of their animosity had been laid when they were teenagers, but it was her involvement in their lives, in their work, and relationship that had caused the rift to become terminal. She felt guilty about coming between the brothers, which was crazy, because they'd had years to make amends with each other and neither cared.

Zara knew what it was to live without family and what it was to want the approval of a parent or the support of a sibling and to be left hanging. Her father didn't contact her anymore, and in years gone by, when she mustered the courage to call home, the conversation was so strained that she eventually gave up trying to force it. Her mother was long dead. Her brother was too busy being a dumbass to think about stepping up for her. To her family, it was as if she'd ceased to exist because she chose to make decisions for herself instead of relying on theirs.

At one time, she relied on CI and on Grant to fill that

hole. Losing both now was like losing an old friend or breaking up with a long-term partner. She knew there was nothing for her here, that she didn't want this life anymore, but it didn't make turning her back any easier.

Her future was with Brodie and the Kindred. What they did was so dangerous, as Grant and Art's deaths had shown, that the void within her was always precariously close to becoming vacant. It could come at any second. Brodie had enemies and one of them could be loitering in any shadowy corner, ready to take her love away from her without any warning.

"I guess I'm early."

Spinning on the spot, all of her thoughts jarred to an abrupt halt when she identified the man who had spoken. "Oh my God," she whispered, forgetting to inhale before she sealed her lips.

"Kahlil Samara," he said, coming into the room with his hand extended.

Her body went into lockdown. She was so stiff, she couldn't move, though her eyes were doing a crazy job of trying to find any troops he might have brought with him. He got over to her and stopped, lifting his hand higher as he smiled.

"What are you doing here?" she asked, casting off her surprise so as not to betray how he'd caught her off guard.

She and Kahlil had met months ago in the Grand Hotel conference room during Grant's negotiations into selling Game Time. But she'd been aware of him before then after overhearing a meeting between her boss and this man. Having believed that she'd made a discreet escape, she was then attacked by Kahlil's security men in the CI parking garage. She'd been green and didn't know how to extricate herself. So it had been lucky that Raven was watching because he'd swooped in to save her ass.

How much Kahlil knew about that night, she didn't know. But Raven wasn't here to save her this time. Grant wasn't even around to offer a buffer. This was her and a terrorist alone in a room. They were probably the only two people in the building who had any idea about Game Time.

Kahlil's master was unsuccessful in his bid for Game Time, so maybe this was him taking a second shot now that Grant wasn't able to hamper the deal.

Kahlil's hand dropped in time with his sigh. "I heard about Grant. I wanted to extend my condolences."

No way that was the honest reason for his visit. Offering commiserations gave him a smokescreen for whatever his true motive for the visit was and it gave her an explanation to feed Julian if he should ask about this meeting.

She had met Kahlil once and their interaction had been brief. He had no reason to care about how she was dealing with the loss of Grant. If the sympathy was a professional courtesy, he should be talking to a board member or one of the company's lead lawyers, like Julian. But she had to accept his offering, even if it was false. The less she did to aggravate the man who had no compunction about causing harm, the better.

"Take a seat," she said, stepping aside and pointing to the guest chair at Grant's desk.

Putting a large piece of furniture between them would make her feel more secure. But she also didn't need his attention on her as she activated the miniature voice recorder in her watch. Darting across the room to close the office door, she used the chance to twist the face of the watch to the one position, setting the tech to record.

She'd found the piece in the manor supply room when she'd gone snooping. At first, she just thought it looked nice and she needed a timepiece anyway, so she adopted it for her wrist. During one of her moments admiring it, she noticed that the face frame moved and that the number inset in the face began to count. Moving the arrow on the frame to different numbers did different things: record, play, rewind, and so on. She didn't know if there was a transmitter that would allow the audio to be picked up remotely. But the point was moot because no one would know she needed them to tap into it.

Having this meeting on tape would be useful, she could play it for the other Kindred members, and hearing it for themselves would mean no detail would be missed. She didn't know how much recording time there was on the device. To maximize what she had, Zara hurried to the desk and sat in Grant's chair.

"Why did you want to meet me?" she asked, spreading her hands flat on the desk to pull herself in.

Kahlil was bright eyed with a clear complexion and a stylish suit that was a faded purple color. His choices suggested he was a confident clotheshorse. But Zara had come to learn that the image portrayed by some didn't always fit what was beneath the choreographed façade.

"We met, in the Grand, on the night of the demonstration," he said.

He was loose, sitting at an angle in his seat, lounging with an arm draped over the back. His positioning suggested confidence. There wasn't any hint of hesitation about bringing up the meeting where illegality had been discussed.

Dancing in this mental parade, she stayed relaxed because she'd learned it was just as important for her to be assured and unhurried. If Kahlil thought she was uncomfortable then she'd cede the advantage, which could be crucial later.

"Yes," she said. "I know who you are."

He wasted zero time getting to the point. "When Grant told us we'd been unsuccessful in our bid for Game Time, we were surprised."

The vultures were circling. Taking her lower lip into her mouth, she licked it and freed it again. It had been months since Grant had made his decision that Sutcliffe was the successful buyer. "I am sorry for that, but that project was tied up long ago."

Pinning his eyes onto hers, he stayed silent for so long that she almost began to squirm. But he was measuring her, testing his opponent, and she couldn't fail his examination. A smile slid to his face. "I have something for you."

He opened his jacket to pull an envelope from his inside pocket. The long white paper was thick and of good quality. When he slid it across to her, she was reminded of the time Grant had given her a check in a similar envelope.

The offering intrigued her. "What's in there?"

Smug yet casual, he was proud of himself. "A new bid," he said and her chin darted up in another bolt of surprise. This one wasn't so easy to conceal. "We know that Albert Sutcliffe did not use the device. Grant returned his payment. Exclusivity is still on the table."

"How could you possibly know that?" she asked, on the ropes.

It was difficult to maintain her cool, but she was doing it. Keeping her expression neutral and her body upright in a pose she'd seen the arrogant business people who did their work in this building use, Zara was thrust from the past to the future. As far as she knew, no one had re-opened bidding for Game Time.

Kahlil was assuming a lot by coming here with an offer already on paper. He probably wanted to get in on the ground floor, guessing that with Grant gone and Sutcliffe ousted, Game Time would be up for grabs again.

"We are not without our own capabilities," he said. "My superior was angry when we lost the deal. So angry that surveillance was ordered on Grant and on Albert Sutcliffe. We witnessed what happened in the Atlas warehouse and know that you are in possession of the device."

"That was months ago," she exhaled.

The Kindred had been so preoccupied by Leatt and what was left of Sutcliffe's legacy that they'd missed the backdoor strike. They were watching the wrong fight! Leatt was long gone, and Rigor could handle any of Sutcliffe's people who tried to return to their former home. Kahlil and his colleagues were coming for Game Time. They needed to switch focus, to find out what Kahlil's boss wanted to achieve with Game Time.

Kahlil had to sense her bewilderment, but he kept the focus on business. "Yes. Grant wasn't interested in accepting our new approach."

So this wasn't completely new. Grant had never told her about a subsequent offer for Game Time. Guessing that Grant had refused the offer without hesitation, she had to wonder about why Kahlil was trying again now that Grant was gone, he had to know that she had no authority over any of

CI's assets or products. But if he had witnessed what happened in the Atlas warehouse, he had to know that she had been the one to drive away from the site with the device in tow.

"What makes you think I will be interested?"

Linking his fingers, he rested his forearms on the desk. "Because you're a woman," he said, looking at her chest, which was concealed behind a conservative, fitted blouse.

Insulting the person you wanted to do business with was not a great starting point for negotiations. Suggesting that her gender made her more susceptible to his suggestion guaranteed that his hearing would not be impartial because she was already affronted.

"So, I'm supposed to do what you tell me?" she said, making no secret of her displeasure. "I wouldn't even consider a deal until you revealed the identity of your superior and his intention."

For a moment, she recalled what Benedict Leatt had said about his superior, and she wondered if they could be answering to the same individual. That idea was quickly quashed when Kahlil made his next admission.

"The players have changed since we last met," he said and for the first time she saw a crack in his nonchalance.

"What does that mean?" she asked, trying to decipher why he would be so affected by a change in his colleagues.

He exhaled and his mouth contorted at the same time he averted his eyes. The confident exterior slipped long enough for her to recognize annoyance. Knowing what ruled your opponent was an excellent way to gain advantage. Changes in his manner and expression could betray those weaknesses, and they wouldn't be recorded by any microphone, meaning it was up to her to catalogue them. Brodie had quizzed her about such things in the past, and she wanted to have all the answers should he do it again.

"I no longer work for the same man."

So it wasn't a change in his contemporaries but a change in his superior that disturbed him. Hazarding a guess that the separation had been acrimonious, she probed in hope of revealing the particulars. "Why not?"

If he'd switched allegiance, then it was possible Kahlil had been the one to reveal Game Time's existence and potential to his new employer, whoever that was. Word about the device was beginning to seep into a wider circle and that was dangerous for CI, and for the Kindred.

The device and corresponding viruses were locked up at the manor. She'd always been assured that the place was impenetrable and for a man on foot with a handgun that was true. But Kahlil had connections. That much was clear from how quickly he'd bounced into new employment and had exposed Game Time to this new party.

"My employer considered me inefficient," he said and didn't seem embarrassed to say it, making her think that Kahlil had an agenda of his own. Did he want to punish his previous associate? Or was this an attempt to impress the new boss in his life while humiliating the old one?

He was guarded enough that she recognized his reluctance to give her details and retreated so as to not aggravate him. "I'm sorry, but I don't have the authority to make deals for Cormack Industries," she said. "Any deal that we discussed—"

"No," he said, shaking his head and letting himself lean into the desk. "We knew that Grant was conducting negotiations privately, using CI as a shield, a front to protect himself. No one else here knew about it. But Grant trusted you, he brought you inside."

"If you saw what happened at Atlas then you know how our association was strained."

"That works in my favor," he said. "You have no concerns about loyalty. Grant is dead. You are free to sell the device."

"Why would I want to do that?"

He smiled and pushed back in his chair again, restoring his confidence. "We know about your connection to the Kindred. About your affair with Raven."

"You heard what was said in the Atlas warehouse?"

"No, we only saw it." She didn't like the knowing slant of his mouth. "But I have inside sources of my own."

If he was trying to charm her into working with him

or surrendering Game Time, then he was going about it the wrong way. "Good for you," she said, pushing away from the desk with designs on rising, but he spoke again before she could get her feet under herself.

"I know the truth," he said and she relaxed her arms.

"The truth?" she asked, wondering what he was going to declare.

"About who your Raven is."

His confidence was warranted and she stayed glued to her chair. Knowing who Raven was changed everything, he could reveal that knowledge and bring Raven's enemies to her and Brodie's door. Kahlil had admitted to knowing what had happened in the Atlas warehouse. Therefore, it was also possible he knew about Sutcliffe's compound and could know how Grant had died. He might even know about who Leatt was working for.

"I'm afraid you'll have to be more specific, Mr. Samara."

"Have many secrets, do you, Miss Bandini?" He arched a brow, but she wasn't biting, so he came nearer to the desk. "I know who killed them."

Again, she wasn't sure who he was referring to, but if he ratted Brodie out to the cops for his work as Raven, it could destroy all of their lives. "Are you threatening me?"

"No. I'm offering you a chaser. Give Game Time to me, you'll get a fortune in cash and the truth of what happened on that boat twenty years ago."

Her lips were stuck together, but they unglued when her shock weighed down her jaw. "The boat."

"Future's Hope, that's what it was called," he said.

That was the name of the boat Brodie and Grant's parents were killed on as the boys watched on from shore. Zara had been focused on what Kahlil knew about the present. She could never have guessed that he could solve a twenty-year-old mystery. But that did explain how he knew who Raven was. If he'd known for twenty years and kept the secret to himself then there was no reason to assume he'd betray it to anyone now. But he had kept another secret all this time, and she couldn't begin to guess how he'd been involved in a boating accident that occurred two decades before.

"How could you possibly know that?" she whispered and there was no way she could disguise her amazement.

Kahlil was in no rush to satisfy her curiosity. "Do we have a deal?" he asked, straightening in his seat to meet her eye.

All joviality was gone and she saw nothing but a ruthless businessman in front of her now. Just as she'd suspected, the charming, stylish friend was a cover.

Sliding her hands together, one went over the other until she was covering the watch on her wrist. Touching it was acknowledging the link to her Kindred colleagues, and she needed a buoy while under Kahlil's scrutiny.

Kahlil knew his opponent. Teasing her with the truth of Future's Hope was a prime weakness he could exploit. Money wouldn't tempt them to release Game Time. "You'll tell me what happened to Future's Hope?"

"You give me what I want and I'll tell you who you're looking for."

Who. The person responsible for taking down Brodie's parents could still be alive. "If you know," she said, curling her fingers around the watch face. "Did Grant tell you?"

Could her boss have known something so profound and always kept it to himself? If Grant had kept the secret, she could think of no reason that he'd confide it in Kahlil. There was no affection between the men, and Grant had dismissed Kahlil's original bid for Game Time suggesting no loyalty.

"No," he said. "Nothing as simple as that."

Both Grant and Brodie had told her they had suspicions about what had happened on the day their parents were killed, rather they'd expressed doubts about whether or not it was an accident. Now she had the concrete confirmation Brodie had never had.

They'd lost Art to keep Game Time from falling into the wrong hands. Grant died trying to steal its power from the one he'd sold it to. She couldn't make promises to surrender it without getting authorization from her chief. But she questioned whether she should bring this development to his attention. Was he so desperate to know what had happened to his parents that he would damn innocent souls? Or would he be pissed that Kahlil was manipulating him and go on a crusade to find the truth another way after damning Kahlil to his grave?

Before establishing what she would do with this information, she had to find out what course it had already taken. "If you offered this to Grant, why weren't you the successful bidder?"

In the end, Grant had proved himself selfish enough that if Kahlil had something extra that interested him, he'd give the man an advantage to gain what he wanted.

"He was never offered this information," Kahlil said. "The man I used to work for was involved in the demise of Future's Hope. He had kept the secret for many years, two decades. He ordered me to keep the secret too. At the time, he had my loyalty, so I did what he said."

"Your boss was involved?" she asked.

"Yes, and honestly, if Grant McCormack found out about his involvement then, our Game Time bid would never have been entertained."

"But when you failed to obtain Game Time, your boss got pissed and fired you."

With a slow blink and a nod, he maintained his calm. "That's right," he said.

"So now you want your revenge?" she asked.

Any information she got from this man would be biased and would downplay his involvement in whatever happened. But he couldn't be more than ten years older than Brodie, meaning he'd have been in his early twenties when this incident occurred. Still, whatever he said would have some thread of truth, and it would give them a place to work from if Brodie decided he wanted to settle old debts.

Kahlil took a second to himself before answering. "My new associates and I have no reason to keep the information to ourselves. The only value the information has to us is its power as leverage. We can barter knowledge for what we want."

And before they could even consider a trade, they

would have to uncover Game Time's ultimate purpose in the hands of these people. "Why do you want it?" she asked. "What's so important about Game Time? You have lost the patronage of your previous superior. Do you plan to turn the device against him?"

He squared the seam of his slacks and cleared his throat before standing up and tapping a finger on the envelope. "Take that figure to your superior."

"You said your new approach would work because I'm a woman," she said, happy to keep her love as far away from this decision as she could.

"I didn't mean to imply that you would be making the decision. But I know you have the ear of your man, the man who will appreciate this information. A man who we both know flouts conscience in favor of his own agenda."

Brodie didn't have an agenda, not like Kahlil did, not like Grant or Sutcliffe. Despite his occupation, he was one of the most selfless of the bunch. "So you think I'll seduce him into agreeing to give up the device?"

"I think women heed emotions and your curiosity is already aflame, I see it. If you want the truth, I am the last chance for any McCormack to have it."

He tapped the envelope with the end of a finger and took shades from his pocket to slide them onto his face before he turned around and strode out of the room. After the door had closed, she snatched the phone from the hook and dialed nine, but before she hit another digit, she slammed the phone back onto the base.

SIX

SHE COULDN'T CALL up Brodie and tell him this. She had to be with him so they could discuss it in person. It was her only hope of tempering his reaction to this revelation. Spurred by this turn of events, she wanted to return to the manor, where they could process the development and construct some sort of plan.

Unfortunately, Brodie's ex would be arriving at CI at some point today and that nixed her ability to flee. Zara needed to stay and use this last chance to make sure that if Kahlil tried to approach CI, without the sweetener, that Cuckoo wouldn't walk into some disastrous deal without knowing what she was selling. Cuckoo wouldn't be interested in Future's Hope, but if offered a bundle of cash her first week on the job, she would probably take it to win favor and prove her ability.

Running to her own office, Zara pulled the box of printer paper from the cupboard and stuffed the reams into the cupboard before locking it again. Returning to Grant's office with the box, she began to fill it. The first thing to go in was Grant's laptop, then she seated herself on the chair and pulled out the key from its secret slot to unlock the drawers.

She put all of the files in the box, along with Grant's personal items and any notebooks or paperwork she found.

Keeping Grant's secrets would be a skeet shoot. Anything that might so much as contain a hint of a secret was put into the box. Once she was done, she left the key in the lock before crouching next to the chair to rip the concealed plastic slot off the underside of the seat. Removing the clue that Grant had something to hide would lessen the chance of Cuckoo's curiosity being piqued.

Content that she had gathered everything from the CEO's office, she secured the lid on the box and went to her own office to pack her own computer and personal items. When the lid was balancing on the overfilled box, she put it in the center of her desk and returned to Grant's office for one last look on the shelves.

Finding nothing of note, she refused to linger because the memories this space conjured were her enemies. Hastening to the exit, she was halfway across the room when a woman walked in, causing Zara to stop dead. The tall Italian was wearing a wraparound dress that clung to her curves. Her long, slender legs were tipped with slick, expensive heels, and when the olive-skinned beauty took her shades from her face, Zara pursed her lips in a smile.

Her tapered eyes had the longest lashes Zara had ever seen, and swathes of black hair hung in large, perfectly sleek curls over her shoulders. "Fuck," Zara bit out in a whisper.

"Excuse me?" the Italian had a vague accent that made Zara more conscious of her own ordinariness. Cuckoo hooked the arm of her shades into her cleavage. Pointing one foot in front of the other, she sashayed closer.

"Ms. Corvi," Zara said, reminding herself to be civil to the new head of CI. "Welcome to Cormack Industries."

The unimpressed glare on Cuckoo's face was well-practiced. "You're the welcome party?" Cuckoo asked, and the curl of her lip made Zara try her best to stand tall.

Mischa had three inches of height on Zara, and that was before she took the heels into account. The European had a tiny waist, generous breasts, and was the epitome of everything a woman didn't want to see in their partner's ex.

Notions of polite civility dwindled. "The copier paper is in the cupboard in the office next to yours," Zara said and opened her hands. "Consider yourself briefed."

Mischa Corvi didn't need anything from her. If there was ever an accomplished woman who could handle anything, Cuckoo was she. Zara widened her tight smile, deciding the only way she could get out of this without being rude was to keep her mouth shut. In an attempt to make a sharp exit, Zara took a step to the side and walked past the newcomer.

Cuckoo had other ideas about Zara's next move because she spoke, preventing Zara from making her escape. "You're not Zara… are you?"

Both women turned in time to face each other again, and while Zara was made more uncomfortable by this truth, Mischa was amused and took her time to examine Zara's figure with a smile on her face that made Zara want to dig her manicure into the European's scalp.

"Yes," Zara said, clinging to her last vestige of restraint.

The confirmation further amused CI's new CEO. "You can't cook, can you?" Mischa asked, wrapping an arm under her bust to rest the other one on it so she could tap her own talon on her bottom lip. "He always wanted a woman who could cook."

So they weren't going to ignore the obvious. Cuckoo wanted to talk Raven. Zara's tongue went to the corner of her mouth, and she had to draw it back in and bite the inner corner of her lip to prevent herself from lashing out.

Never had she so quickly taken a disliking to a person before. She shouldn't be pissed at this woman who was a practical stranger, but she was. Except if Cuckoo knew her, knew anything about her, Brodie had to have been the one who'd delivered the details, and Zara didn't want him discussing their relationship with anyone, but especially not an ex.

That affront, coupled with Art's assessment of Cuckoo, made Zara tense, and had given Mischa an almost zero chance of making a positive first impression.

Trying her best not to be snide, she had to

acknowledge that there were no barriers between them. "Yeah, Mischa, because it's as simple as that," she said, deliberately forgetting to use her adversary's last name.

Out of respect for the company and the family, Zara had intended to remain polite and sidestep their personal connection through Brodie. Mischa had broken the silence, giving Zara permission to take off her proverbial gloves.

Mischa wasn't done with her condescension. "Well, you're peppy. But you American women always are. So… bubbly and bouncy… I'm surprised you're not a blonde," Mischa said, scrutinizing Zara's black hair, which was pulled back in a tight chignon. "I suppose that's one thing we have in common."

"And I would think the similarities end there," Zara said, not wanting to be patronized or compared to this siren.

Perhaps sensing Zara's displeasure, or as a tactical maneuver, Mischa lost her own graciousness. "Yes, I would too," Mischa said. Her new stony expression highlighted her disgust, and to see the woman glare made Zara smile. "He does like to corrupt innocence."

Somehow, it was easier for Zara to keep her cool when she knew Cuckoo was losing hers. "Shame yours was already gone before he met you. He couldn't corrupt what was already polluted," Zara said because if Cuckoo was going to insult her then she wasn't going to take the hit without fighting back. "But you are quite a simple woman, aren't you? Ruled by primitive emotion. Anger. Greed. Revenge. Murder."

Zara knew what this woman was and what Raven had done for her, and Zara didn't want her to get too comfortable. Cuckoo was here to run the company because she was the sole person Brodie knew with the qualifications to handle the responsibility.

As reluctant as she'd been to encounter this woman, Zara was glad that she had the chance to assess her motives and personality. They hadn't been alone for more than a minute or two and already Mischa was revealing herself to have a short fuse, and trouble with receiving insults despite her ease in delivering them.

If it came down to it, Mischa wouldn't be a hard

opponent to beat, not when it was obvious that the Italian had no ability to hide her feelings. She was proud, smug, probably liked to boast, and based on her sultry pose, knew just how killer her figure was.

But Mischa's irritation was turned around with a toss of her hair. "He obviously trusts my capability more than yours," Cuckoo said, pleased with herself. "I am the one here to bail him out. Raven does hate debts and he'll do anything to settle them."

"Yeah," Zara said, not allowing this woman to gain the upper hand when the game was just beginning. She took a lazy step toward Mischa and kept her expression loose. "Maverick is so good for taking out the trash, tying up those loose ends."

Staring at each other, neither woman was ready to relent. "You are cute," Mischa said. Though her lips were pinched, she managed to exude triumph from her gaze. "By the way, your apartment is beautiful."

Zara wasn't expecting that, and her poker face had run out of batteries today. "What?"

"Raven said he would have somewhere quaint for me to stay while I was in town, you know, until I get settled. It's small, but cute, just like you."

Brodie had given her apartment to the woman he used to sleep with. Mischa found it much easier to relax when she knew she'd just knocked one out of the park. "Stay at my place as long as you like, it's not like I stay there often," Zara said, ready to slap Brodie upside his head. "I have better places to lay my head."

Mischa sneered again and was probably gearing up to spit, but Zara had her own bone to pick, so she backed away.

"Where are you going?" Mischa demanded when Zara was just a couple of feet from the door.

Hanging around would just lead to more sniping. Mischa would never admit to needing help from Zara, and so she'd get nothing done if she stayed.

"I'll give you a call in a few days," Zara said. "You know, to make sure you aren't spending too much time on your knees." Mischa's ire grew and that bolstered Zara, so she opened her hands. "You know, spilling the paperclips or whatever. New company, new setup, it will take you time to get used to the way things work. Don't forget that I have every member of the board on speed dial, so don't hesitate to pick up the phone if you need me to call in a favor for you."

She couldn't give Mischa the chance to retort or the women would be sparring all day. So, she left the office and went into her own to retrieve the box from her desk. When she got to the elevator, she pulled her Kindred phone from her purse and speed dialed Tuck.

"Swallow?" he said when he answered.

"Still in the field then," she said because if he was at the manor, he'd have used her real name. "Can you do me a favor? Patch into CI and override security on Grant's office door."

"Want me to add someone?"

"No," she said. "Allow general admission, don't lock it. Make sure my print stays on the CI system, too, even if they think they've deleted it."

"Oh, kay," he said, confused by her request, but she smiled, feeling mischievous.

"And put a few of your little bugs in there, will you? I want the IT guys scratching their heads for a few days."

"You got it."

"Thanks," she said and hung up.

It might seem petty, but her request wasn't part of any vendetta against Mischa because she was Brodie's ex. If Mischa didn't know the setup, she might not add security access prints to the door. But if she did, Zara didn't want to be locked out of there just yet. She still had to go through this box and Grant's computer. There might still be something of use at CI, and she didn't want her credentials off the system before they had a chance to figure out what else they might need.

The elevator got to the parking garage floor, but she lingered for a moment before exiting. This could be the last time she was in this building. After coming here almost every day for five years, saying goodbye to CI was a big change. But sacrificing the past when the Kindred were her future was an easy decision to live with.

***

IF BRODIE HAD handed her apartment keys to Mischa there was no point in Zara going there. It made more sense to her now why Brodie had stayed behind in the apartment that morning. Except that meant he'd known what he planned to do and hadn't clued Zara in.

He'd have his reasons for letting Mischa stay there, but she couldn't figure out why he wouldn't tell her about it when it was obvious that she was going to find out. Zara would let him explain his reasons to her after she had given him the riot act about keeping secrets from her, especially as they related to his ex-girlfriend.

Zara put the box in her car and sped out of the parking garage. A weight lifted from her shoulders the further from CI she got. It had been a huge part of her life, and she'd learned a lot from her job and from Grant, but in so many ways, she felt that she'd learned all she could from that place.

Parking the car in its usual secret location, she carried the box to her jeep inside the grounds and took it into the house. She dumped it on the kitchen island and went to search for her love. He wasn't in any of the recreation rooms, the kitchen, or their bedroom, so she headed to the basement where the Kindred rooms were.

The full gym had more machines than she knew how to work, but when she went inside and spotted him, he wasn't using the cardio ones with all the buttons. He was lying on the bench press and had the radio playing in the background. Without acknowledging her, he lifted the bar up to the rack, which to her signaled that he was done enough that she could talk to him.

Grabbing the towel from the machine nearest her, she dumped her purse and went over to toss the towel to his chest. "You didn't tell me she was the most beautiful woman in the world," Zara said.

"Who?" he asked, sitting up to wipe the sweat from his face and shoulders.

The question was ridiculous because he had to know who she meant, given that Mischa was the only new woman in their life. For a brief second, she considered that he could have taken the opportunity to make some flirtatious comment about their relationship, but Brodie wasn't of the romantic persuasion and Zara was in no mood for playing.

Folding her arms, she tried her best to ignore the glean of sweat on his chest. "Who do you think? Cuckoo!"

A faint glimmer of a smile came and went from his expression. "You like that name. Art did too."

She'd spent two minutes in the woman's company and already Zara knew it was accurate. "He was a smart man," she said. "When did you tell her who you were?"

"I didn't," he said, bending to pick up his sports bottle from the floor to squeeze some water into his mouth. "Never while we were together."

Which implied to her they'd seen each other since they split up or something had changed since then. Irked at herself for not delving deeper into Brodie's romantic history with the woman who was now a part of their world, Zara was frustrated. Except a million questions would lead to a million more and it wasn't like she didn't have a past of her own, so she couldn't go passing judgment or snooping into ancient history.

"Is it your plan to go back to Rigor's?"

"Yeah, tonight. Figured I'd wait around for you and take care of a few things while I was in the neighborhood. 'Cept now you're here—"

"Take care of things? What things? Setting up your ex in my apartment?" Zara didn't want to dredge up the past, but she didn't mind addressing the present. "Why would you put her in our private space?"

Displaying no indication of shame or apology, Brodie's arrogance came so easy to him, it was like it was engrained in his DNA. "We've already got eyes on that place," he said in his usual blank tone. "The cameras are setup. We're comfortable with the layout. There are a bunch of reasons it makes sense. If you've got a problem with it…"

She had any number of problems with the idea of a

viper taking up residence in her nest. But Zara had learned to pick her battles and didn't have the emotional fuel to waste on this one. The truth was, Cuckoo's charming personality and irritating declarations would have to get in line because there was actual business to deal with. Game Time and Future's Hope were more important than Zara being intimidated by the Italian's glowing complexion and presumptive behavior.

This wasn't the time to get bogged down by relationship politics. Telling Brodie about her meeting with Kahlil would have to come before anything else. Mischa was gorgeous and might make many women feel lacking in comparison. But Brodie didn't want to be with his ex and that was the pertinent fact. She was secure in their love and would needle him about his reticence later.

That being the case, if she was given the opportunity to ruffle Mischa's feathers again, she would take advantage. Keeping that woman in her place was fun, though Zara hadn't realized just how much fun it was until the adrenaline of their initial encounter had worn off.

Brodie drank some more water. "I guess if you're home this early, you two didn't get along."

She couldn't imagine he'd believe any other reality, and his own view of the Italian was obviously a pessimistic one. He hadn't invited Mischa to the manor, which suggested he was contending with his trust issues and was happy to keep the harlot at arm's length. Some might wonder why he'd reached out to a woman he didn't trust in his home. The way Zara saw it, bringing Mischa into CI was Brodie's not-so-subtle plan for getting Zara away from the corporation. Brodie's transparent motivation didn't need any discussion, that she could so easily read him was a positive. It wasn't like she could argue that he didn't care when he was showing how much he wanted to have her with him by sabotaging every alternative.

Bringing his leg over the bench, he got to his feet and she went over to rest her forearms on his torso. He might be sweaty, but he was also shirtless, and she liked being close to him when there was an excuse for skin-on-skin contact.

Patting his chest, she enjoyed his strength and hoped

it would endure when she revealed the real news that had come from her morning at CI. "I don't care about that. I don't want to talk about Cuckoo now," she said, because she would get over it. Cuckoo wasn't an imminent threat. As uncomfortable as Zara was with the idea of another woman in her apartment, Brodie was right that it made sense to put her there being that it was under Kindred observation and control. And situations with possible lethal consequences took precedence over petulant ones. "We have business."

"Us or the Kindred?" he asked, resting both hands at the back of her neck.

"Both," she said. Once she told him about her morning, he probably wouldn't be heading to Rigor's. All of their plans were about to change. "You shower and—"

"Talk," he said. For a guy who liked keeping secrets, he was careful about making sure no one else got to keep them.

With him standing here sweaty and distracted, it didn't seem right to have such a sensitive conversation. But the subject wouldn't get any easier to broach no matter how long she delayed talking about it or how clean he was.

His face rested in concern, which wasn't a great starting point because her guess was that his worry would increase when he found out what Kahlil had tried to tempt them with. "This morning, I went to tell Julian about Mischa. It turned out he already knew about her, but he told me that someone had called looking for me."

Immediately, his body grew rigid and Raven eclipsed Brodie. "Who?"

"He didn't know, but when I went upstairs…" She took a breath because she knew he would take this news hard. "It was Kahlil. He wants Game Time."

Brodie's hands shifted to tighten over her shoulders, he said nothing for about ten seconds, then his grip loosened to slide his hands to the back of her neck again. "You told him where to get off?"

Taking her watch from her wrist, she held it up. "I recorded the meeting and I think you should listen to what he had to say."

"I don't need to. I trust that you gave it to him straight," he said, pulling her forward to kiss her hairline. "I'll shower and we can get back to Swift."

"Beau, I…"

He let her go to head for the locker room in the corner beyond this room. If all Kahlil had wanted was Game Time, then she would have shut him down. But she couldn't let this go by without giving Brodie the chance to see what else was at stake. This wasn't about money or about dealing with a lowlife like Kahlil.

Brodie's reaction was the one she'd expected. Except Kahlil's request for Game Time wasn't the whole story. She couldn't conceal the truth because she'd never be able to live with herself if it came out later that they'd had this chance and she'd made a unilateral decision to snub it. Brodie deserved to know that the truth was on the table. It wasn't her choice to refuse. Only Brodie could make this decision, and the rest of them would fall in line for him.

Before the window of opportunity closed, she blurted out two words. "Future's Hope," she said before he took the final step to the locker room.

He stopped. Shouting it out was insensitive, but the urge to say something had clouded wisdom and the words had rushed out on their own. Locking her fingers together, she wouldn't let herself fidget as he turned to set his gaze on her.

"You're good," he said, but there was nothing happy about his statement. "Art's gone. Grant's eating worms… and you're still digging up shit from my past."

If Brodie hadn't given Mischa his real name then he wouldn't have shared details about the demise of his parents with her. Zara's knowledge could only have come from the one other person she'd met with that morning. The ire radiating from him suggested that he'd deduced that much. Brodie didn't like to talk about sensitive topics from his past. The idea that an enemy of theirs could be airing his dirty secrets didn't embarrass Brodie as much as it pissed him off.

"Kahlil offered more than money," she said. As her pulse began to speed, she fought the urge to go nearer and console him. With his mood the way it was, he wouldn't appreciate pandering. Any suggestion that he might be fragile or need support would fuel his anger. Instead of catering to his emotional needs, she appealed to his professional ones by holding up the watch. "He says he knows the truth about what happened to your parents."

His sneer didn't hint at interest or hope. "And you believed that?" he asked, becoming snide. "Maybe you should be a blonde."

Mischa had said that to her. The two of them saying such a thing about her on the same day was no coincidence. "Enjoy discussing me with your ex, did you? Did you have a little chat while you helped her settle into my apartment? The same place you screwed me senseless last night?"

"Yeah," he said. "She wanted to know what was so special about you that you got to stay at my place."

"Did she?" Zara asked and folded her arms.

Mischa had no tact or restraint; Zara had learned that after spending a few seconds with the woman. In the company of a man she was once intimate with, Mischa's insensitivity would be even less subtle.

"It's sure not your ability to call a bluff," he said. "Kahlil dangled that in front of you because he knew you'd bring it to me and try the soft little innocent tiptoeing to cajole me into falling for his bullshit. He doesn't know dick, and you weren't smart enough to notice you were being played. Have you learned nothing?"

Given what she'd told him about her feelings of uncertainty with the Kindred, she didn't appreciate him asking such a question. But she knew him too well to think that he was expecting an answer, though that didn't moderate the initial kneejerk reaction of her emotions.

"Stop it," she said, tensing to take careful breaths because only one of them could afford to be irrational at a time. "You're lashing out at me 'cause talk of your parents caught you off guard. It's okay to be upset. It's okay to be angry about it."

So much for not dealing with his emotions, it seemed they were too assertive to be ignored. "I'm angry that you let this guy play you," he said, pointing at her with his sports bottle. "What you've seen the Kindred do so far, it's been Sunday school. It's going to get harder and dirtier from here. You better up your game if you want to—"

"Want to what?" she asked and scowled after he cut himself off. "Want to stick around? Want to be worthy of you? Thanks, I need you questioning that right now when you know I've been… This isn't about me." She wasn't going to bring up her insecurities when he was in this kind of mood because he might say something they wouldn't be able to take back. "Kahlil says he knows the truth. Maybe he does, maybe he doesn't. Do you want to pass up the chance to find out? Shouldn't you at least talk to him or listen to the recording of what he said to me?"

"I know the truth. They're dead. End of story. Go upstairs and pack your shit. We're leaving in twenty minutes."

When Brodie was done with a conversation, it was over. She wanted to support him, but did that mean respecting his predictable reaction to the news? Or was she supposed to coax him into changing his mind? Kahlil had implied that was what he wanted her to do, but she wasn't going to make the decision based on his recommendation. She wanted what was best for Brodie.

Hearing the name of the boat and the implication that there had been foul play had shocked *her*, and Kahlil wasn't even talking about her parents. Brodie would need time to process this. While he did, she could foresee herself taking the brunt of his emotional journey until he came to a conclusion about what he wanted to do. She wasn't finished talking about Future's Hope, she'd just have to bide her time.

***

AS MUCH AS she didn't want to go to Rigor's with Brodie, Zara went upstairs and did as she was told. All they could do there was sit on their asses speculating about Leatt. There was little else to do about it now that the trail had gone cold.

Given what she'd just told Brodie about Kahlil and his parents' demise, he was angry, and taking that to Rigor would culminate in the two men fighting. With Kahlil, Leatt, and Cuckoo featuring in their circle now, they didn't need any more enemies. Explaining that to Brodie wouldn't alter the inevitable. Reasoning with him was never easy.

Kahlil was supposed to have gone away, back into his hole, after failing to secure Game Time during the first round of bidding. If he was flickering on their radar again, that could indicate other bidders wouldn't be far behind. Sikorski could know the same as he did and he might make his own play for Game Time. On top of that, either group could be in league with Leatt.

With Sutcliffe and Grant gone, there could be a feeding frenzy. Kahlil was right that no one else at CI knew about the device. Both he and Sikorski had put eyes on her. Sikorski was the other failed bidder she'd met at the Grand. Art had said he was a crazy person associated with the Russian Bratva, which was just the kind of guy she needed on her tail.

After packing her suitcase, she put it near the footboard and rounded to sit on the bed, cross-legged, right in the middle. Going to Rigor's was nothing but disadvantages. She'd miss their spacious bed here, and with Cuckoo taking up residence in Zara's abode, all she had to look forward to were the cramped conditions at Rigor's.

Brodie hadn't come upstairs, but she'd packed quickly. In the gym shower, he'd have peace and quiet and might take the chance to reconsider or at least think through what Kahlil was offering, so she wouldn't rush him. Using the time she had to herself, she reflected on her day. CI was her past, Brodie had made sure of that, and by giving Cuckoo her apartment, Brodie was making sure Zara had to stay here with him, and he'd been pushing for that for a while.

She didn't mind giving up CI. Working there hadn't been the same since Brodie came into her life and she saw the truth of Grant's capabilities. Now that he was dead, he could never be redeemed, meaning they could never go back to the way things were. Brodie had shown her that opportunities existed for her to have adventures and make a difference. CI had been a compromise, she'd settled there and convinced herself that she loved it, too afraid to take the chance of finding something more fulfilling.

The Kindred were her future and one she could be proud of, if Brodie didn't lose his patience with her. Kahlil could offer the truth of the most pivotal moment in Brodie's past. Her thoughts on the subject grew to critical mass until a burst of air came from her lips, and she dipped her head into her open palms. They couldn't let this pass them by. If she was curious, Brodie had to be too. If the guilty party was out there, then there was a chance of justice, Kindred style. Brodie wouldn't be interested in evidential proof or courts of law. This was his family. If there were secrets in her family, she would want to know them, so she couldn't believe Brodie was that much different.

A buzzing sound interrupted her reverie and made her frown. She had no idea what could be making the sound in their bedroom, and it wasn't a noise she recognized. Rotating her body, the first thing her attention snagged on was Brodie's nightstand, where they kept the sex toys. His control in bed extended to every aspect of her pleasure delivery.

Crawling to the nightstand, she pulled open the drawer to see if he'd found some way to activate the devices from a remote location. Everything in there was quiet. Brodie wasn't sending her any message that she was to get started on the foreplay solo.

The buzzing got louder and she slunk off the bed in a crouch, craning to follow the sound to a source. Settling on her purse, which was on top of her suitcase, she pulled apart the opening to see her cellphone illuminated in a green glow. Green. It flashed that color when someone was calling her apartment's hard line.

Calls hadn't gone through the physical phone line connected to her apartment for ages. During Brodie's grieving period, Tuck had worked his magic and now they were part of her Kindred phone profile, meaning all calls to her apartment landline were routed to whatever was her current cell line.

The number flashing on the screen brought a bitter taste to her tongue. It was her father.

Clearing her throat, she picked up, watching the bedroom door in case Brodie came in to join her. "Dad?"

She didn't even bother with hello. Pleasant social calls had never been a feature of their relationship. Bad news was the only reason she could figure for this call.

"Zara," he barked, in his gruff smoker's voice. "Good. Thought your number might be different."

Good guess because it had changed more than once. That he was getting to talk to her was a testament to Tuck's skills rather than dumb luck.

"What's wrong?" she asked, backing toward the bed to lean on the footboard. The last thing she needed was a battle with her family. Soon she was going to be working to convince Brodie of the merits of remaining faithful to his own and getting justice for his parents. "You never call, is there—"

"It's your brother," he said, giving her the courtesy of getting straight to the point. "We figure since you've been up in that big city with the fancy job for so long, you gotta have some serious dough, right?"

Money. Well, at least no one was terminal. As bad news went, she'd take financial worries over health woes any day. "I don't… How much do you need?" She wasn't rich by any stretch, but if her father was lowering himself to tapping her resources, they must be in serious need.

"Just twenty grand."

Just… Her mouth fell open. "I can't get my hands in that much. Why do you need it?"

"Your brother got bit by the IRS, bastards, they want paid for doing jackshit or they're taking the farm. That's our land, been in the family for—"

"I understand." Her father cared more for the dirt than he did his own daughter.

Chastising her father and brother for not paying their taxes on time would be redundant and hypocritical. Her boyfriend shot people for a living and had probably never paid taxes in his life.

Still, twenty grand was almost the total amount of her savings, and she was reluctant to hand that over when she knew it would never be repaid. If the roles were reversed, her father would be more likely to give her an earful than a handout.

Elevating her chin, she observed her sumptuous surroundings. She lived in a huge manor house with a man who had plenty of means. Keeping her nest egg to herself in light of the turn her life had taken seemed rather selfish.

"So you'll get it to us?" her father asked. "Has to be soon like."

"Let me see what I can work out," she said, and the line disconnected without any attempt at an awkward goodbye.

Her family was as broken as Brodie's, except the fractures in her relationships with her relatives weren't caused by death, not all of them anyway. Given the losses she'd experienced recently, she should take some time and do something about those fractures before she lost the chance for reconciliation for good. The next time her father or brother got in touch, it would probably be to tell her the other was gone.

Brodie didn't want her out of his eye line, but he and Tuck had work to do, work that they didn't need her for. After Brodie's semi-assertion, she was beginning to see her role in the Kindred as more of hanger-on than as an actual useful colleague. On the plus side of that, it freed up time, so she could deal with these kinds of unexpected personal issues without impacting Kindred progress. Mischa had CI to look after. Zara didn't even have an apartment to clean.

Snatching her suitcase and tossing the strap of her purse across her body, she figured she had to make peace with the past before she could figure out the future. Kahlil and the Kindred would wait. She could be back with Brodie inside a day. Scribbling a note for him, she doubted he'd have a problem with her being independent when it was that ability to rely on herself and face problems that had attracted him to her and kept them all going in the aftermath of losing Art.

If she had her own familial demon to confront, she wasn't going to shrink and hide, she was going to deal with it head on.

SEVEN

SHE'D BEEN SO damn sure about this trip that she'd ditched the man she trusted more than any other to make it. The flight was just a few hours, and it took little time to rent a car and drive to her father's. The heat of the early evening sun joined her as she stood on the sidewalk, staring at the front door of her father's home in the suburbs.

The house she was looking at now wasn't the one she'd grown up in. Her brother had taken over the farm a couple of years ago, and while her father did still work in those fields, he'd moved out of what had been her childhood home in deference to her brother and his new family.

Coming here had seemed like such a good idea when she was sitting in the safety of the manor, and she'd gone on autopilot to make the journey. The moment she'd stepped out of the car and crossed the street to stand on the sidewalk where she was now, the instinct to progress disappeared. Taking in the modest home with its patch of grass out front, she watched the length of the intersecting path stretch. It wasn't more than a few yards, but it was going to be the longest few yards of her life.

She stood frozen, with her suitcase at her back and

her car parked on the other side of the street behind her. Escape was still a possibility. Settling an old conflict was a great theory, but there was a reason she'd never tried to mend her relationship with her father. Experience taught her that he was old school and didn't understand her life choices. She wanted him to tell her that he was proud, to apologize for his behavior, and to admit that he'd loved her all along. Great dream.

Now that she was close enough to envision him in this place, she played the scenario forward. She'd walk into that house, he'd look her up and down, and assume she'd fucked everything up. He'd demand the money, show no interest in her life, and either tell her to leave or to cook him something. Her dreams could only be fulfilled by a paternal figure who wanted to love her. To get what she wanted, her father would have to be a different man, and her taking time to travel here wouldn't change who he was.

Seeing him again would remind her of the heartache she'd gone through after losing him the first time. She'd be reminded that he was a bully who had no respect for her or what she'd been through and she'd end up hating him all over again. It had taken her a long time to get over the disappointment of leaving here without his blessing.

"Don't go in there."

The sound of the familiar masculine voice made her whip around. Brodie was propped against her car on the other side of the narrow street with his arms and ankles crossed. She sighed. "Jeez, you scared me," she said because when she'd stopped here, she'd been sure she was alone, apparently, she was wasn't. She wasn't sure how long she'd been standing here motionless staring at her father's house, but she hadn't heard a vehicle approach. "How did you know where I was?"

Her note had said she was going to see her father, but hadn't said where he lived, or that she was traveling back to her home state to do it.

"You think it's difficult for me to find you?" he asked, pushing off the car and sauntering over to stand with her on the sidewalk. "My best bud can hack any system, and when your name pops on a flight manifest, I know. Hacking the security cameras and running facial recognition takes two seconds." Nodding at the car he'd just left, he hooked his hands in his pockets, leaving his thumbs in his belt loops. "That's your rental car, another breadcrumb... and your phone is equipped with a GPS tracker. If you're on this planet, I can find you. Need me to keep talking?"

If she'd just pulled up, he had to have been sitting in wait to be so hot on her tail. "How did you get here before me?"

"Means," he said. "My cousins are chopper pilots, and I can get a jet to take me anywhere I want to go without waiting at check-in."

Okay, so it wasn't that amazing when he explained himself. Putting her hand on the extended handle of her suitcase that stood just behind her, she turned to face the house. "I have to do this."

"No, you don't," he said, cool and quiet. He wasn't appealing to her; he was stating what he believed to be a given fact. "You could've wired the ransom money and never set foot on a plane."

Amazed that he'd known about her private conversation, she gaped. "How did you...?"

He shrugged. "I know everything."

If he wasn't recording her calls, he might have heard her on audio transmitters that were in the manor. She made a mental note to stop talking to herself when she thought she was alone.

"What the fuck possessed you to come down here?" he asked as she twisted to face the house again. "If you walk in there, he'll think he was right all along, that you've come to grovel. You don't have CI now, but you have us. You have the Kindred. You still feel like we don't need you?"

Exhaling, she conceded that he deserved to know the truth. "I don't have mad computer skills like Swift. I can barely change batteries in a remote. I'm not Falcon. I don't have money to contribute like him, like you. I don't have a useful degree or superior knowledge like Wren."

He didn't flinch. "They don't have your legs."

Tilting her head, she wasn't impressed. "I'm serious,"

she said, scowling at him and letting her hand slide away from the metal suitcase handle. "I'm not Premium Personnel Coordinator anymore. I'm out of CI, I can't give you access. You own the damn building now anyway. You can get it yourself if you need it."

"This isn't about CI," he said. "I don't need dick from there, and you don't need that place either."

She didn't feel any better. "I knew Grant for five years, but it took you telling me about Game Time for me to figure it out. I didn't suspect that you were involved in what happened in Quebec. I didn't see Grant's double cross coming. You were out of the game for months, yet you picked up on it before I did. I was the only one to spend time with Benedict and I had no idea he was following his own secret agenda. When CI landed on you and you didn't want to handle it, you called your ex-girlfriend to bail you out. I'm done. I don't have any skills that can help you or the Kindred."

"And you think walking back in there to Daddy and handing him a bundle of cash will make you feel better?"

"You don't get it," she said, shaking her head. "I'm not here because I'm running back to him. I want to be with you, but I have to confront him, to make him see that he wasn't right. My confidence relies on him admitting his mistake."

"That's not why you're here. You're running. You think I haven't notice that you've avoided going back to the compound? Atlas was easy to avoid; we have no reason to be there. You can't handle the deaths of people you care about because it reminds you of your mother."

Brodie was way more perceptive than she'd given him credit for, and more attentive of her behaviors too. Swallowing, she wouldn't let herself become emotional with him again. "How do you know that?" she whispered.

"Because when I was grieving, I shut myself off and got drunk. Your coping mechanism is to be busy. You always want to feel useful. It's more acute now because you're trying not to face how losing Grant has hurt you."

Biting her lower lip, she held it between her teeth. "I wasn't there for him at the end. I can't fix that relationship."

"So, fixing your relationship with your dad is some sort of substitute?"

Determined, she tried to conjure the resolve she'd had before embarking on this trip. "My dad needs me."

"Your dad needs money," he said. "He's not gonna welcome you without judgment. If you want to stay here because you think he'll make you feel useful, then do it. But it will fuck you up because he's never gonna be the guy you want him to be."

Zara knew that, her optimism had faded. Because she was here, she felt that she should go in to hand over the cash. The Kindred had plenty to keep them busy, and she wasn't an integral part any longer.

Glancing up, she became overwhelmed by the sight of him. Brodie was an amazing man, handsome, smart, dedicated, and he had a purpose, which he'd put aside to come here to intercept her. "I'm of no use to you anymore. We both know it. How long will it be before you get tired of my dead weight on the team?"

His scrutiny made her return her focus to her father's front door. Ignoring her love, she began trying to psyche herself up to start walking. All she could think about was her father's judgment, about how her answers to the questions he asked would never satisfy him.

"That's what your whore comment was about," Brodie said and sighed. "You think if you can't do a job then you'll spend your days sucking my dick." She shrugged because yeah, that was pretty much it. "The first time I shot a gun, I blew out the back tire of Art's jeep."

Despite the randomness of the statement, she drew her attention around to portray how impressed she was because that was a precise shot for a beginner. "Wow," she said, surprised his aptitude had come to him so naturally.

He shrugged. "Thing is, I was aiming for a target six feet to the left and shot wide. Art had taken me to this little African village. He'd been there before and helped them out with a shitty landowner who thought he was God. Everyone in that village was watching me. They were so impressed because they thought that tire was my target. These people worshipped Art and after seeing that shot, they loved me."

Young, triumphant Brodie was a hard thing to picture. "The praise must have felt good."

"Are you kidding?" he said. "I felt like crap. We stayed in that village and ate with the people while they were celebrating my superior skills."

"You could have just faked it," she said. "Made them believe you had full confidence in your ability."

"That's what Art said," Brodie replied. "The thing was, I was shit scared. I asked him, 'What do I do if they call me in to get rid of some crazy bastard? They'll find out I was a fraud thirty seconds before I get my ass handed to me. I'm not as good as they think I am.' I asked how I could make sure that didn't happen, how I could explain to them that I wasn't that good."

Her love didn't often share stories of his past with her, and she relished the chance to hear one now, even if it was an odd time to be sharing. "What did Art say?"

Brodie moved in real close and draped an arm around her, across the width of her shoulders. "He leaned in to whisper and I thought he was gonna reveal some big secret and he said, 'You'll just have to get that good.' I was pissed as hell." She smiled. "I told him it wasn't that easy. Then he asked if I wanted to know the secret to being a good shot."

He paused for long enough that the suspense made her lean until she was almost kissing him. "So, what did he say? What's the secret?" she asked, desperate to know.

He lowered his volume to a whisper, "Practice."

Wilting, she was peeved he'd duped her like Art had duped him. "Hilarious."

Though she tried to cast his arm off her shoulders, he didn't take the hint. "It's not a joke. I'm telling you that you're still a rookie and getting that good takes time. You've been thinking about Saint's death. You want to know who Leatt is working for and what his people are up to, right?" She shrugged. "When I didn't give you the answers you wanted about Game Time, what did you do?"

"Research," she said. "At CI, but I don't have access to—"

"There are other places, other books, other systems. If you want to know who Leatt is, do some research." Her confidence had taken such a knock that she wasn't sure she was capable of taking on that challenge. Leatt wasn't her primary concern since Kahlil had presented his offer. Her eyes drifted toward the house again, and Brodie's lips closed in on the shell of her ear. "Your answers aren't in there. Yeah, you can give up. You can walk away. But what makes you think you'll be any more content in there than you are with me?"

Raising her chin, she apologized with her gaze. "This isn't about us. I love you."

"And how long will that last once your dad has you back under his thumb? There are plenty of eligible guys around here."

It hadn't occurred to her that Brodie might assume she was escaping the Kindred and their relationship by coming here. The last thing she wanted was regular guys and a normal life. Coming home to face her father was supposed to be cathartic, a healing experience that would give her an energy boost.

With Grant gone and Mischa in charge, Zara had no place left at CI. Feeling that she was of no use to the Kindred because she'd failed every mission, it felt dishonest to have the privilege of life at McCormack Manor at least until she could get some validation that her decisions were righteous.

"I feel like I failed you," she murmured.

"We figured out where Game Time was because of you. You gave us the potential buyers. You went to that Grand meeting and charmed their asses. None of them suspected you of wearing a wire or fooling them. You went to the goddamn Game Time drop, even though you thought you were all by yourself. You were there because you wanted to stop it, even if it meant risking your life and revealing yourself. God, baby, it was hot to watch you so confident about doing the right thing."

"Anyone could've done those things," she said.

Grabbing her neck, he pulled her close. "For all we know, the reason Leatt didn't kill us all where we stood was because you made him care about you. You went to Sutcliffe's compound alone. We found the arsenal because of bugs you planted and cameras you carried. You are smart. You're social and you're beautiful. The Kindred need you. I need you. It's as simple as that."

She wanted to believe him and she opened her hands on his chest. "If I lose you… you were going to let Grant kill you just to save my life. I can't… I'm not sure I would've been able to live if I lost you. The guilt of you sacrificing yourself for me…"

"I was never gonna let him hurt me," he said, peering closer until she read the love behind his tough façade. "Swift took you to the floor to protect you. All I had to do was take a couple more steps, and I'd have taken the gun from Saint. Murder in his blood or not, he liked the sound of his voice preaching at me too much. He'd have wanted to deliver another monologue before pulling the trigger, and all I needed was half a second to switch the advantage from their camp to ours."

That was reassuring and something she wished she'd known at the time. But the intensity of her fear remained. "I can't lose you. I can't." But if she didn't trust herself to be useful to the Kindred, she'd never be able to hold onto him.

"Moving back here pretty much guarantees that you'll lose me, baby." She didn't follow. It hadn't been her intention to move into her father's house. Brodie might be able to pinpoint her location, but his tech couldn't read her mind. "If you come back here, I'll end up in jail 'cause there will be a wave of single men in their twenties, thirties, and forties dropping down dead with a single, high-caliber gunshot wound to the head."

She smiled, though she believed his words to be true. "Any male of dating age?"

He nodded once. "Yep. I'll eliminate them all before they become a threat to what we have."

Being close to him eased some of her burden. "No man measures up to you," she said, sinking into his arms when he spread his fingers on her spine to pin her body to his.

A creak made her turn, and she saw her father on the porch, between the door and screen, peering down the path as if trying to make out who they were. "Get in the car," Brodie said, seeing what she did. He pushed her lower back to direct her toward the road as he turned toward the house.

But her love's frown and willingness to address her father made her grab for his wrist to get his attention again. "Are you armed?" she asked.

The glare on his face didn't budge. "Do you want me to kill him?"

No, she didn't, but it meant so much to her that this man would do anything to make her happy. "No. What about the money?"

"Get in the car," he said, bobbing his head in the direction of the vehicle then kissing her hairline. "Trust me."

And although he didn't need an answer, she gave him one. "More than I trust myself," she said.

Before he started toward the house, he smacked her ass, probably in lieu of a kiss, then he strode up the path toward her father who was still loitering. It had been a long time since she'd seen him and he looked older, more weathered, his stance was more hunched and his face more creased. But she recognized him, even if his eyesight wasn't good enough for him to be certain of her identity.

He can't have felt too threatened because he hadn't run off to get his gun. Even if he had, he'd never have gotten a shot off. Brodie would disarm him if the conflict got physical, but her father would notice her love's superior skills. In the event that he did, Brodie would have an explanation, though her father wouldn't hear it because he'd be too busy getting himself riled.

Anything could happen in that house, as neither man was great at holding their temper if the right buttons were pushed. Brodie kept on going up the path and didn't look back at her. Tearing her eyes from the men, she wheeled her suitcase to the car and put it in the trunk before taking a seat in the front passenger side.

She didn't know how long Brodie would be or what excuse he would give to her father for being there. But when the men went into the house, her jaw fell. She'd expected an exchange on the porch, not inside in the bosom of the home.

Brodie hated being social, and her father wasn't much better at it.

Slumping into the seat, she slid her shoes off her feet and drew them up under her. Whatever the men were talking about, she couldn't interrupt, she'd just have to wait until Brodie returned and then query the details. Staring out of the windshield, she thought about what Brodie had said, and it wasn't so much his point about her research as it was his reminder of her being proactive. When Brodie hadn't given her what she wanted, she stood tall and found it out on her own.

An idea hit her, so she bent to grab her purse from the floor. Taking her cellphone out of it, she began to make plans.

EIGHT

HIS COUSINS WEREN'T waiting for him with a helicopter, but there was a jet waiting for them at the airport. Brodie ignored anyone who tried to talk to him, so they eventually gave up. The employees interpreted their choice of transportation as a sign of frivolous wealth and tried to pander as though they were idle and spoiled. They didn't want champagne or canapés. They wanted to get from A to B, that was it.

On business trips with Grant, she'd had the privilege of traveling in a private jet. But the sheen of novelty didn't lessen and enjoying the seclusion of a private plane with Brodie led to some unscheduled activities. Try as she might to press for details, Brodie hadn't been forthcoming about what happened while he was in her father's house, which he had been for about fifteen minutes.

After giving up on that, she tried to address the situation with Kahlil and what he knew about Future's Hope. Brodie didn't want to talk about that either. So instead, they used sex to pass the time and she was happy to cross sex in a plane off her bucket list.

Because he wasn't interested in talking about Kahlil,

he hadn't been interested in discussing her plans either. But he did assure her that they would talk when they landed and regrouped at the manor. Just hearing that they were going to base instead of to Rigor's place soothed her nerves.

Night had fallen by the time they got home, meaning they could open the main gate and drive to the manor house and straight into the garage. Brodie parked and they got out, so she queried his choice of destination.

"Why are we here?" she asked. He'd given up on going to Rigor's without putting up any kind of fight, so the why intrigued her. "I thought you wanted to—"

"When a member of the team goes AWOL twice in the same month, something has to give."

When she moved toward the trunk, he took her hand and pulled her away from the car. "Am I going to be punished?" she asked, traipsing along behind him.

"In private later," he said.

The squeeze of his hand was bruising, and she expected him to take her upstairs to their bedroom. But he didn't. Taking her out through the garage door, they traversed the slope and kept on going until he pulled her into the trees.

Confused by his strange actions, she sought an explanation. "Where are we going?" she asked, but he didn't answer, he just got faster as he shoved branches and pushed leaves aside. Zara struggled to keep up, and it was so dark that she could barely see her own feet, increasing her chances of falling over something. Uncertainty and overexertion made her breathing grow to a pant, but he didn't let her go. "Brodie, you're scaring me, where are we—"

The trees thinned and they broke into a clearing she recognized. Brodie stopped and pulled her forward to reveal the scene. Tall, burning torches had been driven into the ground around the family headstones, lighting up the whole clearing with a warm, yet mystical, orange glow that faded into the mists that hung on the ground. But they weren't the only things of note. Tuck was there, too, beside Zave, who had Thad on his other side. The whole gang was here.

Brodie lowered to whisper in her ear. "I still think Saint was a prick." The Kindred moved aside, and she sobbed when she saw a new headstone next to Art's. Both hands flew to her mouth and Brodie put his arm around her. "This is why we need you. You think like Art. We just have to nurture that."

Turning to gaze up at him, she twisted into his arms and stroked her hands up to his face. "I love you."

"Remember that next time you think about ditching me," he said, taking her chin between his thumb and curled index finger. "The guys have beers over there, and maybe a bottle or two of dry white wine. Want to get drunk?"

Curving her lips, she didn't know if she wanted to laugh, cry, or jump him. "What about business?"

"It will all be there in the morning," he said, dipping to kiss her. "Art and Saint didn't get any send off. Funerals have never been a Kindred thing." Because until recently, the deaths they'd dealt with were ones caused by them. A body would be left where it lay or disappeared, but there was no ceremony attached to that, only evidence removal.

Grieving for Grant was a symbolic way to grieve for her past. Her naivety was gone, along with her CI career, and she needed closure. Being out here, surrounded by Brodie's lost family was a great initiation into her future with the Kindred.

Zara wasn't sorry Grant was gone, the man he'd become was cold and cruel. But she did grieve the loss of his innocence. After losing his mentor, Frank Mitchell, something in Grant had changed and if she'd been paying closer attention, she might have noticed it. Brodie had a support network to help him deal with loss while Grant had no one. At the end, it was clear that there was no going back for Grant, he was too far into his deluded psychosis to see the consequences of his actions. All he wanted to do was win and by doing this, the Kindred were proving that he hadn't won.

They'd spent long enough observing the party from afar, and Brodie slid his hand up her spine to twine his fingers in her hair and take the back of her neck. "Come on."

Guiding her over to the others, she was met by smiles from Thad and a hug from Tuck. Zave nodded at her, which was an improvement over ignoring her. Business had drowned out most of their chances to kick back and enjoy each other's company because when they were together, they all had to be on. Even her time with Brodie had often been cut short or hampered by missions, Game Time, and/or thugs with a plan.

This was a long overdue chance to bond and relax, and she was interested to find out how the Kindred partied when they weren't using it as a cover for something else. If they could all get into the spirit of the night, this was going to be a joyful learning experience.

***

AND IT WAS. Zave didn't drink alcohol, but she did hear him laugh for the first time. Thad was a hoot and everyone shared stories of Art and Grant. Yes, the latter was a twisted maniac who wanted his revenge on them. But he had no one to grieve him. There was no body in the ground.

Sutcliffe's compound had been wiped clean before Rigor and his crew got in there. The Kindred didn't know where Grant's body was, probably in a mass grave with Rigor's fallen men and Sutcliffe's dead followers. Much blood had been shed and for no purpose.

More than just beer was consumed after Thad retrieved supplies from the house. Brodie was persuaded to demonstrate his skills by building a spit to roast the meat that Thad had been desperate to try in the great outdoors—even though they were only a hundred meters or so from the house.

Saying goodbye involved stories and jokes, mostly Thad's, and while Grant and Art were celebrated, Brodie's parents' graves weren't discussed as much. Their loss had become relevant in Brodie's life again, and he was still working through what that meant for him. Toward the end of the night, she caught Brodie staring at his parents' headstones when Thad was singing a song, which he seemed to do a lot of when he was drunk.

At that point, after praising Thad's singing skills, Zara had taken Brodie away from the party. Her goal was to get him to open up, he had other ideas and they ended up making love on the rocks above the crashing waves surrounded by the scent of the sea. By the time they got back to the graves, the torches were out and the others were gone.

Music in the manor betrayed that Thad was still up and partying. But Brodie wasn't interested in continuing festivities and instead took her to bed where they stayed until the sunshine woke her up.

The natural light betrayed Brodie's absence from their bed. Stretching into a seated position, she considered how to tackle Kahlil's offer with Brodie when her gaze snagged on something in the corner. Far left of the bed, on the same wall as the entertainment center, in the corner shadow... Zara smiled. That was Brodie's chair, or Raven's chair, from her apartment bedroom. Cuckoo wouldn't have the pleasure of sitting in the chair that meant so much to her relationship with Brodie.

The piece had probably been there last night when they came to bed, but she hadn't noticed. Exhilarated, she was even more determined to see her love. Given that they had guests, she assumed he was somewhere in the manor with them. So, she got up and ready for the day before she went on the hunt for the others.

They weren't in the kitchen or in the dining room, not that she expected them to be sitting down to a lavish breakfast. Breakfast was more often missed in this house than eaten. The guys were probably hung over, too, making it even less likely that they were indulging in food.

When she didn't find her cohorts in the security room, she sat at the keyboard to activate the motion sensors, so she wouldn't have to wander aimlessly in her quest to locate them. Technology featured more in her life than it had been before. As the system booted her request, one of the screens flickered to a new picture, and she saw her apartment. An initial pang of longing became curious surprise when she noted the unfamiliar interior.

Shifting along to the left keyboard, she typed in the code that brought the picture from the monitor bank and put it on the smaller monitor in front of the keyboard. Zooming in for a closer look, she hunched over the desk. The furniture in the apartment wasn't hers, none of it. She exhaled a laugh and sat back. Brodie hadn't just handed over her personal space and possessions. He'd cleared the place out and had it redressed before Mischa set foot over the threshold.

The motion sensor system bleeped to indicate it was live, so she exited the image of the apartment and rolled her chair sideways to access the system she'd started. But before it could display the results, the door behind her opened, and she spun the chair around to see all four men come in. The door closed behind them and they stood in a row.

Being confronted by four such formidable men would have intimidated her a year ago; these days it didn't make her blink. Tuck, Zave, and Thad went to the table in the corner to sit down.

"Are you ready?" Brodie asked her, though she didn't know what he was talking about, so she could only look left then right as her love went over to stand behind an empty chair at the table where the other men were seated.

All of them were waiting for her, and their intent scrutiny made her self-conscious. "Ready for what?" she asked. This was like getting a pop quiz in high school that everyone else was prepared for, while she hadn't known it was coming. "Is this the initiation or the punishment?"

Calm and patient, Brodie was at peace in an eerie way. "You've been itching to tell me your plan since I got into that rental car with you," Brodie said. "Now's your chance to spill it. Now's your chance to lead."

Brodie pulled out the seat he'd been leaning on and sat down to wait, just like the others. Curling her fingers around the arms of the chair, she scanned each face at the table. They were blank, awaiting orders, there was no judgment or annoyance, but there was a silent expectation and she'd have to meet it. There was no place for whining, complaining, or second guessing herself now. She wasn't performing for her boyfriend and friends, she was presenting to serious, capable colleagues who needed her to step up.

Pushing up from the chair, she swallowed to moisten her throat then licked her lips. She knew all of these men, and she had worked with them, but being in control, that was a different ball game. Here she was, little Zara Bandini in charge of her own army.

Jumping in meant conducting herself with confidence. Art had been an inclusive leader, but the Kindred wasn't a democracy. Brodie ran things and had the deciding vote on all actions taken by their squad. He'd probably instructed the others not to argue with her or disrespect her because he knew about her personal struggle. Even if this little performance was just to humor her, they didn't let it show and gave her their complete focus and trust. Pitching her feeble idea to these experienced men was intimidating because if she made a fool of herself, it would take a long time to win back their respect.

Buying herself some time, she went to the table at the side of the room, poured herself a coffee, and took a calming sip before turning to face them, bolstered enough to fake confidence even if it was wavering a tad.

"Leatt's a dead end," she said. "Hanging around at Rigor's doesn't get us anything. We need to be focused now. Sitting around there waiting for something to come to us is frustrating and counterproductive. Unless we can predict his next move, there's a good chance he'll get the drop on us there. Rigor's place used to be Sutcliffe's, Leatt knows that ground better than we do. Here, we're protected and on our own turf. If anyone tries to come for us, we have the home field advantage."

"So we're supposed to forget about Leatt?" Tuck asked.

Like tennis, the spectators looked at the speaker then back at her. "No," she said, wetting her mouth with the coffee. "We can still keep an eye out and our ears open. But we have an imminent concern."

"Kahlil Samara," Zave said. "You fear him?"

Brodie leaned back and pulled something from his pocket. Tossing the item into the middle of the table, she had to cross the room to see what it was: her watch. "We heard it all."

Everyone was up to speed, so it saved her recounting the meeting. But she was concerned for her love. She gazed at him, hoping for a sign that he was okay after listening to Kahlil bring up his parents in the way he had. Brodie was blank, businesslike, just like the others, and he didn't relax his mask for a second.

Thad broke first and his laugh startled them all. "I particularly liked the part when you told Cuckoo not to spend too much time on her knees," Thad said, his lips twisted in a smile that wanted to be another laugh.

Tuck laughed and even Zave smiled. They'd heard more than just the Kahlil meeting. They'd heard her whole morning. Zara's mouth opened when she fixated on Brodie, but no sound came out. She should have turned the damn recording off before talking to Mischa. Zara hadn't been thinking straight because she was too busy cleaning up after Grant.

She couldn't stay shocked. She might not have realized that the men would hear her initial meeting with Cuckoo, but she couldn't take back what had been said, nor would she if Brodie demanded it. "I won't apologize to her," Zara said, starching herself with resolve. Showing Cuckoo that she was no doormat was important, and groveling would eliminate any possibility of equality between the women.

"Wouldn't ask you to," Brodie said. "You stood your ground."

He didn't smile, but his eyes warmed with pride. "Much as I'm not a fan of the woman, she's doing a job and if she knows her stuff, then she's in the right place," Zara said. "If we can trust her and I'm not so sure that we can. So we should be vigilant." Art didn't trust her and knew she got off on criminality, those facts were enough to keep Zara suspicious.

"So Cuckoo stays put," Tuck said. "What about Kahlil?"

Glad that Tuck was following and supporting her position, Zara was happy to return to business and happier still to stop talking about Cuckoo. "Whether or not he's telling the truth about what he knows," she said. "We have to take him seriously."

"Why?" Brodie asked.

More than a question, she read curiosity rather than

affront. He was testing her; this whole damn thing was a test. He wanted to know how she'd perceived Kahlil and how she'd played this forward.

"Because he's pissed that he got fired for failing to obtain Game Time. So pissed that he went out there and found someone else to bankroll him. Not only is he spreading the word that Game Time exists just by telling his new employer, but he's convinced the new employer of Game Time's value. Kahlil has proven that he's hungry and that he's bitter, that's not a good combination." As Grant had demonstrated.

"There's another hungry party," Zave said.

She opened her hand to him in agreement, then sat down, gulping from her mug as she did. "We have to nip this in the bud. If Kahlil has heard about Grant's death, then Sikorski has too. Both groups wanted Game Time to cause harm, and we shouldn't assume those plans have gone away just because they lost out on the deal."

"She's right," Zave said, and she was surprised that he was turning out to be her biggest ally when he'd never displayed much fondness for her before. She smiled, she'd thought the same thing about Art's opinion of her, and he ended up being her most vehement cheerleader.

Tuck linked his hands on the table. "We have to shut them down before they get off the ground. We have to know who Kahlil is working for now."

So much had fallen by the wayside since the loss of Art, and they were still trying to recover from that damage to their ranks. "He's got to be in town," Zara said.

"There's an email address for contact in the envelope with his offer," Brodie said. She hadn't been aware that he'd seen the envelope. "It's in the box you left in the kitchen."

That's right, the box of Grant's things. Brodie had read her mind because she hadn't given the envelope a second thought. "Can we trace the email?" she asked Tuck.

Tuck shrugged. "I can try if there's activity on it. But it's a free account. I'd guess he won't be accessing it frequently. But I can send out a—"

"What about facial recognition?" she asked, looking

to Brodie. "You said we have access to that, right?"

"You want to look for him in the city?" Tuck asked and stretched his arms toward her as he leaned forward. "We can do that. If he's walking the streets we should be able to find him."

Thinking ahead, she knew they couldn't descend on him in the street in the middle of the day. But if they could track his movements through cameras, they should be able to narrow down the areas he frequented. "We could use it to find out where he's staying, couldn't we?"

"Yes, we could," he said. But it was Brodie's say so that they needed because he was the man in charge and because she didn't want him to be disrespected, especially as it pertained to his own parents.

Making eye contact with Brodie, she hoped for some indication as to his thoughts. "Kahlil is a threat," she said, hoping her love would see how important it was to keep tabs on this man and his intentions. "We might be able to locate him and if he has contact with whoever he's working for—"

"I put bullets in people," Brodie said, showing little empathy for her position. "Don't expect me to get cozy with the guy because he's dangling a carrot."

"But you don't mind if the rest of us keep tabs on him, do you?" He shrugged. That was sort of permission, so she smiled, but it was brief. "We should keep an eye on CI as well, just in case."

"Just in case what?" Thad asked.

If it was up to her, they'd always have eyes on Cuckoo. Brodie had sort of taken care of that by putting her into a place that was monitored by cameras, but Cuckoo could do a lot of damage at CI whether she meant to or not. Beyond Cuckoo, CI held secrets of its own, a legacy left by Grant that could still bite them in the ass.

"Grant kept his work with Game Time a secret. But he did tell us that he'd started Winter Chill again. If those projects are still working—"

"We need to shut them down," Brodie said. At least he was quick to agree with her on one subject.

"You're the man in charge now," she said, lifting her

shoulders. "I brought Grant's computer and if we have to go into his apartment, I can access it. All of his holdings will be distributed as per his will. Julian said that the lawyers were still trying to locate his next of kin, that would be you. If no one has been bequeathed anything yet, that would suggest everything will come to you. Grant didn't have close friends or many girlfriends, none that he seemed to be serious about in any way."

"Always was a charmer," Brodie muttered and while she wouldn't say it, she thought to herself that was another thing the brothers had in common: their inability to connect and commit. They both had trust issues, though it seemed everybody did in today's world. She'd been with Brodie for months, and she had fought a lot of battles with him to get this close to his inner sanctum. Most women would have given up long ago.

She inhaled. "I know you weren't Grant's biggest fan, but we should deal with his apartment as soon as possible. We have to clear it out. We may turn up clues there that will help us figure out what he was intending to do with the new devices created by the recommissioned Winter Chill."

Brodie was unmoved by the notion of emptying Grant's apartment. It had to be done because they had no use for it, they'd have to sell the property. She'd spent time in that apartment as Grant's employee back when she'd trusted him. While remembering how he was at the end, she was struck by the evolution of Grant's character and how quickly the trigger event of losing Frank had affected his psyche.

His whole life had been dedicated to CI. Before his parents were killed, he was being groomed to take over. But he'd said it himself, when he lost all the people close to him, he realized he'd been living his life for them all these years. Now it felt like an excuse, and she couldn't feel sorry for him because there was no excusing his actions. They lost Art because of him and had almost lost each other.

Brodie was a brooder and that could be frustrating for an outsider to deal with, but at least he never hurt anyone when he was struggling with his emotional issues. Grant's go-to position was to take down as many people as he could as though that could somehow ease his pain.

The meeting went on, and she shook herself out of her reflection because now wasn't the time to let her thoughts meander. She didn't want to miss anything. "Grant said he planned to kill Sutcliffe and take over the cult," Brodie said. "So he must have had a plan of his own."

"Yeah," Tuck said. "Those folks were dedicated to Sutcliffe and wouldn't switch their allegiance to Saint without some serious persuading."

"You saw how it went down," Brodie said. "Maybe we're wrong, maybe Saint didn't think it through."

"You think he was nuts enough that he thought showing up was going to be enough?" Thad asked.

"I'd guess his plan relied on telling Sutcliffe's followers that he had the means to facilitate Sutcliffe's plans. That he could give them what they wanted," Brodie said.

"Not all of his people knew Sutcliffe's plans," Tuck said. "Strolling in and telling them that he planned to nuke the world wouldn't have seduced everyone."

"But it would get rid of those who weren't committed to that outcome," Zave said.

All of the men were right, the possibilities were endless, and with Grant in the ground, they had no way to interrogate him about his intentions.

"Even if we don't figure it out, we should kill Winter Chill," Zara said. "I don't trust what Cuckoo would do if she found out that this technology existed."

Tuck nodded. "It doesn't matter what Saint's intentions were. We need to eliminate the threat at the source."

"CI," Zara said. "Cuckoo will be snooping around as we speak."

Art didn't like Cuckoo, neither did Tuck, so she didn't mind reiterating her reservations about having the European at the helm. Cuckoo might know business, but Zara knew a scorned woman wanted leverage. So the last thing the Kindred should do is give it to Cuckoo. They had to decommission Winter Chill right under Cuckoo's nose, without revealing their actions to the woman Brodie had put in charge.

"It will take her time to settle in," Zave said. "We should take advantage of that window."

"Because once she's confident in her role and in the systems, it will be harder for us to get in," Tuck said. "I can limit what she can see, but if she figures out what we're doing, we might just make her curious."

"Mischa won't cause trouble," Brodie said, and he was so blank that Zara struggled to read if he was serious or how he could be so sure.

Brodie had been intimate with the woman and so knew her better than the others in the room. Cuckoo hadn't made a great impression on her, but Mischa's attitude toward her may have been motivated by sour grapes. Zara had the man Cuckoo had once loved. Either Cuckoo wasn't as despicable as Zara believed her to be or Brodie was confident in his ability to control her.

Asking more questions in this environment, in front of their audience, wasn't appropriate, this was a business meeting. Trusting Brodie, and their love, meant although she was curious, she had no real reason to question his assertion.

While she was examining her man, Thad piped up. "What is your plan for Cormack Industries?" Thad asked Brodie. Zara was glad that she wasn't the sole person at the table invested in that answer. "What's your plan long term? You can't mean to keep Cuckoo there forever. She has her own company to run."

And the last thing Zara wanted was Cuckoo in their lives full-time. Brodie's answer didn't assuage those concerns. "Mischa gave up full time responsibility at her father's firm a couple of years ago. She flips around different boards, different companies, different countries," Brodie said. "She doesn't have a great professional attention span."

Zara could hope that meant Cuckoo would eventually get bored at CI. But for the woman to drop everything and run at Brodie's command, it suggested she was interested in more than just the McCormack firm.

"Why did you bring her into CI then?" Thad asked, and she appreciated that he probed for the answers she wanted but couldn't request without coming across as a jealous girlfriend.

"Because she's the only person I know who has the experience needed to run a multinational like CI. And she has the reputation to support her being given the position," Brodie said. Forcing Brodie into a corner was more likely to get a person killed than satisfied. That he gave these answers without appearing pissed made Zara think he'd anticipated the questions and maybe even rehearsed the answers in his head. "I just needed it off our plates and so I put it on hers."

The doctor wasn't done and started to speculate. "You could absorb it into Knight Corp," Thad said, twisting to Zave, who was at his side. "You could take over."

Tuck laughed. "When was the last time you set foot in the Knight building?" Tuck asked Zave, though Zara didn't know what Knight Corp was. "Have you been there in the last ten years?" Zave just shrugged. "It's running on its own steam and that steam will run out. You don't get the rep of being the ghost director by showing up for work every day."

"What's Knight Corp?" Zara asked.

"Zave's company," Brodie said. "He started it when he was a kid. He made his first million before he was sixteen."

That was impressive and as her brows rose, she watched Zave's annoyance grow. "It keeps us in chopper fuel," Zave grumbled, and for the first time she saw him get riled, though he tried to conceal his annoyance behind an angry glare and a clenched jaw. "I don't want CI. I don't even want KC."

"Which I knew," Brodie said, giving a logical explanation for why he hadn't done what Thad suggested. "CI can wait, let's just forget about that and focus on finding Kahlil and shutting down Game Time."

The rest of the group were happy to move on; they'd gotten all the answers they would get from Brodie today. "I'll set the system to monitor his email and search facial recognition until we get a hit," Tuck said.

"Zara and I can go through the paperwork that's upstairs," Thad said.

She appreciated the doctor's support, and grunt work was all she was good for given their current situation. "I'll take his computer," Zave said. "When you're done, Swift, we'll go hunting."

"Sounds good," Tuck said and everyone began to rise.

The group began to disband and she crossed to intercept Brodie. "What are you going to do?"

"Clean the rifles," he said, brushing his thumb across her chin. "Always gets me in the mood for a fight."

NINE

THAD WAS A LOT of fun. Working with someone who made jokes and was easy about showing his emotions was refreshing in comparison to what she'd been surrounded with of late. She and her workmate spread out in the dining room they'd once all eaten in to go through all of the files from Grant's office.

Every once in a while, Tuck came in with a pile of printouts from the laptop and added them to their in-tray. As he and Zave pulled more data from Grant's computer they brought it up for a second look, since the two techies were tasked with retrieving, not analyzing, the data.

"You've held up well, given all that's happened since you joined the Kindred," Thad said, putting a file into the done pile.

"It's been tough," she said, still reading. "You and Zave always show up right on time."

"Brodie's the only one Zave trusts," Thad said, picking up another pile of papers to pull them over to him.

Thad was always so chipper, but she saw the flicker of disappointment he tried to hide by turning his head down. She could only imagine the kind of missions the cousins had been on together and how each one would have affected familial politics.

"Zave trusts you," she said, feeling the need to be discreet about her reassurance. "You're almost always together."

The length of time they spent together and the proximity of their homes made her think the men had made a conscious decision to be close to each other. It had always perplexed her how they enjoyed each other so much because their personalities were polar opposites. She'd never inquired about the details of their relationship with Brodie. Other things always came up before they had the time to delve too deep into the particulars of his family.

Just as always happened, something got in the way of her gleaning more from the doctor. Tuck came in, and she expected more documents for them to trawl through. Except, this time when he got to the table, he had no papers. Propping both arms on the back of the black scroll top chair, Tuck bent to rest his forehead on them for a second.

Tuck was a go-with-the-flow type of guy, who rarely got ruffled. Either he was just tired or they'd found something serious enough to affect the aloof hacker and that put her on alert.

"What's wrong?" she asked.

He looked up. "We got a hit."

"That's great," she said, maintaining her restraint until she found out why he seemed so conflicted. "Was it the email or did you find him? You can't have located all Winter Chill locations yet, can you?"

"I'm not talking about Saint's computer. I'm talking about the facial rec. It's Kahlil," Tuck said. "We've got him coming out of CI."

Her request for the search had proved fruitful, but tracking down Kahlil at the company responsible for Game Time was unexpected, and she understood Tuck's reticence. "It's after nine at night," she said. Confusion merged with concern when she recalled Grant's after-hours meeting with Kahlil. Leaving her seat, she snatched her purse from the floor. "I have to get over there."

"Whoa! Whoa," Tuck said, catching her shoulders when she tried to hightail it past him. "CI isn't your racket anymore. What are you gonna do after you rock up there?"

"I…" He might be right, but that didn't mean that she should sit here and let Kahlil strike up a relationship with Cuckoo, who until now hadn't known anything about Game Time.

"Have another bitch off with the new boss?" Tuck asked. "She's not gonna tell you what Kahlil said."

There was still a chance that the two hadn't met. Kahlil could've shown up looking for her and left when he was told she wasn't there. If he'd been told she no longer worked there, then he may have spoken to Cuckoo instead and that could lead to any number of potentially catastrophic outcomes. They couldn't have Cuckoo knowing about Game Time or searching for Winter Chill; the Italian couldn't track it down before they did. The Kindred had to stay ahead, knowledge being their only advantage.

Kahlil and Cuckoo could've been working together all along. If they had been then the Kindred had played into their hands. "If she's working with him then we gave them everything they needed when we anointed her queen at CI. The game's already over."

Zara couldn't argue the notion that she was the best person to get answers from Cuckoo, not after their showdown in Grant's office. The need for debate vanished when Brodie came into the dining room. He noticed that she wasn't working and was in the clutches of his best friend while his cousin observed.

His scrutiny became a scowl. "What?" Brodie asked, focused on Tuck's hand on her shoulder.

"What's pissing you off, beau? That Tuck might be hurting me or that he might be making a move?"

Tuck released her and retreated with his hands up. For all the times Tuck had bailed her out and saved her from danger, she hadn't broached the topic of his personal life with him. Through Brodie, Zara knew that Tuck had broken up with the woman he loved after Art's death. Tuck would never hurt her or seduce her, and she knew Brodie knew that. His preoccupation was irrational and primal. He just didn't like anyone getting too close to her.

"I'm pissed that there's panic on your face," he said, closing in. "What's going on?"

"Kahlil just left CI," she said. "He has to be working with Cuckoo. You've put her in the perfect place to control Winter Chill. We have to go in there and stop—"

This time, Brodie was the one to get in her way when she set the exit in her sights. "You're not going anywhere," he said, seizing her neck and pulling her back.

"But someone has to—"

He raised his voice. "You remember what happened the last time you busted up one of Kahlil's late night meetings in that place?"

His features set to stone when she didn't shrink. "You kissed me."

That wasn't what he was getting at, but that didn't prevent his eyes from falling to her mouth. It was true that the night she'd first heard of Kahlil ended with Brodie kissing her for the first time. But he was referring to her being accosted by Kahlil's men in the parking garage when he'd had to swoop in and save her ass.

Reminding her of the danger Kahlil and his people could pose was supposed to scare her into staying here at the manor where she was safe. Being facetious soured Brodie's already sensitive mood.

"That's not what I fucking meant," he growled.

"But you did, do you remember?" she said, looping her arms around him to bunch her fists in his shirt at his back. Of course he did, but his scowl didn't fade. "With you at my back, I'm invincible."

Grabbing her wrists, he pulled her arms away and walked her backward until she pressed into the table. "And in this house, you're untouchable. You're safest here, so this is where you'll stay." He used to tell her that the safest place was on her back and under him, but flirting with him now wouldn't gain her any brownie points or result in mutual orgasms, not when there was so much work to be done. He let her go and backed away. "Stay with Tuck," Brodie said to her. "Wait until you hear from me."

The pals exchanged one of their secret looks, and Brodie sprinted from the room. Tuck was an ally, but his loyalty to Brodie trumped his loyalty to her. If Brodie gave him an order then he was going to follow it. She needed her own secret ally and preferably one without a penis.

****

WHEN SHE NEEDED a female perspective, there was only one woman she trusted: Bess, Art's sister, Thad's mom. Bess knew about the Kindred, although she didn't travel with them and so probably didn't know too many of the gorier details.

Brodie was still out. Tuck and Thad were still working on their tasks, but Zara had taken a break and stolen a few moments of privacy to come down to the security room and talk to Bess via secure video link.

Zara had relayed what was distracting her to the patient real-time image being beamed from the other side of the country while hoping that Bess would support her point of view. As ever, Bess smiled and listened, but she hadn't been as empathetic as Zara might have liked her to be.

"So I'm just supposed to sit here and pretend it's okay that he's going to confront his ex?" Zara asked after hearing Bess' perspective. "I know what he's like when his temper heats up."

The others were focused enough on their research that Zara was confident they wouldn't be interrupted, at least until there was something significant to report. During Brodie's dark period of grief, Zara had spent a lot of time talking to and consoling Aunt Bess, who lived most of her life in Zave's island home.

Bess was calm and warm. Zara could tell she was used to staying neutral. Offering an ear to whichever member of the Kindred needed to vent, Bess was the non-judgmental matriarch who had no interest in vying for a top spot. She had the respect of all of the men and knew enough that no one had to watch what they said around her. On some nights, sitting in the security room talking to Bess was like sitting in the confessional.

"You trust him and he is protecting you," Bess said, just the sound of her mothering voice was soothing. "I know it's hard, but you've been through plenty together. He loves you. You don't think he's going to betray you and be intimate with her."

It had been a long time since she'd had a mother figure in her life. Even when her mother was still alive, she'd been sick so often that long, heartfelt conversations were rare. Once she'd begun to bond with Bess, after Art's death, Zara had latched onto Bess' encouragement and acceptance. "No," Zara said, huffing and dropping her chin into her hand. "But I don't trust her, what if she hurts him? Or manipulates him into doing something we're all going to regret?"

"Brodie isn't a man who has regrets, you know that. You said he took Zave with him, they'll keep each other safe. It's priority one."

Zara knew Brodie didn't mention regrets. But he'd replayed that day in the Atlas warehouse through his mind's eye on a loop, thinking of ways he could have gotten them all out of there alive. Guilt was a large part of his struggle to come to terms with losing Art.

Bess was right that watching each other's backs was a priority, but Zave wasn't a marksman and hadn't contributed much in terms of physical force to their previous missions. She didn't know how he'd hold up in a fight or how far he'd be willing to go. Brodie was happy to beat the crap out of men who deserved it, and he'd have no hesitation about using fatal force if he needed to. Tuck had once told her that no one was full Kindred until they'd killed. Somehow, Zave didn't seem like the sort to get his hands dirty, not out of any righteousness, just because it would be inconvenient and taxing.

Zara wasn't as worried about their relationship as she was frustrated by how quickly Brodie had benched her. "I don't like it when he treats me with kid gloves."

"He wants to protect the woman he loves. You can't fault him for that. And you've abandoned him twice in the last month, so you can't blame him for wanting to keep you at home either."

Like she was some sort of disobedient filly, Zara sighed and looked into Bess' soft face with its generous laughter lines and crow's feet. She wasn't as keen as Art or as reserved as the younger generation. Knowing Bess helped her to understand where Thad got his easy smile and positive attitude.

Brodie had done enough chasing. It made sense that he didn't want to do any more. "I guess not."

"You know that if you need to get away, you can come and visit us here. We'd love to have you for as long as you want to stay."

"Thank you, that's kind of you." It was, but a vacation wasn't much of a priority.

"Where is that spirit?" Bess asked, adding some pep to her voice. "My brother told me you weren't scared of anything."

"I'm not scared."

"Of losing Brodie?"

She conceded that with a nod of her brows as her head tilted. Identifying her grievances was the only way to address them. "It's embarrassing," Zara said. "I'm not worried about losing our relationship. But I guess that what Cuckoo said is still bugging me. She was right, when Brodie was in a pinch, he called her."

"And that insulted you?"

"He didn't consider letting me deal with Cuckoo and Kahlil tonight. How can I be a vital part of the Kindred if Brodie can't rely on me?"

"You kept him alive for three months, he knows you're capable."

"Of making soup and picking up after him?" she asked. "I'm not his mother."

"So this is about sex?"

Growling in frustration, she pushed the chair back into a brief recline and ran her hands into her hair. "It's not about sex. We have plenty of sex."

"You don't know what to think, do you, dearie?" Bess asked. Sorrow took her over, and Zara leaned forward again, bending to rest her head on her arms when she crossed them on the desk.

"He's been gone for hours," Zara said.

Worry for Brodie made her itchy, it made her fidget and over think. She just needed him back with her to give her a grounding. She wouldn't be able to rest until he was with her. He'd be pissed at her for checking up on him, but she was pissed at him for dismissing her, so as far as Zara was concerned, after this, they'd be even.

"Don't get yourself into a tizzy," Bess said.

Zara turned her head to glance at Bess' image and read the time in the corner. "It's after midnight. Hold on."

Shoving herself along the desk in the wheeled chair, she tapped the farthest keyboard to bring the CI cameras up. She didn't get much from them. There was no direct video link inside the building, though she had various external views. Glancing up at the monitor bank, she watched one screen change, but instead of bringing up a picture, it was a blank, black space.

Intrigued, she frowned. "Hmm," Zara hummed.

Removing the CI image from the display, she tried to locate the hidden embedded code on the faulty black screen to bring the feed onto the monitor in front of her.

"What is it?" Bess asked. The video link was still active on the first screen while Zara worked on the third of the trio of screens at the security workstation.

"One of the cameras is out," Zara muttered.

"Someone will be getting their ass handed to them," Bess said on a laugh. "Who's responsibility was the check this morning?"

They'd been drinking last night, so it was possible that whoever it was had been too hung over to do it properly. Zara thought for a moment, and she figured it out just as she input the embedded code and the data log popped up. Marrying all of the information together, she sat up straight, slowly. Bess had to see something in her expression because she became serious.

"What is it? Zara? What is it?"

"Brodie was on security check this morning," she

whispered.

"It's not like him to be absent-minded."

"No, it's not," Zara said.

"Which camera is faulty?"

Distant, she tried to temper her distress. "It's not faulty," she said. "The data log shows it was manually overridden and disabled from here."

"I've never known any of the boys to do that. The cameras are placed where they are because the locations they monitor are vital."

"I know," Zara said, unable to find her volume switch.

"So, what is that camera watching?"

"My apartment."

Bess didn't have anything to say to that and neither did Zara. Why would Brodie want his ex to have privacy that he wasn't interested in his current girlfriend having? He didn't apologize for monitoring her apartment when it was Zara's permanent residence.

"I'm sure he has his reasons for—" Blinking her disbelieving eyes at Bess, Zara quieted the sheepish woman. "What are you going to do?"

She wanted to go over to her apartment and find out if the reason Brodie had been so long with Cuckoo was because he'd taken her home. But a dramatic confrontation would just embarrass them all. Zara had to trust her boyfriend. She was too aware of his commitment to the mission and to the Kindred to doubt his professional loyalty. If Raven had to get close to Cuckoo under false pretenses of romantic interest then Zara might have to just live with that.

He'd done it to her, that was how they'd become involved in the first place. The process worked, and he'd been honest about sleeping with women for information in the past. But if that was what he was doing, she'd have to lay ground rules, the first of which being he had to be honest with her about it.

When the door opened, she spun in the chair to see who was coming in, hoping it was Brodie returning to base. It wasn't. Tuck was storming toward the security desk so fast that she leaped out of the seat, knowing he'd need it.

With a blank, intent stare, he swung himself into the seat and began to type faster than she'd seen a person type. "What is it?" she asked, putting a hand on the back of his chair to look at the screen just in front of the keyboard, but he didn't answer her. He just kept on typing.

She glanced at Bess, who was frowning. "I'll let you get back to work," Bess said and blew her a kiss.

"Take care," Zara said, managing a smile before the woman left the screen.

Without slowing in what he was doing, Tuck reached to the keyboard on the right and tapped the code to kill the audio feed she and Bess had been using. "We have something," he said to her after a few more swipes.

"Is it Brodie?" she asked, panicked that something could have gone wrong while he was away from the manor.

"Nope," Tuck said and reached to the left keyboard to bring up a still on the monitor in front of it.

She crept around him while he returned to his typing and crouched until the picture was at her eye level. It was Kahlil, going into some building she didn't recognize. "You found him," she murmured.

"Yep."

Tuck was a man of few words when he was intent, so she left him to his work and speculated. The picture was dark, but it was nighttime. She couldn't pick out many specifics, and it was just lucky that Kahlil had looked over his shoulder at the right moment to be picked up on the traffic cam.

"Fuck, yeah," Tuck said, pleased with something. He banged his hands on the desk then pushed the chair away from the desk to get up.

"Where are you going?" she asked, blocking his route. He searched her expression like he'd forgotten what a human being looked like. He spent so much time with computers, she wouldn't be surprised if he did forget sometimes. "Where is he? Where's Kahlil?"

Tuck turned to point at the picture he'd left on the screen. "That's an apartment block in a shitty part of town. But there's a hotel opposite one side, it's a crappy place that rents rooms by the hour, you know? But I'm gonna check it out. If Kahlil is staying in that block, we might get eyes on him, and if we can surveil his movements…"

"We might see who he's working with," she said and smiled. "I'm coming with you."

His eyes widened a fraction. "No, you're not," he said.

"Brodie told me to stay with you, and it's dangerous out there. You shouldn't go alone."

"Kahlil has seen you. He'd be able to ID you."

"Not if I dress right and we go into that hotel together. You'll raise fewer eyebrows if you walk in with a hooker, and I'm the only woman on the team."

His jaw clenched and he said nothing, he just stood there, static, as though he was processing potential scenarios. After about a minute, she started to get uncomfortable but was impressed by just how thoroughly he switched off.

"You've got five minutes to get changed. Dress—"

"Slutty, I know," she said, squeezing his arms then whirling around to rush upstairs to change.

Having something to do helped keep her mind away from Brodie and what he was doing. Zave was with him, and Bess was right, the men would look after each other. But that didn't explain Brodie handing over her apartment then shutting down the surveillance on it. Personal issues would have to wait because she had Kindred business to take care of, and she was glad of the distraction. Being patient wasn't her forte.

TEN

"WANT ME TO JUMP on the bed?" she asked, and Tuck took his eye from the scope to glance at her.

"I don't think anyone gives a shit what we do," he said and went back to his scope. "But knock yourself out."

They'd rented a room in the seedy hotel for the night instead of the hour. From the way the guy at the reception desk window looked at her, she was confident he bought that she was a streetwalker. Tuck had left his equipment on the rear fire escape and retrieved it before they went into the room. It was a dark, dirty space with little more than four walls, a bed, and a desk. There wasn't even a television or a lamp.

The double bed had a wooden headboard that was screwed to the wall and a threadbare comforter on it. On a positive note, the sheets were clean, at least to the naked eye. Tuck had been doing his best to examine the block opposite through their grime-covered window, trying to figure out where Kahlil was residing. He'd brought a laptop that somehow patched into the city cameras, and he kept a constant eye on the program it was running. As far as his system knew, Kahlil hadn't left that building.

At that moment, Tuck was sitting on the wooden chair that had been at the desk, peering through his fancy black telescope. Hunkering down when he raised the angle, he examined every window of the cheap apartment building the system had caught Kahlil going into.

"Shit," he muttered, and she shifted to the edge of the bed behind him where she'd been seated while he worked.

"What?"

He inhaled and leaned back, leaving the scope pointing upward. "You need a new client."

"Why?" she asked.

When she glanced at the window, she didn't see any movement or figures, but she was farther away and had a lesser view from her angle. Her job was to provide cover that let Tuck enter and transact like he was any other john using the premises to facilitate his need of amusement. So far, she'd been doing her best not to make a nuisance of herself. Now that he'd located their target, they needed to strategize.

"He's in there, but he's on an upper floor. One down we could've lived with, but the angle's too sharp for us to see anything from here. He just came to the window and left again. He's up there. We need a room on the floor above this one, one unit right."

She understood. "Okay, Wren's still at the manor. We can call him, and I'll meet him on a street corner, make it look good."

Taking his eye to the scope, Tuck adjusted something and his cellphone began to ring on the desk. Moving back just a couple of inches, he glanced down at it. "I think it's for you."

Sliding off the bed, she reached forward to grab it from Tuck. All the screen said was 'unknown' but she'd had calls from that guy before. "Hello," she said, ensuring to sound upbeat.

"Now you've gone and run off with another man," Brodie's growling voice wasn't amused, but she laughed.

"That's funny 'cause it's kind of true," she said and sat down on the floor to look up at Tuck. "This loser can't afford another hour. I need you to meet me. Bring your wallet."

"Tell him to ask for room thirteen," Tuck muttered.

Thirteen, ironic she thought, but it wouldn't be an unlucky number for them. The Kindred worked best when they were focused on a common goal, and she was finding her fire again. Brodie didn't argue when she gave him the address or explained the setup. Zave had probably found the data that had brought her and Tuck here anyway, so Brodie would understand what was going on.

Brodie wouldn't take long to get here, this was where the mission was centered, and there was a chance of action, which was her love's specialty. There was no way he'd want to miss out on observing Kahlil, and that she was present for him to chastise was another bonus to hurry him along.

***

SHE WAITED IN the mouth of the blackened alley for her love to come into view. He hadn't asked her many questions. He listened to her spiel and had spoken to Tuck for a minute before they hung up. She'd waited with Tuck as long as she could before leaving to stand in an alley just around the corner from the hotel.

Kahlil wouldn't be able to see her from here even if he looked out his window. But her revealing apparel and thigh high boots weren't standard CI uniform. So even if, by some miracle, he did happen to see her, he would never recognize her.

Thick red lipstick stained her lips, and her hair was backcombed into a voluminous style that would take her an hour to calm when they got home. Then again, if this was Kahlil's safe house, they might be spending a lot of time here until they got what they needed. Gaining the upper hand would rely on them finding something out that Kahlil didn't want them to know.

Brodie could arrive at any minute, sooner would be better for her. She didn't like being on the street alone in this garb. Her shoulder maintained contact with the alley wall as she twisted to fall against it. This wasn't a great neighborhood, but she had her gun in her purse, as she always did. With a panic button on her phone too, there wasn't anything to worry about. If something happened to her, Tuck could be downstairs and at her location in less than a minute.

A laugh deep in the alley made her push away from the wall and straighten up. That wasn't Brodie, no way, but there was something familiar about the sinister tone of that satisfied sound.

"You have come a long, long way, Miss Bandini."

"Fuck," she exhaled and folded her arms just as his face was lit by the light coming from the street. It cut a harsh diagonal across his face at almost the same angle as the gnarly scar on his neck. "Griffin Caine."

"At your service," he said, dipping his head in a false sign of civility.

If she took that statement as truth, she'd tell him to go and jump in the Atlantic, preferably from a ship that was a thousand miles offshore. His intention wasn't to serve her, he had his own agenda and always had a reason for popping up when he did. "What the fuck are you doing here?"

"You know me," he said. "I like to pop up at inconvenient moments, when you're at your weakest."

When he took another step toward her, she opened her arms to hold up her hands, indicating to him that she wanted him to stop. "Don't you come near me."

"Oh, you're not afraid of little me, are you?"

There was nothing little about the tall, muscular man with the blue eyes so cold they could turn the warmest heart to stone. "The last time we met, you held me at gun point."

"I don't have a weapon," he said and showed her his hands, turning them front to back.

"Then you've made a major mistake because Raven is on his way here; he'll be here any second." Just because Caine wasn't holding a weapon in his hand didn't mean he wasn't carrying one somewhere on his person. She wouldn't relax based upon his unreliable word.

"A reunion. Excellent."

It couldn't bode well that Caine was being so jovial tonight. "We left you in Sutcliffe's place with Leatt, how did you get out of there? Was it you? Were you the one working with him?"

"No," he laughed.

It amazed her how he could be casual, yet so terrifying at the same time. She was scared of him because he was the type of loose cannon that could explode at any second, and she didn't want to be in his path when he did. But she wasn't scared enough to pull her gun, because they'd met several times and he could have killed her on any of those occasions. Some part of him didn't want her dead, and he'd have his own, probably demented, reasons for that.

Using the chance he presented by showing up, she wanted to know what he knew. "Who was? Do you know that?"

"I do now," Caine said, strolling closer. Zara kept herself tense but wouldn't weep or run. Caine was a sadist; he just exuded that kind of psychopathy. A doctor didn't need to diagnose his evil. It shimmered around him, warning the world that he was the devil's blood relation.

"Who?"

He stopped and leaned back as he put his hands in his pockets and tipped his head back a few inches. "You think I'll tell you just like that?"

"Maybe." If it caused aggravation for the Kindred, he would. Sometimes Caine was funny, sometimes he was threatening. The lone certainty was that no one could predict his next move.

"Tell you what, I'll be fair. If you get down on those sexy knees, wrap those shiny red lips around my cock, and give your boyfriend a real show to walk in on, then I'll tell you."

It was her turn to laugh. If Brodie walked into this alley and saw that, Caine's life would be over before either of them knew he was there. "You think I'm that desperate to know? The only thing that would get you is suicide by Raven."

He began moving again and got closer than she'd like him to, but he kept on coming until he was in her personal space. "I'd prefer it by Swallow," he murmured.

Intimidation was his dominant field, and he knew how to exploit any situation. She was dressed like a whore and so he treated her like one. Sex wasn't something he'd requested from her before. He took the setup and used it to his advantage, probably banking that she would feel uncomfortable in her appearance, so he promoted her self-consciousness to increase her discomfort.

She wouldn't give him the satisfaction. "What do you want, Caine?" she asked, matching his assured stare with her own. "You pop up when it's inconvenient, but you also pop up when you want something. What is it this time?"

"Just wanted to let you know I was around. I'm sure you were worried about me."

"Beside myself," she said, but she hadn't given him a second thought after leaving him in Sutcliffe's place with Leatt.

"And I wanted to tell you that…" She'd never seen him hesitate, but he did it now. For half a beat, there was something human in the way he averted his eyes.

"Tell me what?" she asked and took a hand to his elbow, which snapped him out of whatever held him back.

Ripping his arm away, he retreated. "You'll never match up to her in his eyes," he said and smiled just before he stepped into the shadow that had delivered him. "Just like I could never match up to him."

Searching for meaning in what he said, it took her a few seconds to put the pieces together, and when she looked up, she couldn't see any flicker of movement. Cuckoo. Art had told her that Caine's feud with Raven was rooted in a situation involving a woman. Caine wanted her, but she didn't want him. Cuckoo.

The woman, who Brodie had just brought into their lives, was the whole reason that these men hated each other. If there was ever a time for Caine to snap, this was it. Brodie was happy with a new woman but had still managed to get the old girlfriend to jump on his command—the old girlfriend Caine no doubt still pined for.

The situation was already complicated enough, but Caine was a grenade with its pin pulled. He had to know that

Cuckoo was back in their lives and his warning was either in sympathy or in hate. Either way, another explosive variable had just been added to this mission's unbalanced equation.

ELEVEN

"BABY?"

Spinning around, Zara saw Brodie at the top of the alley in the same spot she'd been waiting for him before Caine had drawn her deeper into the darkness.

Her ears were ringing with the shock of Caine's revelation that had blasted her like roving shrapnel. "You looking for a date?" she asked. The tease she'd meant to accompany those words was absent.

Brodie noticed her stupor, but she couldn't shake it. "What is it?" he asked, furrowing his brow. "You sound like you've seen a ghost."

"Not my ghost, yours," she said. The ghost of Brodie's Christmas past. If Caine's admission was meant to throw up more questions, he'd succeeded. Instead of going on the offensive out here in the open where Caine could still be watching, Zara chose to focus on the chore Brodie had been doing before this new need arose. "Are they in league?"

The answer to this question was important. Learning whether or not Kahlil and Cuckoo were in cahoots would affect their strategy going forward.

"No," he said. "Talking can come after we get off the

street."

If he was a john, they wouldn't chitchat, he'd proposition, there would be a price, and then they'd go somewhere private. "Come on. I know somewhere we can go."

Getting cozy with her lover wasn't as appealing as it usually was, not while she was still processing the new information Caine had delivered. But for display purposes, she let Brodie loll his arm around her and curled her fingers around his wrist while pasting a smile on her face. That he walked on the curbside gave her protection from the building opposite when they turned the corner. As they ambled into the hotel, she laughed and tipped her head back so onlookers would believe she was trying to tempt her client.

Checking in with Brodie was different to checking in with Tuck. For one thing, Brodie never tried to smile, and he grew rigid when the guy on the other side of the plastic window checked her out again. The proprietor winked to indicate that he recognized her, but he didn't ask any questions. Her second client of the night might not appreciate that her first customer was still in occupancy upstairs. The hotel owner wouldn't mention that because as long as she brought clients here to ply her trade, his pockets were being lined. And in a place like this, he was probably used to all sorts of shenanigans.

Room thirteen was more expensive, apparently it had its own bathroom and a couch. It was the highest caliber of room this dump had, though the owner at the desk didn't put it like that. Zara kept up the pretense of whispering flirtatiously as they traversed the stairs and the hallway to the room that Brodie had requested. But as soon as they got inside, she dropped the act and put some distance between their bodies.

The room was indeed bigger but not by a whole lot. The bathroom was to the left of the narrow space they entered. Leaving the confined entryway, the accommodation opened out with the bed to the left and the couch to the right on the same wall as the desk and chair that were perpendicular to the long narrow window opposite where she was standing now. The couch was covered in stains that made her bypass it and head for the bed, choosing that as the safer bet.

"I'll text Tuck to tell him we're here," Brodie said, taking his phone from his jacket pocket. "He'll pack up the gear downstairs and bring it up. After that, I'll get Zave to come get you and take you home."

"I'm not going," she said, sitting on the end of the bed to unzip her boots.

"You're not—"

"We have to talk," she said. She hadn't gotten as far as taking her boots off her feet, though she'd unzipped them both. Leaning back on her hands, Zara looked up at him. "Us this time."

"Talk about what?"

He wasn't that dumb and try as he might to clear his expression of guilt, she was sure that she read it on his face. Until now, she'd trusted that he had his reasons for acting shady about Cuckoo, but it turned out she had a limit to how much freedom she would give him when it came to keeping secrets from her and Caine had just taken her to it.

"I can't cry on your shoulder about being useless to the Kindred because I miss all the pertinent signs and then ignore them when I do recognize them just because you're the guilty one," she said.

Affront smacked him. "Guilty? What the fuck?"

Kicking off her boots, she clambered to her knees on the end of the bed because it gave her more height than standing on the floor would. "Why did you bring her in to take over at CI? You thought she was great at business, fine, I didn't like it, but it made sense. But that doesn't explain why you turned off the camera in my apartment after telling me you put her there to keep an eye on her."

He didn't need to hear a name to know whom Zara was talking about. "I did, we had the hardware set up—"

"You turned it off," she said, demanding the truth while she still held onto the trust he'd worked so hard to gain from her.

"What makes you think I turned it off?"

"I was talking to Bess, one of the screens came up

blank. I thought it was broken so I checked it out. The data log shows it's not broken, it's off, and you were the one to turn it off." His hands went to the back of his head, and she could tell he was cursing the day she was taught how to use the manor security system. "Why would you do that unless you wanted to…" She couldn't bring herself to make the accusation.

"Unless I wanted to what?" he barked, storming to the end of the bed and grabbing her shoulders to haul her to the absolute edge. "Don't stop there, lay it out for me. What do you think I've got cooking? You think I'm screwing around on you?"

"Are you?" she asked, sorry that Caine had managed to get in her head.

Too many things were stacking up that suggested she should be suspicious. Maybe she wasn't great at the mission stuff, but as a woman, she could tell when her boyfriend was hiding something from her.

He gritted his teeth behind the pinch of his narrow lips. Praying he'd say something to alleviate her worries that could explain the inconsistencies, her heart bounced from her throat to her gut, but she made herself seal her lips and wait.

Brodie tightened his grip on her shoulders until she winced at the pain of his power. Opening her lips to release the gasp of pain, she tried to twist herself out of his hands, but he was too strong. With a brutal thrust, he threw her body away from his, tossing her so far that she landed on the pillows.

Striding away from the bed, he went to the window. "If that's what you think then yeah, I am," he said.

Grabbing the chair from the desk, he turned it around to straddle it, leaning on the back so he could look out the window across to Kahlil's location.

Releasing the tension in her body, her arms fell and she straightened her legs. That didn't sound right. Brodie's sulk was infuriating and it solved nothing. Caine might not have her best interests at heart, but he'd posed a possibility she couldn't ignore. She had every right to question her love on it.

If something else was going on here, she deserved to know. The Kindred deserved to know. He had enough integrity that if he wanted to end his relationship with her Brodie would have revoked her clearance for the manor and told her to clear out. He wouldn't have given her the floor to direct their latest mission.

Except Brodie hadn't been forthcoming about why he'd involved Cuckoo in their lives and this latest development was too significant for her to allow him to continue being evasive.

Setting him in her sights, she pulled her legs up to cross them as she took her weight off the headboard. "You turn around and look me in the eye when you lie to me," she asserted and awaited his next move.

Slowly, he turned until only one of his forearms was left on the chair back. "What makes you think I'm lying?"

Without expression or nuance, she matched his intensity. "I'm pretty much all the woman you can handle, Rave," she said. "I keep you plenty busy." His brow rose before he returned his stare to the window. "She was the woman, the one who got between you and Caine."

"Don't know what you're talking about," he mumbled.

"Art told me there was a woman…" Zara braced for his reaction to the next truth. "Caine told me it was her."

Brodie had to be wondering if there was any person who didn't reveal the secrets of his past to her, but he didn't react as strongly as she'd anticipated. "He tell you that in front of Saint or when he had the gun on you?" he muttered like he didn't care which of the answers were correct.

"No," she said, because neither of them was true and she wouldn't hide her encounter with his foe. "Five minutes ago in the alley downstairs."

This time when he turned to glimpse her, he wasn't passive or casual and despite her heart being on overdrive again, she didn't blink. "Motherfuck," he grumbled. In one fluid motion, he stood up, hooked the back of the chair in one hand, and spun to hurl it across the room into the opposite wall where it splintered in a thunderous crash before its pieces scattered on the floor. "Motherfuck!"

"Calm down," she said, soothing with open hands as she climbed onto her knees. "Nothing happened."

"Nothing?" Flying at the bed, he grabbed her to haul her off and up against him. "We didn't even know if the motherfucker was still alive. Now we know he's alive and tailing you again!"

"Rather me than you," she said.

She didn't want Caine around to rile her lover because that was what he wanted, and he was managing to do it by using her as the conduit. Questioning whether she should have confessed, Zara knew she could only be honest. She couldn't ask for it and not return it.

"Where the fuck you come up with that logic?" he asked, shaking her. "If he's on you, then you're in danger. And when you're in danger and I'm not there…"

"What?" she asked. His long fingers dug into her upper arms, and he held her so close and so high that her forearms were squashed between their two bodies. Opening her hands, she stretched her fingers to stroke what she could reach of his jaw. "It pisses you off?" That much was obvious from the shattered furniture.

For the longest time, he searched her, but she didn't know what to give him, didn't know what would relieve his torture.

He came lower. "I'm doing this because of him," he hissed. "I called her in to take over at CI because of him."

"I don't understand."

He exhaled. "I'm sick of him on my tail, on your tail. Before you, it didn't matter, he was just a bug on the windshield that I could flick off if he got too annoying. But he's a sick fuck, baby, and as long as he's around, I can't let you out of my sight. I've been stupid to think I could, and tonight proved that."

There was pain in his words, though it was difficult to decipher from the anger that crackled in them. "We didn't know if he was alive, just like you said. We could never have predicted—"

"The guy has more lives than a cat. We didn't have

confirmation, but I was sure he was still fucking out there, waiting to cause shit. I can't have that. I can't have him on our backs. It puts you in danger. I wanted it done, over. Meesh is a surefire way to force his hand."

"You're using Cuckoo to draw him out?"

"The fucker doesn't come for me like a man, he's resorted to stalking my woman because he knows you're the way to get to me. All I need is ten seconds with eyes on. One if I have my weapon in my hand."

"So, the next time I see him, I should shoot him?"

"Oh no," he exhaled and perverse amusement twisted his features. "I want that pleasure all to myself."

"Does that mean you want him to think you're sleeping with Cuckoo? Is that how you'll tempt him out?" The plan had sort of backfired if she was the one curious about the relationship and Caine was still on her tail.

"This is my problem, and I'm gonna deal with it my fucking way. The camera isn't off, it's routed to my phone because these crazies are my problem."

So he'd been keeping things from her, saying nothing to the others, because he was embarrassed or carrying some kind of guilt about what had gone on with Caine and Cuckoo in the past. "You don't have to deal with anything alone. You're Kindred," she soothed. "How long have you been thinking this way about Caine?"

A knock on the door saved him from answering the question. It was the same combination of knocks used on their motel room door during the last mission, so she knew the person on the other side would be Tuck. Brodie went to the door, the men exchanged mumbles, and she sat on the bed expecting both men to come in.

But when the door closed, Brodie came back alone. "Where's Swift?" she asked.

Brodie took the large black bag to the window and hunkered down to open it and pull out the kit. Laying the scope and other pieces out, he zipped it and kicked the bag under the desk, though it wasn't empty.

Next, he pulled the couch out and across the worn carpet to the window, which was high enough that the couch wouldn't be visible from outside on its own. Once he had the scope setup, he closed the curtains over the window, just letting the lens peek through the other side. Pulling off his jacket, he tossed it onto the desk beside the couch and sat down to put his eye to the scope.

Swift wasn't here and she didn't know if he was coming back. Brodie didn't want to answer more questions about Caine and Cuckoo, so she'd give him time to calm down. The furniture wouldn't withstand another outburst. Leaving the bed, she went to the couch, staying behind it to reach over and squeeze his shoulders. Bending lower, she massaged his neck and down his arms. On their return, she curled her fingers to scrape her nails upward.

Edging an inch away from the scope, he didn't look at her, but she knew he'd registered her act. "Why would you want to fuck the guy who's fucking around on you?" he grumbled. Scratching him aroused them both and was often her greeting or her first step toward seducing him. The act itself tended to be enough. Once he knew she was turned on, he took control.

Putting her hands on the back of the couch, she lifted one leg over and then the other. Squatting behind him, she rested her chest on his back with her legs open on either side of him and her hands on his shoulders.

"I'm sorry, beau," she said, rising to kiss the nape of his neck. "I didn't think that. I was just confused."

Snatching her wrist with his opposite hand, he yanked her around enough that he could glare down at her. "I fucking love you more than life. You think my dick would be happy in some inferior pussy?"

Shaking her head in a slow, shallow arc, she tried to push up to kiss him, but the arm she was pressed against moved, and he captured her jaw in his powerful hand. "I love you," she whispered, hoping for a kiss. "I worry about you. You're not alone, beau."

"By now you should trust me to handle shit," he snarled. "I withhold information, I lie to you, to protect you."

But she didn't want his protection on those terms. She wanted to know it all, everything there was to know about him, about his past, his fears, the future, everything. "I'd rather be in danger than shut out," she said, and he grabbed her up to seize her mouth.

Throwing her arms around him, she felt his body twist to come down over hers, and then his hand was up her skirt stroking her sex. "You fucking belong to me," he said, nipping her lip. "And I'm your guy, nothing busts this up, hear me? You get that shit out your head."

"Uh huh," she rushed the words, and he plunged two fingers into her. Yelping, she reared up and undulated against them.

Reaching for his groin, she pressed her palm into the solid dick behind his fly and rubbed it while moving her hips. Tearing his gaze from hers, he took his eye to the scope. While he was distracted, she pulled her top over her head and freed him from his jeans.

When she squeezed her fist around him, he took his attention from the scope, and it fell to her naked breasts. "Swift will be coming back," he said and glanced around in the direction of the door, but she was already climbing onto his lap.

"I'll be quick," she panted, she was already wet enough to suck him in deep, and he grabbed her waist to hold her down on him.

He filled her so completely that she squirmed with the need to push him out and pull him in, both at the same time. It felt so good to have him crammed so deep that she could feel his length throbbing inside her, pushing the limits of her swollen center. But as she whimpered and bit her lip, he wouldn't let her move.

"You think you want this?" he demanded

"I need it," she said and tried to move, but he clamped an arm around her pelvis, pushing her clit into his groin until she yelped at the desperation that made her writhe against him. "Please... please, baby."

"I want you to remember this," he said. "You feel my fat cock all the way up inside you. It feels good, doesn't it? You dirty girl, you love this, pretty baby."

"Yes," she cried. "Please."

His precision focus on her eyes increased her need. "You'll be begging and apologizing for a long time. You'll never forget your duty to my dick. It's your job to keep it happy, plaything. No one else gets to play."

His palm pressed to her cheek and he pushed her hair away to gather it in his fist. Pulling her head back at an angle that allowed him to suck her pulse point hard, the burn prompted her to dig her nails into him and call out his real name.

They made eye contact, and she was apologizing all over again. They had aliases for this reason, so they didn't have to use real names in what was potential enemy territory. "I'm sorry, I didn't mean… I shouldn't have—"

"Always knew you were naughty," he said, grabbing and fondling her breast. His other arm loosened and he smacked her ass. "Now you can ride it like the dirty whore you're playing."

Using his shoulders to steady herself, she moved up and down, back and forth, working herself over him. He wrapped an arm around her waist, she thought to give her traction, but he pulled her to the side and peeked through the scope again.

It was impressive that he still remembered they were on a job given what they were doing. She smiled. "Am I distracting you?" she asked, and he smacked her again.

"Is that sass?"

"I don't know," she said, speeding up as the heat of pressure grew in urgency. "Would that piss you off?"

His eyes slunk to hers. He sat back and considered her. The pride she read in him made her work harder. Just as she found her rhythm, he thrust both arms around her and stood up, sending the scope onto the floor, but he didn't pay the equipment any heed. With their bodies still engaged, he carried her to the bed and threw her off his cock onto the mattress.

"Think riling me is hot? Think pissing off a guy who trades in pain is smart?"

His jeans were loose over his hips, and he pulled his belt from the loops and halved it to snap the leather. The sound was abrupt enough to startle her, but she stretched her arms above her head and her legs down to her pointed toes. She wasn't afraid of him, and he would never hurt her. He snapped the belt again.

"Suck my cock," he said, holding himself and coming close to the bed. She flipped over and crawled to the edge to take his shaft from his hand.

Opening her lips, she licked her taste from him and sucked him as hard as she could, her head bobbing as she tested her ability to take him to her throat. He scooped her hair out of the way and held it tight. But she worked hard at her task, squeezing her thighs together when she heard the whisper of curses come from his lips.

She assumed he was close to climax, so she doubled her effort. He let go of her hair and looped his belt around the back of her neck. He slid it into its buckle but didn't fasten the pin. With his hold on her improvised leash, he pulled her away and retreated.

"That's your job, plaything. My dick's your full-time occupation."

She nodded and smiled, he let go of the belt after a yank backwards and she fell onto the bed. He lay down over her and she opened her legs to accept him inside her. In a powerful move, he pushed himself through her juices into her slick passage. "Raven," she whispered, arching up into his invasion.

The insistence of his member grew. It forged its advance, opening and closing her internal space, forcing her body to stroke his, to stimulate nerves, to pleasure him as he needed. He was using her to sate his desire. The stimulation drove her to an insanity of chemical overload that made her scratch at him, to grasp and claw her resolve to take him all, to own him and be owned.

"Every name, whoever I am, you're the only one I touch. You're my woman."

"Yes," she exhaled, working hard to move with him, but she was beginning to tire.

Lowering to lick her earlobe, his breath warmed her. "You like that? You like it when I fuck you?" he growled into her ear and kept pumping his hips.

"Mm," she mumbled her approval and he boosted himself up again.

"Swallow," he said and the name made her eyes pop open to lock onto his. "Fucking say it."

"You're my guy," she cried out, close to her own climax. "Oh, God, yes! Fuck me, Raven!"

The noise of banging on the wall didn't shatter the haze of her hormones that made her call out when she came. Brodie clamped a hand over her mouth to quiet her as he expanded and jettisoned his seed within her. The banging came again. She and her lover weren't calling out for each other anymore. They were just panting into the humid air they'd created, trying to find their equilibrium again.

TWELVE

SHE FOUND SOMETHING comforting about the moisture he left inside her as he withdrew. There was no time for lying together, no cuddles and reassurance. Brodie went straight to the scope, pulling his jeans up with one hand as he picked up the fallen equipment and took a look through it.

Happy to relax and enjoy her own afterglow, even if Brodie didn't have a permit to join her, Zara just breathed and let her body stay heavy. "Can you see him?" she asked, looking at the water-stained ceiling.

"He's in bed," he said and glanced at his watch. "Swift and I agreed to give him an hour, then we'll go in."

"What?" she said, sitting up. The weight of his belt fell into her cleavage. She'd almost forgotten it was around her neck. Picking it up, she loosened it to pull it off over her head.

Brodie was on his feet, fastening his jeans, so she got up and went over to stand in front of him. He frowned down at her. She smiled and began to thread his belt through its loops. "I love you," she said, putting both arms around him to get it through the loops at the back.

"You're not in one of your smiley, happy moods now, are you?" he asked, peering down at her like she was contagious and so should be avoided.

He might be Mr. Assassin tonight, but she'd just been fucked good and hard, she loved it when they played their games. "Maybe," she said. When she was finished with the belt, she elected not to fasten it and chose instead to leave it loose. Gathering his tee shirt, she lifted it up to kiss his ridged abdomen, then pulled it higher and kissed his chest.

"I meant it when I said Swift was coming back," he said, taking her wrists to pull her off his body. "We're in for an all-nighter, but not the sort you're looking for." He scanned south then dropped down on the couch. "Put your tits away."

She didn't even know where her top was. Seeking it out, she found it on the floor and bowed to pick it up, ensuring to turn and bend at the waist so he could get a view of her ass in the G-string that wasn't hidden at this angle because her skirt was so short and loose.

"You're gonna tease me all night, aren't you?" he asked and spanked her before she stood up.

"I'll try to be good," she said, looking through her hair over her shoulder as she pulled on her skimpy halter-neck.

"You better 'cause we're working," he said and slumped in the couch, appearing none too happy that they were constrained by circumstance.

"What are you going over for?" she asked, sitting beside him, right beside him, so their bodies were in full contact. "You said that you and Tuck had agreed to give Kahlil an hour before you are going in."

He glanced down at her to register her proximity, despite the vast length of couch on her other side, then sat forward to peer through the scope. "We can bug the place while he's asleep."

Frowning, she thought of all the things that could go wrong. "Is that smart?" she asked. "He might have gadgets of his own or men watching the door."

"Possible," Brodie said. "We know what we're doing. We'll be careful."

She sighed. "And I'll sit here looking through the scope, hoping you're not decapitated by his crazy friends. He had two guys with him at CI the night he met Grant, don't forget what happened in the CI parking garage. I would guess he'd have more if he's staying here in this shady area. He could have bodyguards in the next door apartment or something." Brodie didn't respond. Her thoughts came to a new conclusion. "It would make more sense for me to go in."

Now she was sure he was listening. "How in the fuck do you figure that?" he asked, giving up the scope.

"You're the sniper. So if I get in trouble, you can eliminate the threat. You've shot people right next to me before. Hell, you shot Tim when he was on my face. I've only shot one person, and he was so close it was impossible to miss. If you and Swift go over there and get into trouble, I'll be more likely to shoot the old lady two floors below than be any help to either of you. Also, Kahlil knows me, and his men might too. If they catch me I can vamp, tell him I'm there to talk about Game Time or something, see if I can't get him to talk about Future's Hope."

She preferred using the name of the vessel than referencing his parents. Brodie didn't need it spelled out. He was considering her suggestion, he didn't dismiss her, and that sign of respect bolstered her need to be useful. To be a part of the Kindred, she would have to do jobs like this. She didn't have experience, but practice was the way to get that, Brodie had said so himself.

"We'll leave Swift here to spot," Brodie said and returned to his spying.

She didn't mind if Brodie was the one with her, she just wanted to understand the decision. "Why?"

"Because they've seen me come to your defense before." In the CI parking garage. "And if they watched Atlas play out, they saw us together. I doubt they noticed Tuck, and we don't make our people show their faces unless they have to."

He cared for his cohorts and that made her love him more. Bringing her hand to his face, she stroked it as she twisted her knees onto the couch under her to lean in and kiss him. He accepted the kiss until she tried to slide her tongue into his mouth. Then he took her arm to pull her away.

"Seriously, Swallow, sit your ass down."

That he was so serious about her keeping her hands to herself tickled her, but she had to respect his wishes. They were on a job and she could be a professional. She always had been before, then again, she'd never been boning her boss before. Choosing to lie on the couch, she pressed the balls of her feet into his thigh and drummed her toes.

Brodie kept one hand on the scope and dropped the other to her bare ankles. She appreciated the nod to their intimacy, even though they were being responsible. "How did you meet Caine?"

He glanced at her but answered as he went back to work. "In a bar," he said. "It was… years ago… five, maybe ten, I don't know… whatever, we met in a bar."

"And you became friends?"

"We were never friends," he said, leaning around the arm of the couch, he pulled the bag from under the desk over to the floor at his feet. "It was a poker game, a big deal, major odds. He was just another guy there, least he was to me. Someone told him of my legend, and it was after that he started hanging around, showing up in places we were, even shot a couple of my kills."

"He took jobs from you?"

"No," Brodie said. Opening the bag, he pulled aside the edges to reveal a case—Maverick. "Back then he was trying to impress me, wanted in on the inside. He stalked who we stalked and would set up to try and take the kill shot before I did."

"Did he?"

"I said he shot them, not killed them," he muttered over his shoulder and opened the case to take the pieces out and put his closest ally together. "He shot shoulders, took off one guy's ear, he shot another guy in the hip, no idea where he was aiming at on that one. A couple of times he missed completely, making the target and others scatter. Pissed me off 'cause it meant I had to work faster, and if it was in public, people panicked, it caused mayhem."

"You ever miss?" He stopped what he was doing to turn his glare on her, and it was enough to make her grin. He didn't appreciate his skills being questioned. "Did you tell him that he was being a pain in the ass?"

Brodie continued building Maverick. "Confronted him more than once, but he just liked the attention, he was an eager puppy trying to please his master."

"But Cuckoo changed that?" she asked, watching how efficient he was at putting the weapon together.

"He knew her before I did. Fucked her before I did too. She heard about me from him. I think he was trying to impress her with his knowledge and didn't think the game through to the end, always was his problem," he said. Holding the weapon upright, he gave it a once over, then flipped it around in a quick motion and laid it down on top of her. "She's not loaded, but don't touch her."

Raising her arms above her head, Zara flopped them over the arm of the couch she was resting on. He was more protective of Maverick than he was of her. Zara wiggled her toes against him, it was the only available avenue to tease and show him affection with a rifle on top of her.

Trying to peer down the barrel that was pointed at her, she arched to lift it and give her a better view. This weapon had seen her up close many times when Brodie was aiming to keep an eye on her. It had taken lives and protected her.

Brodie was busy with something else and she moved up and down, testing the hardware. The weight of the weapon surprised her, and the metal quickly heated with the warmth of her body. It was a formidable piece and would be terrifying if turned against a person. But all she could think about were the times it had saved the lives of people she cared about, including Brodie's.

"Fuck."

She expected Brodie's exhaled exclamation to be directed at something out the window, but the scope had been moved away from the window and there was another tripod in its place. "What?" she asked, unsure why he was scowling at her with such a keen appreciation.

Taking her foot, he pulled it over his thigh and pressed her toes into the erection in his jeans. "I told you not to fuck with me."

She massaged him with her toes. "I'm not fucking with you. I'm just admiring your hardware," she said, tracing a fingertip down the long barrel of the rifle. "You're the one that put her on top of me. Two females laid out and ready for your choosing, beau."

"Don't make me choose," he said, and she was disappointed when he took the rifle from her to attach it to the tripod.

Something settled over his expression when he looked through the telescopic sight and began to adjust various knobs and dials. She didn't think there would be a better view from the weapon than there had been from the prop that was there before, but when he was done fiddling, he seemed more at ease with his trusted companion set up.

Zara sat up, crossing her legs under her and stroking her hands over his thigh to get his attention. "Can I look?"

As far as she'd seen, he hadn't put any ammunition in the rifle yet, so there wouldn't be a better time. Picking her up, Brodie pulled her onto his lap. He settled one hand on her hip and the other on his gun at the same time she leaned forward to look through the sight. The image was so much clearer.

"Put your cheek here," he said, pressuring her cheekbone to position her. "It's a little high for you."

The lines and markings were different and the green of the nightlight was sharper. Kahlil was there in his bed, unaware that he had such a powerful firearm pointed at him.

Brodie had been doing this for years, these kinds of experiences were mundane to him, but she had never been party to such a thing. Lifting a hand, she didn't get the chance to touch the weapon because Brodie caught her wrists and pulled her hands around to the small of her back, which forced her ass to slide against the lump in his jeans.

"I just cleaned her," he said, but he'd had no problems with using her body as a weapon rest.

Zara smiled and focused on the gun sight again. "In all these months we've been together, I never realized."

"Never realized what?"

When she lay back on him, he released her hands. Her form relaxed on his torso until her head was on his shoulder and she was gazing up at him. "All this time I've been the other woman."

"You're way sexier."

She squinted. "Hmm, not sure I believe that," she said, and it was his turn to kiss her even if it was against all the rules.

His mouth opened and when his tongue brushed hers, she didn't shut him down. Twisting her body one way while he went the other, he got her on her back on the couch again and insinuated himself between her thighs.

"It's wrong that you're so turned on by this, baby," he mumbled into her mouth, though he was the one grinding his solid dick against the dampness that lingered from their last union, proving that she wasn't the only one who was aroused.

He pushed her arms over her head again and kissed the pulsing column of her throat all the way down to her cleavage. Her top hung loose, and the stubble on his chin rasped on her sensitive breast when he pushed aside the material to breathe in her nipple.

"I like being naughty," she said, closing her eyes to arch into his mouth.

He reared up to kiss her again. "I've known that since the minute I laid eyes on you."

"You're dangerous, beau," she whispered before he slanted her mouth to kiss her again.

"I'm not the only one," he said. "You're dangerous now too."

"Only when you're watching over me."

Brushing his nose on hers, he made her look at him. "Mav and I are your dedicated servants."

"Oh, baby," she murmured.

He'd loosened his hold enough that she could free her hands to skim them down onto his face and hold their mouths together in a devouring kiss. She'd never heard anything so hot in all her life, nor had any man ever looked at her with the devotion Brodie had in his eyes. He would do anything to protect her, give up anything to make her happy, she'd been insane to doubt that for even a second.

Sliding his hand down her body, he caressed her thigh before letting it continue to her shin where he pulled her limb higher, curving it around him to deepen their intimate connection.

Spurred by his advance, her hopes rose. "If we're quick—" A knock on the door stopped her words and when she wilted beneath him, he exhaled a laugh into her mouth and kissed the end of her nose before vaulting up onto his feet.

She sat up and snagged his wrist. With a forlorn sigh, she eyed his groin. "I'll get the door. You deal with that."

Tuck wouldn't appreciate being welcomed by the bulge in Brodie's jeans. Using the strength in his arm, she pulled herself up and darted around the couch.

"How do you want me to do that?" he called after her.

"Think about something unarousing, like Wren."

"That'll work," he muttered.

Snagging a pillow from the bed as she passed, she tossed it at him and it was a good thing he caught it or she might have KO'd his beloved Maverick, and he'd have no sense of humor about that. Opening the door to Tuck, she allowed him to slip in carrying a big black sports bag and a couple of paper bags that smelled like Chinese food.

"You brought food," she rejoiced, snatching the bags from him after closing the door.

They moved out of the space in front of the bathroom. "We won't have to worry about jumping on the bed now, will we?" he said.

The aroma of their joining still filled the space. It was either that, her flushed face, or the mussed bed, but something gave away what she and Rave had been up to. While Tuck was being snide in a teasing way, she smiled and took the food to the bed with her.

Sitting in the center cross-legged, she began to take food from the sack. "Just doing my duty," she said.

Brodie linked his hands on the top of his head to lean back and look over the back of the couch. "Folks next door got no sense of humor," he said.

Tuck dumped the bag on the floor between the bed and where the couch had been and frowned at his buddy. "Paper walls?"

"Should be all right, she was loud… even for her."

Tuck relaxed and took off his jacket to grab a couple of boxes of food and join Brodie on the couch. "What does that mean?" she asked, taking the chopsticks from their paper and separating them.

"You're loud," Tuck said, opening up his box to inhale the scent of his food.

"Okay," she muttered, grabbing up some noodles. "I like to make my point."

"We get it already," Tuck said around a mouthful of food. "You like sex."

She liked sex with Brodie and as they ate, she tried to think if any of her exes had commented on her volume level, though none came to mind. Comparing Brodie to the men who'd come before him was a bit like comparing this dime-store Chinese food to Art's homemade spaghetti and meatballs. They were both designed to do the same sort of thing, but the end result wasn't the same. One left her satisfied and sated while the other would leave her nauseous and hollow. Laughing at her own comparison, she ate more and told herself not to be so harsh on her exes, not all of them made her feel sick at the time, but in retrospect—

"What are you laughing at?" Tuck asked. Both men were twisted to examine her enjoying her own little world.

"Nothing," she said because if she said sex, the jokes would never end. She chose instead to change the subject "What did you bring?"

Casting her food aside, she clambered off the bed and kneeled beside the bag Tuck had discarded. "Supplies," Tuck said.

She unzipped it and found clothes, towels, snacks, weapons, playing cards, everything they might need to fill the long night ahead. "Swallow and I are going across the street," Brodie said. "After we've eaten."

"Copy," Tuck said, sucking down a noodle.

Leaving the bag, she retrieved her food and went over

to flop down on the couch between the men. "If we go across the street, you'll have to leave Maverick here with another man," Zara said, peeking into Brodie's food box in case there was something she wanted, but that left hers open and he snagged some chicken from her box with his chopsticks.

"He's handled Maverick before," Brodie said. "He knows what he's doing. She'll be in good hands."

Except she wasn't allowed to touch… she didn't even begrudge that rule, the black metal monster daunted her. "I hope you don't share all of your women with him," she said.

Brodie didn't give her a laugh, but he winked at her before he stood up and put his food on the desk. Pushing her head down onto the couch, he gave himself the space he needed to vault over the back of it to cross the room. The bathroom door closed, and she reached over to swap her food box with Brodie's.

"Can I ask you a personal question, Swift?"

"I've never slept with any of his women," he said, snagging her legs to pull them aside, so he could sit where Brodie had been. These men shifted her around like a ragdoll. It was warming that they were so comfortable with her and it suggested a closeness, but they'd all seen death together so that made sense. "Not since we hit our thirties anyway."

That modifier drew a brief scowl from her, but he was too busy dipping into the food she'd left on the desk to notice. "That wasn't what I was going to ask," she said, pushing her skirt down as she moved to a perpendicular position with her legs crossed.

"Okay, shoot."

Probably not the best thing to say while they had a rifle peeking through the curtains, and it was when she saw the slither between the two rectangles of fabric that she realized why they hadn't turned the lights on: it would make their position obvious.

"Is sex different when you're in love?" she asked.

Drawing his focus around, she wasn't sure if he was surprised or affronted. Whichever it was, the food certainly wasn't as enthralling for him as it had been a moment ago. "You were a virgin before you had sex with Raven? I never read that in your file."

"No!" she said, pressing a hand to his shoulder. Every member of the Kindred had to know she'd slept with Brodie before she knew he was Brodie. All she knew was his alias. It would have been quite a leap for a virgin to take from pure to vixen in the space of one kiss. But if there was any man who could've done it for her, Brodie would've been it. "I mean is it different for a guy… like you."

"For a guy like me? No." He snickered and scooped some more food into his mouth. "You mean for a guy like Raven."

She'd just been making relevant conversation; she didn't know he'd take her question so seriously. "Okay, yeah, so I mean a guy like Raven."

Twisting toward her, he wasn't buying it. "No, you want to know if he was with any other woman the way he is with you."

She hadn't thought to frame it that way, but yeah, she guessed that was what she meant. What had been a casual question was turning into something she didn't like. "Forget it."

"Why do you think I would know?"

"Because," she said and dug into her food again. "You loved Kadie."

He loosened and didn't show surprise, but she could tell her words had caught him off guard from the way his face blanked. "Loved Kadie." He turned his head toward the window but wasn't anywhere near the sight. "Yeah. I loved her."

Zara hadn't meant to bring up a sensitive subject, she'd sort of avoided it, but she couldn't ignore how forlorn he was now. She lowered her food carton. "You shouldn't have broken up with her, you know. She's stronger than you think."

She and Kadie had never met, but he didn't point that out. "Kade is as strong as women come," he said, wearing a distant but proud smile.

"What's she like?" Zara asked. "Does she have family?"

"Never knew her dad, her mom ran off when she was a kid, she has an older cousin who looks out for her. He's everything a good guy should be."

"What did he say about you dumping her?"

"Dempsey will be looking to tan my hide, no doubt about that," Tuck said on a hissing inhale then glanced through the sight.

His return to form gave her a reprieve, except she hadn't thought he was the type to cut and run like a coward. "So you didn't see him after? You just broke her heart and split?"

"Listen!" His shout made her jump, he wasn't as at peace with her presumption as she thought. "You don't know squat about Kade or about our life, stay out of shit that's nothing to do with you!"

She'd never heard Tuck shout or been the subject of his scrutiny like she was now. "Sorry," she croaked, bending to put her food on the floor.

The bathroom door opened and she did her best to leave the couch with composure. Making a beeline for the room Brodie had just vacated, she snagged her purse from the floor and didn't make eye contact as she went into the bathroom and locked the door.

THIRTEEN

DROPPING HER PURSE to the vanity, she fell against the locked bathroom door. "Stupid," she hissed at herself.

Art and Brodie had both told her that Tuck was a private person. She'd always assumed they were exaggerating because he was open with her. Now she saw that he was open about the Kindred, open about Brodie, all things that involved her. His life beyond the Kindred was a closed book, and she should have taken the advice of those who knew the hacker better than she did.

When she got to the bathroom mirror, the reflection staring back didn't look like her. Her hair was a matted mess. Her makeup was smeared. She'd taken on the appearance of the persona she wanted outsiders to think she was. It was no longer an orchestrated façade, instead she was one hot mess. Random, rough sex and backcombed hair were a recipe for a grooming disaster.

Turning on the faucet, she washed her face and took her comb from her purse to try to tease her hair into some semblance of order. The battle was a losing one, it would take serious time to score victory and she didn't have that to spare. Her scalp was beginning to hurt, and she was already grumpy enough after her dumb misstep with Swift. If she went back into the room with a headache, her bad attitude would probably get her into an argument. In close quarters with these guys, for an undefined period of time, Zara didn't want to test their tempers any further.

She pulled her hair into a ponytail and fastened it with a tie from her purse, then she took out her rolled ballet flats and put them on. Wherever she and Brodie were going, being covert was going to be more important than being sexy, so the thigh-highs just wouldn't do. Content that she'd done the best she could, she psyched herself up to leave this room and apologize to Tuck before departing with her love.

With a deep breath, she opened the bathroom door and dropped her purse to the floor again. Striding into the body of the room with her mouth open ready to launch into her apology, she came up short when she saw that Tuck was the only one here.

"Where's Raven?" she asked, deflated.

"Doing a job," Tuck said and slid along the couch. "See for yourself."

He'd ditched her? She was supposed to be going on this job with him. She was more than a little pissed and disappointed that she'd been left behind when she hadn't been in the bathroom for a prohibitive period.

"No," she said, hurrying over to sit on the couch and peek through the lens to see her love inside Kahlil's bedroom, hunkered down right next to the bed. "Why did he—"

"He thought we could use a minute alone."

It made her feel somewhat better that she hadn't been cut from the team for fear she might be incompetent, but that did leave her facing an awkward conversation in her immediate future. "Oh," she said, slumping. As soon as her spine hit the back of the couch, she was inspired to jump to her feet. "You should be sitting there. Keeping an eye on him ready to… you know."

Her conversation with Tuck could happen wherever she was in the room, but Brodie still needed someone to watch his ass while he was prowling in enemy territory, and if someone needed to take a shot to save his life, Tuck was a better bet than she would be, as she'd explained to Brodie already.

"He's nearly done," Tuck said but moved over to seat himself behind the rifle, and she appreciated him being there even if he was just humoring her.

A serendipitous side effect of him leaning forward and paying attention to Brodie was that she felt more comfortable about what she had to say because she didn't have to look him in the eye. "You were right, Swift, I should've kept my nose out of your private business. I wasn't judging you, I… I should've respected your boundaries."

She gave him time to process and kept quiet, praying he would forgive her prying, and that they could move on without things becoming awkward between them.

"She always just understood me. Kadie. She always understood me," he said and because he didn't move away from the rifle sight, she guessed that he, too, was more comfortable having this conversation while they had the job to distract them. "For the first few weeks after we split, I had to keep telling myself not to hack her email or her phone like I did when we were together."

That was an odd admission but fit with who Tuck was. Zara often wondered what he did during all the hours he spent gazing into his different laptop screens. This confession was beginning to answer that question. "She was okay with you doing that?"

He wasn't embarrassed or hesitant about discussing his invasion of Kadie's privacy. "It was a game," he said, lowering his chin. "She knew I did it and encouraged it by acting all affronted when I spoke about things I could never have known without accessing her personal data. Getting her riled always ended well for both of us, if you get me."

Zara's guess was that teasing and banter were a part of their foreplay. "I get ya."

Tuck was fixated on a single point just beyond the scope. "If I didn't do it, if I didn't track her movements and conversations, she'd get so pissed. Violating her privacy was a way of… showing how much I cared, I guess. She liked that I couldn't help myself, that I had to pry into her life because I loved to feel like I was a part of it. We couldn't see each other every day, but I always knew what she was up to."

Zara wasn't too sure of what else to say. One thing was clear. "You don't have anyone to talk to about how you feel… about her."

He'd broken up with Kadie in reaction to his grief over losing Art. Zara could understand how that tested his security in his own mortality. But Tuck was a bit of a loner. During Brodie's seclusion, Tuck went off on his own. Zara always thought he was going to Kadie or going to other friends or family he might have. Now it seemed to her that he'd been dealing with his bereavement and his break-up by himself.

He cleared his throat. "Told Rave when we were through."

"That's not the same thing," she said, sliding over to take his hand from his thigh. He chose to watch their physical connection rather than to meet her eye. "I didn't mean to upset you or to take liberties talking about her… It's just… I'm in a kind of unique position to understand her… I know what it is to love a man who could disappear one day."

"She doesn't know what we do."

"She knows what you do, doesn't she? If she knows you can hack her email…"

"Doesn't matter," he said and took his hand out of hers.

He'd shut down, and Zara had learned her lesson about pushing him. "I'm sorry I was an idiot. But if you want to talk… I can keep a secret. You should hear the soppy shit Raven says to me all the time. I never tell anyone about that."

This time she got a laugh, and she appreciated his smile. "That I'd love to hear."

"You and me both. It's wishful thinking on my part," she said. "Seriously, the most romantic thing he's ever said to me is, 'On your knees, bitch.' Honestly." Tuck laughed again, and she appreciated it when he put his arm around her neck to pull her forward.

He was still laughing. "We always wondered how he seduced you."

The time for serious discussion was over. She wanted to return to their ease, so she kept joking. "There was a lack of sleep involved, alcohol, too, I'm sure. He definitely took advantage of me when I was at my weakest."

"Ah, now it all makes sense."

The knock at the door caused Tuck to let her go, giving her clearance to answer it. Zara went over to open the door to Brodie, who moved to come inside, but she didn't budge out of his way, keeping him in the hallway. "Newcomers must submit to a strip search."

He groaned. "I knew you were in this kind of mood. I just knew it. I should know better than to fuck you on an empty stomach."

"Maybe you should've let me swallow," she said, walking her fingers up his torso.

Grabbing her wrist, he spun her around and marched her into the room, slamming the door behind himself. "I paid the room for the rest of the week," he said, keeping her arm loosely twisted up her back all the way over to the couch. "I told him we were gonna party, there might be noise, music, banging—"

"Banging?" she asked, elevating her chin in hope.

"Yes," he said, squeezing tighter and wrapping his other arm around her waist. "You're in for a wild ride this week, baby. Any time we need cover, we're calling on you to do more of that screaming."

"You're calling her for that," Tuck said, turning away from them. "The mark hasn't lifted his head, you got in and out clean."

Brodie lowered his lips into her hair. "What did I tell you, baby? We're pros and we're in for the long haul."

***

WHILE THE MEN setup the audio equipment to monitor the bugs Brodie had planted, she laid herself down on the bed. She must have fallen asleep because the next thing she became aware of was the light glowing through her eyelids. She yawned and stretched, dropping a hand onto the torso of the man lying beside her.

"Wrong guy," a voice beside her muttered.

A strong hand took her wrist to shunt her hand back over to her own side. As soon as he released her, she sat up in a flash.

Tuck was the one lying beside her, fully clothed but still asleep. He rolled over, putting his back to her and continuing to snooze. Whipping her attention around, she saw Brodie on guard duty with one hand on the back of the couch so he could check out the sleeping pair.

"Why didn't you move me?" she whispered, grabbing her pillow and schlepping across the room to sink onto the couch on her side.

Putting her head in his lap, she hugged her pillow for warmth, drawing her knees up around it.

"Because when your mouth is that close to my dick I get distracted," he said but stroked her hair away from her face while she slipped into slumber.

"What's the plan today?" she asked on another yawn.

"Swift and I will keep watch. Tracking Kahlil's movements will give us more information, and he might lead us to the other players."

It beat sitting around and waiting for attack. Brodie needed to be doing something practical that didn't involve him thinking too hard about what he did or didn't know about his parents' death.

"Did Wren and Falcon find out anything more from the data at base?" she asked. They'd gone through most of it before facial recognition had brought them here. But if Grant knew something about Future's Hope, they needed to know it too. That answer would weigh heavily on their ultimate decision of how to deal with Kahlil.

"Wren took a commercial flight back west this morning," Brodie said.

Her eyes were still closed, but she presumed he was still watching Kahlil. "That's a shame," she said, because Thad was a fun guy to be around and he always injected a bit of humor into tense situations. With guys like Brodie, Zave, and even Tuck, she was often left smiling alone.

"He asked if you wanted to go with him. Something you should tell me?"

She smiled. "Bess invited me to visit."

"What did you say?"

"I didn't commit to anything. I had other things on my mind."

"Do me a favor," he said, coiling his fingers in her hair. "Check with me before you jet off. I want to check Zave's calendar to see what he's got going on before I let you go over there alone. There are certain times that his place is just plain off-limits, hear me?"

Rolling to her back, she opened her eyes. "Are you ever going to tell me what it is he does that makes you say these cryptic things?"

"You know me, baby," he said, sliding his hand down to her breast so he could toy with her nipple through the sheer material she wore. "Cryptic keeps you on your toes. I like that."

A loud bear yawn from the bed made her sit up in time to see Tuck get up and stretch to the ceiling. "What's the update?" he asked, opening his arms to each side. The ripple of the muscles in his arms reminded her of Brodie, and she recalled the first time she'd laid eyes on Tuck, when he happened to be shirtless.

Brodie's fingertips crossed her face to press her opposite cheekbone until she was facing him. "What?" she asked, but he just glared and went to his sight.

"What we got?" Tuck asked, rubbing the stubble on his jaw.

Brodie settled back, bringing his hands up to the back of his head in a relaxed pose. "Guy just started jerking off. We're good."

Shocked and interested, she hadn't considered what would happen if their subject got intimate with himself or others. "Seriously?" she asked, clambering onto Brodie's lap to peek through the sight.

"Least he's up, we might get some action," Tuck said.

"This takes invasion of privacy to a whole new level," she said, knowing that she should be more demure but intent on the movement of the bedclothes over Kahlil's lap. As disgusting as it was to watch, it was useful. His ability to intimidate dwindled with every jerk of his fist.

Brodie's hands held her hips, they slid around to her abdomen and up under her top to cup her breasts. She grabbed his arms to try to tug them away. "What?" he asked, countering her strength without breaking a sweat.

His hot, entitled hands shouldn't be touching her in intimate places during this spectacle. "Don't stimulate me while I'm watching… this," she protested.

"You're the one choosing to watch," Brodie muttered. "You want the full stereo experience?"

He tapped a button on the laptop, and Kahlil's pants and grunts echoed into the room. That enhancement was more than she could stomach. The foul performance made her close the laptop to cut off the audio. Flopping back on him, his hands pressed into her breasts as she tipped her head to look at him.

He'd succeeded in his goal of grossing her out, so she took a turn at doing the same to him. "Want me to blow you and we'll see who finishes first?"

His face distorted in disgust and his hands disappeared from inside her top. "Okay, that's just wrong."

Tuck laughed and ran his hands through his hair. "I'm gonna jump in the shower, then I'll go out for coffee." He pointed at Brodie. "You okay for a bit, Bud?"

Brodie waved him away then opened up the laptop and logged it in. "I'm good."

Tuck grabbed some things from their supplies bag and went into the bathroom. The shower went on ten seconds later. It was on for less than two minutes, and two minutes after that he was bidding them goodbye. She was still curled in Brodie's lap. They hadn't even spoken to each other.

"He's quick," she said after the room door closed.

"Speed is required for necessities," he said, holding her body when he leaned forward to check their subject again. "If you can't be quick, you don't shower."

"Do you want to shower?" she asked, stroking his shoulder and nuzzling closer to his neck, but he smelled clean and given what they'd done last night, she was surprised.

He explained before she asked. "I showered before Tuck got into bed with you. I'll get naked when there's someone on watch."

"I can be on watch," she said.

"Yeah, but if I'm naked you'll be watching the wrong thing. We're not doing surveillance on my dick." She wouldn't mind that job, and when his lip curled, she knew he was aware of her thoughts. Pushing her onto the couch, he got up. "I'm gonna wash my face. You keep watch while I do that."

He was humoring her, giving her a chance to steer the car while he still worked the pedals, but she would pay her dues and do grunt work. It took time to work through the ranks, to prove she was capable of protecting these formidable men.

"You won't be naked?" she called over the couch when he walked toward the bathroom.

"No, I won't," he said, and she was glad to be amusing him. "When I am, you're distracted, and you need to focus."

Pointing at the window before he went into the bathroom, she followed his silent instruction and turned to peek through the sight. She'd missed Kahlil's climax but was completely okay with that. On the desk beside her was a notebook with notations in it and the computer with a program open, the background was black, and there were a bunch of options along with the main audio visualizer.

She leaned forward, expecting to see Kahlil getting ready for the day. But what she saw was Kahlil walking toward his front door. Grabbing up the headphones, she plugged them in and hit record just before he opened the door.

One of the guys in the hallway shoved Kahlil inside, and the other came in to close the door. "Did you get it?" the first goon asked and she squinted to peer closer. These were the guys from the parking garage.

"You can tell your master to go fuck himself," Kahlil spat out, and for a man wearing nothing but underwear, he showed a surprising amount of gumption.

This pair had been on Kahlil's protective detail when

she'd met them. Seeing that they were on opposing sides now corroborated Kahlil's story that he'd been cast out by his former employer.

The goon didn't appreciate being disrespected, and he threw his fist into Kahlil's face making her yelp and Kahlil fall on his ass. "Get dressed. We're going on a trip," he barked.

Throwing the headphones from her ears, she scrambled off the couch and ran to the bathroom. This wasn't news that could wait. Bursting through the door, she saw that Brodie was bent over the sink splashing water on his face. It ran down his neck and onto his bare chest when he stood to clock her reflection to the left of his.

"He's leaving," she said, holding the door in one hand and the frame in the other.

He snagged the towel from the rail and rubbed his face as he came out. She walked backward in front of him as he dried off and moved into the room. "Two guys showed up, said they're taking him on a trip. They're the guys from the parking garage. The ones that attacked us. Except they're not protecting him anymore." Brodie bent to pull a tee shirt from the supplies bag. He pulled it on then went over to grab his jacket from the desk.

"Why do you think that?" he asked, bending over the back of the couch to look through the sight. "He's getting dressed."

"The bigger guy punched him in the face," she said.

Brodie leaped over the couch and began to take Maverick apart. He pulled out the case and put all the pieces inside but left the case and took a handgun from the same bag.

"What are you going to do?" she asked.

"I'm gonna follow them," he said, standing up and checking the clip of his gun before digging it into the waistband at the back of his jeans.

"Is that smart?" she asked, again walking backward in front of him as he came around the couch with the door in his sights. "You haven't slept. There's three of them. And if they have a vehicle—"

"They will. Kahlil's vehicle is the silver coupe parked down the street. But they'll probably have their own transportation. My bike is parked around the corner. I'll tail them."

Pushing her aside, he opened the door but paused long enough to tip her chin up with a curled finger to kiss her. "Stay here. Swift will be back in a minute."

"Be careful," she said, but he was already out of the room.

Closing the door, she paused then rushed over to the window, but there was nothing to aid her view now. The original scope they'd used was still in the bag. Rooting around until she found it, she picked it out and propped it on the tripod they'd used for Maverick. Kahlil was putting on his watch and picking up a cellphone. He lifted the cellphone to his mouth, and she put on the headphones to listen to what he was saying.

"Possible final recording," Kahlil said into the device. "GPS activated. TTX poison secreted in timepiece. If I get close enough, I will eliminate the enemy."

Enemy. Poison. Damn, she wished that Brodie had stuck around long enough to hear those facts. Kahlil tucked the phone into his side pocket then touched the watch on his wrist. Zara stood up with the scope and tried to see if Brodie was on the street, but she couldn't see him.

Kahlil went through his apartment to the door where his chaperones were waiting. When the door closed, she lost her view, so dropped the scope to the couch, and grabbed her cellphone. Ringing Brodie, she closed her eyes and begged for him to answer. He didn't. Kahlil was packing a deadly toxin. A gun wouldn't keep Brodie safe from an attack like that.

Prevention was out, so the next option was cure. Hanging up on Brodie's line, she pressed Thad's speed dial. It went to voicemail, but at least he had voicemail. He was probably still on a plane, but she needed him working as soon as he landed. This situation needed a hasty response.

She waited for the beep. "It's Swallow, nothing to worry about, but I need an antidote for TTX poison on hand." Didn't that sound ridiculous, keeping her voice breezy and telling him not to worry while asking for a cure to a deadly poison that she'd never heard of before. "Can you put something together for us on the down low? Call me back."

She hung up and tried to see any of the players through the window. She spotted the trio of men from the apartment emerge onto the street. Kahlil was bundled into the back of a black car near the building entrance. One of the goons got in the front, the other pushed in beside him.

The car was moving a breath later and as the sound of the car engine faded, the engine of a motorbike revved as it shot past the hotel. He gunned the engine when toying with her, but as she flopped onto the couch, she didn't feel like smiling.

Brodie was out there following people who could kill him in any number of ways. He might be lucky and get a bullet through and through, or he could die a painful death all alone languishing in the effects of a toxic substance. All she could do was sit here and wait for coffee and for Tuck.

She wished that she'd been the one to go for the drinks. Pushing the balls of her fists into her eyes, she cursed herself for not taking Tuck's place. The two men should be together, looking out for each other. Her cellphone chirped, and she sat upright to snatch it to her ear. "Rave?"

"Having some trouble locating your boyfriend, are you?" Cuckoo drawled down the line.

Like she wasn't having a bad enough day, now she had to deal with the ex-girlfriend too. "We're just fine," she said and sighed. "What do you want?"

"I had an interesting meeting last night."

"If you've called to tell me about how Rave just couldn't stay away, it's fine, I know all about it, okay?"

"I doubt that," Cuckoo said with her accent so thick even Zara had to admit it was sexy. "But I wasn't talking about our mutual lover."

Past for Cuckoo, present for her, but Zara wasn't in the mood to rise to the bait. "What are you talking about?"

"I want you to come in. Meet with me."

"Meet with you?" Zara asked, surprised by Cuckoo's stern tone. "At CI?"

"Why not? It's a safe space for you, if you're afraid of me."

Narrowing her eyes in a glare, Zara was glad of the opportunity to vent her current frustration. "I'm not afraid. Just don't see why I should take the time out my life for that place or for you when I'm no longer on payroll."

Cuckoo returned to doing the sexy thing. "Trust me, you want to come to this meeting."

It was probably engrained in Cuckoo to flirt and seduce; she used her allure to her advantage. Shame for her that Zara was immune. "I don't think I do," Zara said, glancing at the door, wishing one of the men would come back so they could get on with tracing Kahlil. "I'm busy today, getting my nails done, you know."

"Be here at noon. The future of the world may depend on it."

The line died before she could get in another word. She threw the phone down on the couch and shot to her feet. "Damnit!" she shouted in the same second there was a knock at the door.

Hurrying over, she pulled it open and grabbed hold of Tuck to pull him inside. "Something wrong?" he asked her.

She took the tray of coffee and the bag of food away from him. "You have to go after Raven."

"Where did he go?" Tuck asked, switching from jovial to serious in a heartbeat.

"Kahlil went out," she said, stepping aside to let him rush across the room. "Two guys came and took him; said they were going on a trip."

Tuck began to pack everything up, and she fizzed with the need for him to hurry up. "Will you please go after him, you'll have him on GPS, right?"

"I have him," he said. Taking his phone from his pocket, he typed on it while the laptop they'd been using for audio surveillance shutdown. "We can't leave evidence here. I'm not leaving the kit and I have to take you home first."

"I can pack everything away," she said.

He stood straight. "You have to stage the place. The room's still ours, and we might need to come back if Kahlil does."

"I will," she said, witnessing his conflict.

"What about Caine? What if he's lurking?"

She didn't know he knew about that, but it was probable that the men had spoken into the night while she slept. "Caine approaches me at night. I will deal with this place and go back to the manor, I swear to you."

"Okay," he said, grabbing up the bag with Maverick in it. He'd leave her alone but wouldn't risk abandoning Brodie's first love. If she wasn't so worried about her love, she might laugh at his innate priorities.

"Hurry," she said, holding the door open. "Swift, come on, you know, be quick like the name."

"Straight back to the manor," he said. Striding over, he ducked to kiss her cheek. "And if you need me, call."

She nodded and gave him a nudge out the door. With two men out there to worry about, she should probably be twice as concerned. Instead, her panic halved. They would look after each other, and that made her feel better about their safety.

Facing the room, she took in the view. Stage the place to look like there had been a party, then get home to the manor to tame her hair before she had to face Cuckoo. Cake.

FOURTEEN

BRINGING THEIR THINGS back to the manor gave her something to do that didn't involve worrying about Brodie and Tuck. It also prevented her from thinking too much about what Cuckoo might want from her. Zara didn't see Zave at the manor, but she didn't seek him out either. If Brodie or Tuck had gotten a reprieve from what they were doing, they no doubt would have clued their teammate into what was going on, if he needed to know. Given that he was hardly a Chatty Kathy, Zara couldn't be bothered trying to force a conversation that would just be awkward for both of them.

Zave was a world-class mind, she'd seen evidence of that herself in the gadgets she was given on a regular basis. Zave was the one responsible for building the Kindred tech that got them out of jam after jam, so she was grateful for him. There was no alternative; they needed him. But the guy still made her uncomfortable. It would just come off as peculiar if she made a point of trying to hang out with him while no one else was present.

She made a note to ask Bess how she managed to live with the guy. Thad had his own place and his own job, so Bess and Zave had to spend most of their time alone in the manor that matched Brodie's. It was probable that the kind, warm woman left the master of the manor alone as Zara had chosen to do. Despite what might be considered negative opinions, Zara did respect Zave. One of the most positive things about his character was his refusal to make himself out to be something he wasn't.

Zave didn't put on false airs or make bullshit conversation. If he had something to say, he said it. If he had nothing to say, he stayed quiet. Her awkwardness came from his unvarnished manner. He was never mean, though some might consider him rude. But Zara liked knowing he would never present himself in a lie, even if he did do stoic better than anyone else she'd known.

Her own curiosity made her want to quiz Brodie about his brooding cousin. Every once in a while, someone made a comment about Zave and all those occasional tidbits did was intrigue her further. When all of this was over, she and Brodie should get the chance to take a vacation, depending on how it all played out. Then there would be time for lingering conversation, and that was when she planned to get her answers.

Brodie might not like her chatter, but there would be nowhere for him to run and hide if they were overseas together, providing that she didn't make so much of a nuisance of herself that he ditched her in some foreign corner.

Thoughts of Zave dwindled while she showered and worked to return herself to her usual appearance. Seeing herself in the mirror again was refreshing and gave her the invigoration she needed to face the new head of CI.

If Cuckoo's meeting was company related, Zara would take pleasure in showing the superior bitch how things were done at CI. Even if it turned out to be another gloating session, Zara was happy to partake, it beat sitting around the manor waiting for Brodie to return. One thing she'd learned about watching Brodie charge into potential danger was that she wasn't good at being idle.

Just as the cab dropped her off outside CI, her cellphone buzzed in her purse. Retrieving the device from beside her gun, she hoped that the caller would be her love.

When an actual phone number flashed up on the screen, she knew it wasn't him.

"Hello?" she answered.

"Miss Bandini," a voice said, and although it was faint, she recognized it.

"Mr. Samara?" she asked, assuming he'd want an answer for his proposal. Though if Brodie and Tuck had been captured, this mission could be taking a grave turn.

Hurrying up the external concrete stairs that led to the CI main entrance, she diverted her trajectory away from the grand CI doors. Instead, she stayed outside and went to shelter herself in one of the steel arches that towered around the lobby of the skyscraper. Wishing that she'd heard from Brodie or Tuck, she didn't know what they knew, which could lead to her making a mistaken assertion. Still, if her cohorts had been made, as she'd previously considered, this could be Kahlil calling to issue his demand of ransom.

"I trust you've had sufficient time to think about our offer," Kahlil said. "Have you discussed it with your colleagues?"

Taking a silent moment to appreciate her relief, she felt her heart return to its normal pulse. Kahlil wasn't angry or accusing, he was a man making a business call. He could be playing her, except she couldn't fathom any reason he'd have to deny discovering the Kindred tail.

Talking business, whether legal or not, was something she had plenty of practice in, so she cleared her throat and matched his efficient, professional tone. "Yes," she said. They'd talked about it, but they hadn't come to any conclusions.

She anticipated he would request a definitive answer. "I would like to meet to discuss it. I tried to contact you at CI yesterday and was told you'd been terminated."

Well, that was one way to put it, and at least she didn't have to worry about Cuckoo begging her to come back to work. A meeting with Kahlil also bought her time to vamp and to maybe find out some new information from him.

"New management," Zara said. Cuckoo might not be within earshot, but she wouldn't pass up a chance to make a jibe. "You know how it is."

"Yes," Kahlil said, showing no concern for her lack of a position at CI. But he knew the Kindred had Game Time. CI was a conduit for him to get in touch with her, to get the wheels moving on this deal. They didn't need the corporation, and Zara appreciated that she didn't have to explain why she no longer worked there. "Can you meet this afternoon?"

Yes, she could, she was out and about anyway. Lining up another meeting after her one with Cuckoo gave her a great excuse to depart CI on her own terms. Whatever Cuckoo wanted from her, Zara didn't imagine it would take any longer than thirty minutes.

"There's a bar down the block from CI, Purdy's. Meet me there in half an hour."

He agreed without hesitating. He had to be within thirty minutes of Purdy's, he might have followed her here or been watching CI. Zara scanned the plaza for any signs that her colleagues might be around. If they'd been tailing Kahlil since this morning, then they should still be with him. If Kahlil was nearby, her people wouldn't be in plain view, unless they wanted her to see them.

Now she was thankful that she hadn't heard from Brodie or Tuck, their lack of contact was inadvertent confirmation that they were still on Kahlil. They didn't have time to talk and plan, but she'd been on enough Kindred missions to know the deal. Following Kahlil to the meeting meant that she would have backup because they'd be around to observe the meeting.

Putting her cellphone away after disconnecting the call, she took out her compact mirror to reapply her lip-gloss. Facing Cuckoo's perfection armed with a tube of lip-gloss wasn't much of an arsenal. Their firepower might not be a match, but Zara was here now and refused to let this woman affect her emotions.

It didn't matter that this building was no longer her place of employment, it still felt like her territory because she'd graced its halls for more than five years. In the lobby, she got smiles and waves from the reception girls and security men. She was recognized, connected, and Cuckoo wouldn't have the same relationships with the staff as she did.

Holding her breath in the elevator, Zara reminded herself not to turn her lips into her mouth because of the gloss. There was no point in swiping it on if she was just going to lick it all off. Pressing her thumb to the security panel, she closed one eye and waited to see if it would flash or not. It did.

The elevator began to ascend, and she smiled. Tuck was good, she'd have to get him a gift for fulfilling her personal request. Cuckoo might have tried to revoke her security credentials, maybe it was her goal to cause embarrassment when Zara had to go and request a guest pass. Tuck had made sure to thwart that objective.

The moment she stepped out on the executive floor, she turned the face on her watch to record. She doubted Cuckoo would say anything relevant to their mission, but Zara was learning to be prepared for every possibility. Brodie would also want to know why she'd come here, and Zara didn't trust Cuckoo to be honest.

In that brief pause just outside the elevator door, Grant's other assistants spotted her and began to surround her. It started with one noticing her, then another, and another. They came from offices and desks until she had pulled a dozen women into her orbit. But she couldn't stop and answer all of their questions, it wasn't her job to do that anymore.

She kept on trying to walk and got as far as the CEO's office, where she was pleased to see the blinds were open. Cuckoo would be able to see how people around here trusted and respected her. Zara knew her former colleagues well enough to understand they wouldn't take to Cuckoo's superior attitude kindly.

Her entourage couldn't come into the meeting with her. She had a time limit here, as Kahlil would be waiting in Purdy's for her soon. "Hold on!" Zara called.

Some of the women were asking questions, others were shaking papers at her. They all wanted answers, and she was so unaccustomed to this type of concentrated attention that for a moment she felt like a celebrity being hounded by the paparazzi.

She didn't like to see these women floundering, full of questions. Losing their beloved CEO was enough of a shock for them, now they were working without their director. Under Grant, she'd delegated tasks and guided staff. They could always come to her for help or advice, except it wasn't her responsibility anymore.

"Sorry, guys," she said, raising her hands to squeeze out from the throng. "Direct all of your queries to Ms. Corvi. Good luck."

Pushing into the office, she was greeted by Cuckoo glaring across the room from behind the desk. Her tight expression betrayed how unamused she was. "Isn't that cute," Cuckoo said.

"You should get someone into that office next door," Zara said, nodding toward her old office. Pretense fell and she sidelined her ego. Zara did care for this company and those people. Someone needed to be looking after them. "They're used to working from one set of instructions. A single go-to gal, you know? Do they have those in Italy?"

"My focus is not so narrow. I have worked in corporations all over the globe. I was educated at Oxford. I'm far more worldly than you," Cuckoo said, folding her hands on the desk, but her shoulders were too tense for Zara to believe she was relaxed. "And they do work from one set of instructions, mine."

Cuckoo was on form, so Zara donned her snide cloak again. Cuckoo wasn't interested in putting their differences aside for the good of the company, all she wanted to do was play games. "Grant never had time to delegate all the things he needed done to run this office smoothly," Zara said. "I suppose you're not quite up to speed. You probably don't have that many balls in the air. The board is probably going easy on you, you know, because you're…"

"Italian?" she offered.

Zara began to walk across the room. "No, not that."

"A woman?" Cuckoo offered another option, but Zara shook her head and continued to ponder until she reached the desk and sat in the guest chair.

"A bitch," Zara said with a triumphant smile. "That's the word I was looking for."

"Raven didn't think so last night."

Scanning the room, Zara understood that this woman didn't like to be ignored and was used to commanding attention, so the less of it she could give her, the better. "He's been distracted recently with real life. You know, actual important concerns. He doesn't have the time to consider your attributes negative or otherwise."

"If you're not curious about the time we spent together last night, why did you come?"

Now Zara couldn't avoid looking at the European or absorbing the satisfaction reeking from her. It was pungent beneath the expensive perfume she seemed to have bathed in. "I came because you told me the world depended on it. If your preferred topic of conversation is Raven's cock, I think the sun will rise tomorrow whether we discuss it or not. I'm going with not."

Preparing to stand and leave, Zara began to think about her next meeting. Cuckoo spoke before she was all the way up. "Game Time," Cuckoo said, and the temperature dropped in the room by twenty degrees.

Sinking back into the seat, she watched Cuckoo push back and unfortunately, she had everything to be smug about now. "What?" Zara asked, and the time for playing was a distant memory.

"Tell me everything you know."

She owed this woman nothing. Cuckoo was the perfect example of a person they didn't want to be in command of Game Time, so Zara had no intention of telling her anything that may titillate her unwanted attention.

"Not a chance," Zara said, exhaling a snicker behind her words.

"You have an obligation to this company—"

That was a joke, it had to be. "I have no obligation to you," Zara said. "If you want to get the majority shareholder in here, he can ask me all the questions he has and I'll answer every one."

Brodie knew everything about Game Time and would

take Zara's side in this fight. Cuckoo didn't appreciate being reminded of her former lover's allegiance.

Zara sensed anger simmering around the frustration. "I am in charge here," Cuckoo said.

Examining the fraught nerves trembling below Cuckoo's perfect exterior, Zara noticed the lock grip of her interlinked fingers was making her knuckles white. Zara would like to take credit for causing Cuckoo's state, but it had come too quick and too intense to be all her responsibility. The only person who would have the skills to affect the European so deeply was Brodie. This random meeting and Cuckoo's insistence took on new significance.

Zara smiled. "You asked him last night, didn't you? At the meeting you're so desperate to pretend was something more than it was. You asked him about Game Time, and he didn't tell you anything, did he?"

"Why would you think that I—"

"Because you would never ask me for a favor, and that's what this is," Zara said. "You'd rather rip off every one of those acrylic fingernails and set your hair on fire than admit you needed something from me."

From the tension radiating up to Cuckoo's jaw, Zara knew she was right. Resting back in her chair, she crossed her legs. The power was shifting. Zara could take her time and enjoy erasing the smugness from Cuckoo's aura. Tilting her head, she was going to recount the play-by-play of what she envisioned had happened last night.

"Let me see if I've got this right," Zara continued. "You hear those two words somewhere, I don't know, maybe you hacked a computer or someone came in asking about it. Then just as you get interested, you're intrigued, Raven shows up. Wow, you think you've scored, he'll tell you everything, right? He resisted, maybe reacted the way I did and laughed in your face. So you offered a little incentive, you got on your knees, maybe did a bit of rubbing, batted those sultry eyes at him, it always worked before, didn't it? This time was different. He shut you down or he had no reaction to you. He wouldn't be manipulated. Not only did he refuse to give you answers, but he refused to screw you too. It's driving you crazy that he won't give you what you want." Zara smiled but furious fury was building in her adversary. "Isn't it? Cuckoo?"

"Do not call me that!" Cuckoo exclaimed, flying up from her seat and smacking a hand on the desk as she lunged over toward Zara.

Zara took her time to breathe and admire the beauty with her feathers ruffled. "Art was right about you all along. You are a complete nut job. You agreed to come here, to manage CI, because you thought Raven would come back to you. That he'd owe you one, so maybe he'd take you along for the ride when he was working. But it's not working out, because he has me and we have something real. Something that involves actual emotion."

"You don't know what you're talking about," Cuckoo said, lowering herself back into her chair and smoothing her blouse. But she'd already cracked, the damage was done, Zara had seen her true jealous, erratic nature.

"Don't I?" Zara asked. "Which part? The part where I said he loves me or when I said he couldn't get it up for you?"

It took a bit of time, but Cuckoo surrendered a smile. "I should feel sorry for you. He might be interested in you now, but it won't last. We're a part of a vast web of darkness that you don't understand. Our paths intersect and then we fade from each other's lives, but we always come back."

Zara had not gotten specifics on the last time Raven had been with Cuckoo, but she knew not to trust this woman. After letting Caine get into her head, she wouldn't fall for the same ploy again. "Like you and Griffin Caine?" Zara asked. Bringing him up startled Cuckoo, which was the response she was going for. "You fucked him before you fucked Raven. How many times have you come back to him?"

"You think my not getting back together with Caine somehow proves that Raven and I won't reconnect?"

Yes, that was Zara's point. Raven had said his feud with Caine had started because of Cuckoo. The temptress had chosen Raven, and Zara couldn't blame her for that, but it had left Caine vengeful and obsessed with his rival.

"I don't think that you and Raven are destined to be

together," Zara said. "He won't come back to you."

Cuckoo wasn't discouraged. "Do you know where Caine got the scar on his neck?" she asked, stroking her throat in the place Caine's scar was. Zara didn't but said nothing and let Cuckoo continue. "He got it from Raven. Caine walked in on us having sex in his bed, and the lunatic lost his mind. He tried to attack us, tried to attack me, and Raven got between me and Caine's blade. He took the knife from him and in the struggle… he cut Caine's throat."

Her words slowed as the story progressed, not out of disgust or regret, her smile grew in time with her satisfaction. Cuckoo was enjoying this. Zara's sixth sense twitched, warning her of danger. She might not have liked the woman before this story but watching the pleasure Cuckoo experienced while recounting it revealed to Zara what Art had seen in this woman. Mischa was cold. Unable to feel remorse for getting between the two men. She saw nothing wrong in what had happened and rejoiced in retelling the tale like it was something to be proud of.

"Caine loved you," Zara said. Although he hadn't gone the right way about expressing it, she did feel sympathy for Caine in that moment. Walking into your own safe space and finding your girlfriend wrapped around your idol's idol must have split Caine's heart in two.

In much the same way as she imagined Brodie would react if he walked in on her screwing another guy, Caine lashed out. It probably hadn't been Brodie's intention, but the scar he'd left on Caine's neck was a constant reminder of that day, of that betrayal. One that Caine would see every single day in his reflection. It was no wonder the man had been driven half mad. Every time he looked in the mirror, he probably replayed that experience. Remembering how he felt when he opened that door and absorbed the sight before him.

"Men often do fall in love with me," Cuckoo said, lifting a hand to comb her long digits through her luscious locks.

"How terrible for you," Zara muttered, quite at a loss as to how one person could love themselves so much.

"You're wrong though, unfortunately."

"Wrong about what?"

"Caine and I did not separate forever… after Raven left me, we reconnected," she said, appreciating her own symmetry.

"Caine and you did not separate forever," Zara repeated, not believing the beauty for one second.

"No, we didn't. He's a dutiful little puppy dog. He sits and stays and begs on command. Whenever I have use for Griffin Caine, all I have to do is snap my fingers. I haven't even had to demean myself by having sex with him for the last three years. He just does my bidding if I pout, it's entertaining. He's desperate to please me and drools all over himself until I give him a command." Cuckoo laughed and swung forward and back like they were gal pals exchanging salacious gossip. "At first, I had to force myself into his bed, I had to make up some of that ground to get him back to the land of the living. After losing me, he turned into a hopeless disgusting drunk who just whimpered and moaned and cried. There's nothing manly about him, nothing attractive."

Zara began to listen. She'd been listening before, but Cuckoo's ranting was giving Zara the chance to make connections. "Why would you go back to him if you weren't attracted to him anymore?"

"I was never attracted to him," she insisted. "I needed to find someone, someone who could do what needed to be done. I needed the best and once I heard Caine was the closest follower of the man I needed… Sleeping with him was just the easiest way to get what I wanted." So a relationship that Caine thought was real had just been a ruse on Cuckoo's part to tempt out Raven. "The plan worked perfectly, Raven came to me and we… came together."

She smiled as her focus drifted, and Zara told herself not to yak all over Grant's carpet.

"Caine walked in on the two of you, got his throat slit, managed somehow to survive, but lost the will to live and so turned to despair. While you and Raven were cozy, you didn't think about Caine again. You didn't care about him… until Raven left you."

Cuckoo picked up a letter opener and squeezed her

hand around the handle. "It was his ridiculous chief. I know it was. We were happy. Then suddenly, poof, he was gone. On another job he said, but he never came back. The bastard."

Zara wasn't sure if she meant Art was the bastard or Raven. But admitting that Raven didn't return to her contradicted what she'd said earlier about them always coming back to each other.

"That's when you went looking for Caine?"

"Found him lying in a pool of his own vomit, it was foul."

And from the sneer on her face, Zara would guess that Cuckoo didn't enjoy the memory, which was odd given how she'd enjoyed recounting the story of her infidelity. "Why did you go looking for him?"

"Caine had skills. A unique skillset that I needed. He had experience that no one else could boast."

Zara's mouth opened a good three seconds before she managed to talk. "He could track Raven," she whispered in a single slow breath.

After learning who Raven was, Caine had followed his work, both Art and Brodie had told her that. At the time, he'd probably been young, impressionable, and over-eager. But having been Raven's groupie once gave him the knowledge that Cuckoo needed to track the man who'd scorned her.

"Yes," Cuckoo said and she was smiling again.

"How long have you had him on a leash?" Zara asked, bouncing to the front of her chair. Cuckoo didn't answer, but the proud jut of her chin that enhanced her cleavage told Zara all she needed to know. "It's you. Caine isn't following Raven because he's waiting for his time to strike. He's following Raven because you've got him wrapped tight. It's you... isn't it? You've had him watching Raven, reporting back to you with everything. You told him to come into Purdy's and threaten Raven in front of me because, why? You wanted to see what I was like? Wanted to see what I would do?"

"I assumed that you would whimper and hide under the bed. You can't imagine how annoyed I was when it brought you closer to my man."

"Your man," Zara said and almost wanted to laugh, but she settled for slouching instead. "Yes, he's your man, if the qualification is the duration of obsession. My God, you're so narcissistic that you wouldn't even stalk him yourself. Why waste your own time when you can waste someone else's? You've got Caine putting his own life on hold to do what you're too lazy or busy to do. How the hell do you get a guy to do something like that and for years no less?"

"He has an obsessive personality," Cuckoo said. "And he's pathetic, serious self-esteem issues. He believes that I think more of him for being so ridiculous. He honestly thinks we have some kind of relationship, that I value him."

"But you don't. He's worthless to you."

"His worth is what he tells me about Raven's life. You can't imagine how overjoyed I was when I found out his absurd keeper was dead," Cuckoo gasped in joy and opened her hands on the arm of the chair that rocked in motion with her excitement. Zara bit back her own fury. Art's death wasn't something to be happy about, except for Cuckoo who'd seen it as an opportunity. "The stage was set… but you just wouldn't go away."

"You sent Caine to me every time. You told him to call Grant and offer protection after the Purdy's raid. You sent him to that bar to pick me up. It wasn't Grant that wanted me in Sutcliffe's house. It was you. You've been watching us since the beginning."

Coming close to the desk, Cuckoo bent over and decreased her volume. "I have been watching Raven since long before either of you knew the other existed."

"And Caine just follows your orders."

"The best part about it is, I don't have to be in his physical company," Cuckoo boasted. "He does his work and reports to me by email or telephone. He has to be where Raven is."

"And that's nowhere near you," Zara said, her jibe earning an eye roll. Cuckoo was an even more despicable person than she'd initially thought.

"A few sexy words, a quick flash on a webcam, he's

putty. He has no mind of his own; he's a drone who does as he's told."

"You told him to come to me last night, to cause friction between Raven and me."

"Raven and I haven't had much alone time recently. I didn't want Caine around, so I made sure he stayed on you. Caine's loathing of Raven is real. I don't want them in the same room together with me, it would become a pissing contest. Caine doesn't know how to control himself, he's a lunatic when it comes to Raven."

Sure because the guy had been conditioned by this wench who used sex to take over his existence. "You've had Caine watch me when he can't get to Raven. Why? Wouldn't it have been easier to kill me?"

"It may have come to that, but watching Raven destroy you would have been much more fun. He will leave you eventually, and I plan to be there to see it. Caine had to stay close, I had to know when Raven was ready. Without his uncle to restrain him, it was only a matter of time before he emerged. Once he returned to missions, I knew that would be our time to be together. I'm sorry, Zara. You can't get between us."

She wasn't sorry, but Zara wasn't dubious about Cuckoo's delusions. They would never come true. "You think that I'll be Caine, that one day I'm going to walk in on you two fucking in my bed?"

"He did put me in your apartment. It's poetic. I had hoped that last night would be the night, that's why I sent Caine to watch that blasted house of his."

The manor would put a kink in any stalker's plans because the best they could do was watch from a distance, and it would be quite a distance because the manor was covered by heat detectors, motion sensors. Every toy Falcon had ever built was guarding their home.

"But Raven left you unsatisfied," Zara said, pleased that she'd been the one to receive his satisfaction. "So you sent Caine in to stir up the pot."

"He will leave you—"

"You keep saying that and yet here I am, completely

unconvinced."

"I love him and he loves me," Cuckoo said.

It was a shame that Mischa seemed as certain as Zara felt. Only one of them could be right. "And you're just using Caine. You'd flush him if Raven did come back to you."

"When Raven does come back to me, he'll take care of any unfinished business Caine and I have. Taking out the trash, as you put it."

"Maverick," Zara said. This woman had no compassion, no ability to feel. She had used Caine for years, and if she did achieve her goal—which Zara knew she wouldn't—she planned to have her new boyfriend put a bullet in the old one. To Cuckoo it was clean and simple. Caine wouldn't see it that way, and neither would Brodie. "You've used Caine for years, you plan to terminate him when he's no longer of use…"

Cuckoo was not dissuaded from her position. They were at an impasse and enjoyed their stalemate for a few seconds before Cuckoo spoke up with a toss of her hair. "Now I have given you something. You must return the gesture."

Zara hadn't made any deal; Cuckoo had spoken on her own. One positive quality most narcissists shared was loving the sound of their own apparent righteousness. It made fact-finding easier when the mark started spilling details all on their own.

"Sorry, Raven has a mind of his own, and I don't auction off sexual favors from my boyfriend to women who have interesting information. I can't make his dick dance for you."

Cuckoo exhaled unimpressed impatience. "I don't need you to tell me how to arouse him. I've done it more times than you have."

That could be true, but she and Brodie had had a lot of sex since they'd been together. The comparison was stupid anyway because she planned to be with Brodie for a long time, so her odometer would tick past Cuckoo's in due time. Zara also had the pleasure of falling asleep in Brodie's bed in his house, and she could call out the name he was given at birth while doing it. Cuckoo was not going to succeed in belittling Zara into doubting the certainty of her future with her love.

"So, what do you want from me?" Zara asked.

"Game Time," Cuckoo said, much as she had at the start of their conversation.

"I don't have it."

"Caine says different."

"Caine thinks you're some kind of goddess," Zara said, mimicking Cuckoo's earlier eye roll. "He has issues with reality." Leaving her seat, she glanced at her watch, estimating the time it would take her to calm down and get coffee at Purdy's. Kahlil would be there soon. She was in demand today. "Now if you excuse me, I have another meeting."

"I'm going to keep pursuing this," Cuckoo said, leaving her chair. "I will get my hands on it."

"Yes," Zara said, calling over her shoulder as she went to the door. "You will get your hands on Game Time on the same day Raven admits his love for you and dumps me."

Turning full circle as she opened the door and swung around it to witness the European's frustrated satisfaction, Zara made a beeline for the elevator, trying not to make eye contact with anyone who might bring her CI work.

She got to the lobby and out into the fresh air. After she gasped in a heaving breath, she panted out her amazement. Caine wasn't who they thought he was. His motivation was almost the complete reverse of what they'd suspected, and now Cuckoo wanted Game Time. From Zara's perspective, the reason Cuckoo coveted it was because other people did.

Cuckoo was immature, selfish, and crazy in love with Raven. Though Zara couldn't fault her for the last one, she could fault her methods. Getting this meeting with Kahlil out the way was the next point on her agenda, and then she had to get back to Brodie because boy did she have news for him.

FIFTEEN

FOR THE FIRST time in a long time, she was relieved and relaxed when she went into Purdy's. The time of day no doubt had an effect on her mood. It was lunchtime. The atmosphere was relaxed. Daylight still shone outside, lessening the likelihood that there would be a criminal attack or an amorous admirer trying to seduce her into revealing her secrets.

At least, that was what she thought.

"Zara!"

When she twisted in her chair to see who was calling for her, she wished she'd gotten something stronger than a coffee. "Julian," she said in greeting, and he came over to sit at her table. "I'm waiting for somebody."

"Oh," he said. "A date in the middle of the day so close to work?" He didn't quite nudge her and wink, but the shift of his brows was enough to make her force a smile.

"It's not a date. It's business. And I don't work at CI anymore."

He lost his cheer. "Yes, I heard you had a run-in with the new CEO, what a shame. She's great."

It wasn't a surprise to her that Julian liked Cuckoo. He liked a woman who looked good in business wear. "It was time for me to move on."

"Is that what you're doing here? Do you have an interview?"

"No," she said.

Julian took her hand from her cup. "I will be sorry not to see you at work. You're capable and beautiful, and if there's ever anything you need…"

This presented an opportunity, one that she hadn't considered until he just made this fortuitous offer. Turning her body toward his, she tightened her grip on his hand. "There is one thing that I need, something you might be able to help me with… if you can keep a secret?"

He blinked; he hadn't expected her to ask for something. "What do you need?"

"I need a list of Grant's personal accounts."

Julian was intrigued, which was a better reaction than suspicion. "His personal accounts? Why?"

"His personal accounts as they link to CI. I think he was funding a company project with personal funds."

"That's messy," Julian said. "And would be frowned upon by the board and the IRS."

"I know. That's why we have to keep it a secret, to protect his memory," she said. If Grant was a faultless party, she might feel guilty about suggesting altruistic motives. "But he was the CEO, he could do whatever he wanted. This was an important project for him, a bit of an obsession."

"What is it you're looking for?"

"I wouldn't want to betray his confidence. Is it something you can help me with?" Using the techniques Brodie had nurtured during her seduction of Leatt, she blinked and maneuvered her arms to enhance her cleavage. Julian noticed, more in passing than anything else, but it was enough.

Julian's attraction to her became an advantage to the Kindred. This was the last piece of the puzzle and quite possibly their last chance to stem future work on Game Time. When in relation to death and destruction, Zara was happy to manipulate whoever needed to be manipulated.

"His accountant has been involved in executing the

will," Julian said. "I've been in a few of those meetings, I should be able to get those accounts for you without answering too many questions."

"Thank you," she said.

It was hard to believe that just a few days ago she was doubting her ability and her right to be part of the Kindred. Today proved that when she maintained her focus, she could achieve many things.

"I'll email you with what I find out," he said and left the table. "Enjoy your meeting and keep in touch."

It was sweet that he would miss her. Life at CI was so frenetic that she was sure she'd be forgotten in a few days, not because she didn't have an impact there, but because life moved on quickly in business. There was little time to mourn. With Grant gone and her distanced from the company, she was allowed a new perspective on what her life had been pre-Brodie.

There was no permanent monument to her work at CI, she would fade away just like every other employee who moved on. During her time there, she'd believed she was making a difference in the world, now she could see that was an illusion.

She'd been with the Kindred for less than a year. But if she left their ranks tomorrow, she wouldn't be so quickly forgotten. For one thing, she was sleeping with the chief. He couldn't ignore her loss and he'd proved that by coming back for her then chasing her to her father's doorstep. She had rapport with Tuck, more so since their clash that morning. Thad was a bright beacon who wouldn't let her fade away. Zave was just Zave. Even she was becoming accustomed to what that meant.

Choosing Brodie and the Kindred over Grant and CI had been a drastic decision for her. But as she sat sipping her coffee while waiting for Kahlil, she knew she'd made the right choice.

"Oh, I love you, beau," she murmured, tucking her head down to hide her smiling lips and silently wishing that he was in her ear to support and torment her.

Purdy's had been a stable, recurring location in her

life since she started at CI almost six years ago. It had been a place for her to reflect and be grateful for the freedom from the oppression of her father's house and his ideas about what her future would hold.

She had become the strong, independent woman that she had striven to be, and with Brodie and the Kindred, she was fulfilling her childhood dreams of adventure and doing something worthwhile. No matter what Cuckoo said or tried to insinuate, Zara wouldn't give up her man, or the life they had together, without a fight.

Her coffee was almost finished by the time Kahlil came into Purdy's. It didn't take him long to pick her out in the quiet space with its smattering of customers. He came straight over without ordering at the bar and sat down opposite her.

She waited. This meeting was happening at his request; it was his responsibility to explain why he'd called it. Aloof and brooding worked for Brodie, so she tried to mimic his success by waiting for Kahlil to speak first.

"I have had a busy morning and I don't have time for games," Kahlil said, but he seemed more impatient than stressed, suggesting his meeting this morning didn't upset him too much.

But his mussed hair and the bruise on his chin spoke to the pressure he was under. "What happened to your face?" she asked, indicating the bruise. She might have seen the blow that caused it through Maverick's sight, but she wouldn't reveal that to him. Asking outright put him on the spot, and she waited to see what lie he would come up with.

"A disagreement with an old colleague."

His choice not to lie was a surprising one. The explanation was enough to allow her to move on without rousing suspicion. "Are you ready to tell me who you're working for?"

Brodie and Tuck might already have that piece of information if they'd witnessed the morning meeting. But Kahlil had been honest with her once, so she took the chance that he might do it again.

"Keeping my employer's identity secret is imperative

to the success of our mission."

"What is your mission?" Any details she had about Kahlil were related to his previous employer and even those were vague.

"I plan to protect all the puppies and kittens of the world and open my own unicorn sanctuary," he said, not in a show of dry wit, but in continuance of his impatience.

She wasn't impressed. "You're only going to get what you want if I sign off on it," she said, pushing her cup aside.

Kahlil might like to think he was in charge here, and it was obvious that he didn't like dealing with her, maybe because she was subordinate to him in the grand scheme of things, maybe because she was a woman, or maybe just because he didn't like her personality, which she could identify with. Kahlil was hardly a treat himself. It was something about the men in this game, they were so caught up in their own importance that civility and charm were often the first personality traits sacrificed.

"Does that mean you're open to a deal?" he asked.

Coming in not as an adversary, but as a client, would have been a better strategy for Kahlil. Her own curiosity grew, and she became eager to get to Brodie to find out what Kahlil had endured that morning. "Yes. We'll deal. Give us the story first, money on delivery of Game Time."

"Raven comes to the drop," Kahlil said. "I want him there with you when we make the exchange."

Most people wouldn't want their seller to have superior numbers in this situation. "Why would you want him there?"

"I know what his primary skill is."

That made sense. Kahlil knew that Raven was a sniper, so unless he was right in front of the buyer, Kahlil would have to assume he was lying on the top of a building somewhere ready to take the shot.

"Tell me the story now," she said. It would be recorded on her watch, meaning Brodie could hear it for himself. Getting the details without her love present would spare him the pain of having an audience when the truth came out.

But Kahlil shook his head. "I will be in touch with a time and a place. I will bring the money. You will bring the device."

"I will have to consult with my colleagues before we commit to where and when."

"Good. But make it soon. I want to get out of this city. I have plans of my own that don't include hanging around here."

Could his boss be local or was he just desperate to get on with outdoing his old boss? It didn't matter to her either way. The Kindred hadn't agreed to sell the device to Kahlil, but Zara was determined that Brodie would know the truth about his parents. If there was retribution to be had, she would make sure the Kindred were dedicated to getting it for him.

He'd lost his parents, Art, and Grant. No story could bring any of them back. But finding out the reason for their deaths would bring closure. Losing her own mother had been devastating to her teenage self, but at least she knew how it had happened. Brodie and Grant had both suggested to her that the blast, which killed their parents, was no accident, and they had the chance to confirm the veracity of that and get some details.

"We'll be in touch with the details," she said, and although he was perturbed, she couldn't feel intimidated by his arrogance, not after what she'd seen him doing this morning.

"I brought someone with me, my partner. He insists on seeing you. He thinks his presence will reassure you."

She didn't like to be blindsided, and when a shadow moved across the table, she glanced up. Her instinctive gasp revealed more of her surprise than she wanted it to. Coming to Purdy's during the day was supposed to be safe, now she wondered if she'd been wrong.

Shoving to her feet, he was blocking the path she'd need to travel if she wanted to reach the door. He'd spared their lives once, she couldn't bank that he'd do it again.

"Benedict Leatt."

"What happened to Ben?" he asked, having the gall to smile. "I'm not your enemy, Zara. Sit down and let me explain."

Trying her best to don her Kindred mask, she sank back down onto her chair and watched Ben sit in the perpendicular place. "You were working for Kahlil all along?"

"He wanted Game Time," Ben said, not answering the question. "I didn't know what it was, but he was willing to pay a serious amount of money to find out where Sutcliffe was keeping it."

From that explanation, she guessed he'd hooked up with Sutcliffe as he'd said he did. Kahlil would have seen Leatt's strategic position and turned to the physical therapist. "Is that why you stayed at the compound after murdering Grant because by then you were on Kahlil's payroll?"

"We didn't know where Game Time was. We knew that the Kindred had emptied the bunker, Grant told us that. But we wanted to check the place out just in case he'd hidden it anywhere on the property."

They knew that the bunker was empty, they didn't know what had been in it for the Kindred to take or what Sutcliffe had kept closer to home. "You didn't find it. We have it."

"We know," Ben said. "And we knew that was a possibility, which was why you and yours weren't eliminated like your former boss. He was of no use to us. We realized after he tried to take power that he wouldn't be worth dealing with. We couldn't ask him to rebuild Game Time for us, he proved he had his own agenda." Ben nodded toward the silent Kahlil. "My friend here said he had leverage with your people."

All along, Ben had been playing her. He'd known about the Kindred. About who killed Tim and why. He was good. "So you held the story as backup?"

Ben nodded. "When we didn't get Game Time from Sutcliffe. We scratched an alliance with Grant McCormack off the list. That left us with you. And here we are."

"And here we are," she repeated. "How did you two get involved with each other?"

"Sutcliffe came to me as a legitimate patient. My friend here approached me, he didn't give me all the details at first, just guided me in how to talk to Sutcliffe. I soon figured it out. That was long before I even met you, Zar. I'm sorry I couldn't tell you."

"Why would you—"

"Money," Kahlil said. "I paid him well for his loyalty."

Money gave access, forged an alliance, and ultimately got Grant killed. Kahlil had been fired by his previous employer then begun a crusade to usurp what Sutcliffe had won. Except no one knew where Game Time was and Sutcliffe was a paranoid bastard, though with good reason it seemed.

"Sutcliffe lost his arsenal," Zara said. "Grant tried to take over, and you took him out before he could get in your way."

"I'd think you'd be grateful for that," Ben said. "He was going to kill your friend."

Brodie was more than her friend, but she didn't need to remind them of that. "You spared us because you wanted to use us. If you couldn't find Game Time on the compound, you planned to get it from us. How could you kill a man for that?"

"I care about you, Zara. You were upset, I thought I was doing you a favor," Ben said. "Your boss man would've been a much bigger problem for all of us if we'd let him take control out there."

"That's why you killed him? He'd served his purpose and was going to get in your way?" she asked. "I thought you were a good guy. I thought—"

"Everybody thinks they're the good guy," Ben said. "My motivation is money, power. Kahlil's is revenge. What's yours?"

Her motivation was to do what was right. Game Time was under Kindred control, so if it got out there, it would be on them. Zara didn't like these two men being affiliated, between them they had quite a conniving mind. Brodie had his answer on who Leatt was working with, Rigor could rest easy because Sutcliffe's compound was old news to every other party.

"We'll let you talk to your people. We'll come to a mutual agreement about the terms of the exchange," he said, and she was still thinking about how Brodie and the others would react to this when Ben took her hand, forcing her to look at him. "I hope this will make you feel better, knowing that I'm involved. I would never hurt you. You and your friends aren't our target. The time we shared, Zara, that was real to me."

Real that they got along or real that he developed feelings for her? Brodie had already said that Ben might have. If this was Grant or another man who might be declaring their intentions toward her, she'd put them in their place without blinking. But this man was a potential client and one she might have to work, depending on Brodie's orders.

"I was hurt and confused," she said. "When I thought you were with Grant and were going to hurt us."

Ben smiled. "You don't have to worry about that." He took her hand to his lips. "No dog will come near you."

That would be reassuring, if she didn't suspect that she was being played all over again. This game was complicated, and she needed more practice. Kahlil got up first but was closely followed by Ben. The men made stilted goodbyes and left her alone with her coffee. She hung around in Purdy's for an extra few minutes just to make sure Ben and Kahlil were long gone and that Julian was back at work.

She didn't need any more meetings today. The one conversation she was interested in having had nothing to do with Game Time, which was in itself refreshing.

Ben being back, with Kahlil, was shocking. But at least they didn't have to worry about Ben sneaking up behind them when they weren't looking. Brodie would have more answers, and she was eager to find out what he and Tuck had witnessed.

But it was her conversation with Cuckoo that she was determined to address with her love. Kindred business should always take precedence over their personal matters. But Cuckoo wanted Game Time, maybe because Caine had told her about it or just because she wanted to play with the toy that everyone else wanted.

Zara had to know if Brodie knew about Caine's motivation and how it might change their approach to the guy. She had to get to base, to seek out her love and to give him a truth they'd all missed.

SIXTEEN

SHE WENT TO the manor security hub before going anywhere else. There she checked her messages and was pleased to see that she had one from Thad, until she read that there was no antidote. A list of questions followed this statement, asking why they needed such a thing and if he should be worried. The Kindred were in the midst of a mission, they should all be worried.

An email from Julian explained that he'd meet with the accountant later in the afternoon and should have answers for her by this evening. Progress, it made her feel good. The last message was from Bess, who apologized for taking Zave away from the mission, stating he had urgent business that had just come up. That guy was a puzzle.

Because she was in the basement anyway, she checked the gym, the shooting range, and their weapons room. Brodie wasn't in any of them. She checked the kitchen, but he wasn't there either. Running up the stairs to their bedroom, she was confident that if he wasn't here, he would be at the hotel staking out Kahlil or maybe still on his tail. If either of these were the case, she would want to get changed and pack some supplies before heading over to spend another night on the stakeout.

Pressing her fingerprint into the circular security panel on their doorknob, she smiled when it flashed to grant her entry. She still got a kick that her print worked on his bedroom door. The first time she'd come up here, she hadn't dreamed that one day she'd be this ensconced in the life of her mysterious bedroom intruder.

Closing the door, she exhaled all her worries when she saw his familiar form sprawled in the middle of their bed. She wasn't just established in his life, she was entrenched in his trust too. Being this exposed, alone in bed, asleep, gave her the opportunity to hurt or take advantage of him if she wanted to. But he trusted her enough that he could be this unprotected without any worry she'd hurt him.

This was the same man who kept his jeans on anytime he wasn't at home, just in case someone attacked while he was vulnerable. After hearing Cuckoo's story of them being caught in the act by Caine, Zara guessed that was where Brodie's compulsion to remain semi-dressed if they were having sex off-base began. If he'd been wary before that happened, then having a guy come at him with a knife while he was naked and getting busy would increase his paranoia level to eleven.

Tuck had slept last night and wasn't around in the manor. He was probably at their stakeout location, or he was the one still tailing Kahlil. This was Brodie's time to rest because he'd no doubt be on the nightshift again.

She should let Brodie sleep because the more rest he had, the quicker his reflexes would be. So she considered calling Tuck to discuss the developments with him. But cutting Brodie out just because he was unconscious was too reminiscent of how they'd coddled him during his grief period.

Sliding her shoes from her feet, Zara stripped off all of her clothes and crept over to the bed. Picking up the blanket, she slid beneath it. She wasn't exhausted but if she got a nap and synced her pattern with his, then she could keep him company tonight if they were watching Kahlil again, though whether they were or not would depend on what information Brodie and Tuck had discovered that morning.

Insinuating her flat hand between his chest and the bedcovers, she stroked down Brodie's solid body from his collarbone to the head of his dick. Since her hand was there anyway, she curled her fingers around his cock and he grumbled. His eyes didn't open and she wasn't here to wake him up, she was here to sleep, so she let him go.

Brushing her hand down him again, she stroked his thickening dick and kept on going until it was at full salute. Kissing his pec, she rubbed her cheek on the solid muscle beneath and barely contained her enthusiasm. He was unconscious, and his body was reacting to her insistence. It seemed a waste to ignore her effort, so she carefully peeled back the covers and pushed them down to his shins.

He was a magnificent man, all those hours in the gym kept him in shape for anything the job might require. His form was like art. Even marred by the odd scar and his tattoos, she thought he was perfect. Clutching her handiwork, she crawled down the bed and kissed the head of his dick. Opening her lips, she licked and sucked, working his balls in her other hand with a gentle caress. Forcing herself to take him deeper, she hummed and shifted angle to let her nipples graze his thigh as she bobbed her upper body in time with her suck and withdraw.

Blinking her eyes up, she was surprised to see his were open to slits, observing her work. Smiling around her toy, she pushed one hand up his torso to stop on his abdomen. "What are you doing?" he grumbled.

Pulling back enough that his head stayed just between her lips, she held him there with her free hand and swirled her tongue around him. "I would've thought that was obvious," she mumbled with her mouth still full.

"Come here," he said, opening his arm.

Taking him out of her mouth, she kept him clamped in her fist while she slid her body up on top of his. Working her hand around him, she felt the increased beat of his heart through her ribs until he got his hands between them to fondle her breasts, which separated them a little.

His rough hands were assured in their possession, he squeezed the sensitive flesh, and caressed her nipples with his broad thumbs. In time with her first whimper, he bent a knee, drawing it up between her thighs to her damp core. "You always get distracted when I'm naked," he said. Snatching a handful of her hair at the back of her skull, he pulled her body away from his and rolled her onto her back.

With his fist still locked in her hair, he forced his mouth onto hers. Just a few seconds ago, he'd been sleeping, and now he was alert and firing her to be ready for anything. Tugging one nipple, he stroked her abdomen and over her clit to press his digits into her opening.

"You gonna wake me up this way every day, plaything?" he asked, sucking on her lip and neck, near to the spot he'd already branded as his. "Get that hot, hungry mouth wrapped around my cock to suck me awake?"

If that was what he wanted, then that was what he would get. Grabbing her inner thigh, he pressed it to the bed and let go of her hair to grab his dick. Watching their joining, he forced himself into her, pushing in and sliding back until she'd expanded to fit around him. The wicked twist of his smile flashed to her, and she crunched up to drive her nails into the pec she'd been kissing minutes before.

Brodie grabbed her by the throat and thrust her down, pinning her there while he fucked her body with the cock she'd worshipped awake.

"Beau—" His other hand landed on her mouth, and she couldn't speak a word, all of her concentration went to breathing through her nose because his weight was concentrated on two vital parts of her body.

"I love fucking this body. I love playing with it, watching how you heat up the faster I go. You love taking my cock. You couldn't keep your damned dirty hands off. Soon as you get close to my dick, you can't keep your mouth closed or your legs shut. You let me fuck you any way I want to."

Whimpering behind his silencing hand, she wriggled and bucked. He was so hard and long inside her and was moving so fast that her insides were burning in carnal friction. Her body clenched, orgasm tore through her, and took over her senses with concentrated pleasure. She couldn't relax, just clenched again at the second spasm that impeded his speed.

"Relax," he demanded, wearing a frown. "Relax that pussy. Take my cock like a good little plaything." But she was struggling to control her own body. The weight of orgasm was forcing her body to close around his. "Feels like I'm ripping you in two, it's so damn tight in here."

He gritted his teeth and when he lifted his head, it felt like he grew, enlarging the passage he was fucking. One whispered curse became a hiss, then he fired into her all the spunk he cooked up just for her.

Letting her go, he flopped to his back beside her and exhaled. "You took that one hard, baby," he said, resting an arm over her abdomen so his hand came to rest over her core.

Taking his fingers from between her thighs, she squeezed them together and purred in the shocks of pleasure still thrumming through her. Bending his elbow, she brought his hand to her mouth. "Sex with you is incredible," she panted. "You turn me on so much." Her whole body was still hot, trembling, and conscious of every touch of his flesh and the fabric of the bed she lay on.

Rolling over, she thought nothing of lying on top of him, and she closed her eyes. "I'm obsessed with your pussy, my dick can't get enough."

"You'll sleep better now," she said, because she could already feel the change in his breathing. "Can I sleep with you?"

"That's a crazy question, this is your bed and I'm your guy, where else would you sleep?"

She laughed and twisted onto her front so her breasts were squashed into him and her lips were on his sternum. "I meant, did you need me to do anything? It's the middle of the day. You're my chief, too, so if there are any orders…?"

"Orders," he said, bending enough to grab her ass so he could shunt her higher. He licked her lip, and she opened for the invasion of his tongue. Parting her legs over his hips, she squirmed against his pelvis. "How about you tie yourself to this here bed so you're always available when my dick needs a distraction?"

The implication that he might have wanted her here when he first got into bed was an ego boost. "After this mission, I might just do that."

"After this mission, I'm taking you somewhere hot and relaxing."

"You wouldn't be happy just lounging around on a beach all day. We could go sightseeing in cities or hiking somewhere if you like."

"Hiking?" he asked. "You're into that?"

His definition of hiking and hers were probably two different things. "I have endurance, so as long as we start off with something easy, I should be Okay. No Everest on my first day."

"Okay," he said, gathering up her hair to hold it in a bunch at the back of her neck.

Considering the possibilities for where they could go and what they might get up to on this global trip they'd discussed before, she realized it wouldn't always feature five-star living. "I've never been camping, but I should be fine with it. It's just sleeping outside, isn't it? You're not going to make me eat a snake or anything?"

"Only the one you can't chew," he said, elevating his hips to grind his dick on her. She laughed and stroked his face. "You've never been camping? I have a lot of work to do with you."

To get her up to speed with his life experiences would take decades, but she wouldn't shy from the challenge. "Art taught you well."

"He did," Brodie said and kissed her again.

This time was supposed to be for sleeping, for recuperating for what would come next. She had his attention and given that they were alone, she decided to take the opportunity. "What would you do if you walked in and saw another guy having sex with me?"

Tightening his hold on her hair, he drew them apart enough that he could frown at her. The question was unexpected, but that didn't stop him from answering it. "I'd cut off his dick and make him eat it. I'd cut off his hands and skin him alive while he was screaming his apologies, then I'd slit his throat to shut the bastard up. Why do you ask?"

His matter of fact words were concise, like he'd given

this some thought, or it was something he'd done before. She mustered one word. "Wow."

"If you were getting fucked by another guy it would be rape, and any man who dares hurt my pretty baby doesn't get a quick, easy out."

Such graphic words, yet her heart sang and she had to kiss him again. He was right, of course, that she would never screw around on him. Brodie would be the last man to have the pleasure of her body. The question had been a reference to what Cuckoo had told her about Caine, and she'd thought it was a way to ease him into finding out that she knew about his past.

"I love you so much," she said and dug her teeth into his jaw as she scratched her nails into him.

"I'd never let anyone hurt you. You don't have to be afraid of being hurt by—"

"That's not why I brought it up."

"So why did you bring it up? Did someone proposition you? Was it that fucking lawyer from CI? He's been slobbering to get into your panties for months. I'll give him the scare of his life, we'll get Tuck to hack his address and I'll—"

"No. I have to tell you something," she said, running her hands up over his jaw to tempt his eyes to hers. "And I think it's going to shock the shit out of you… I'm not quite sure how to say it."

"Just say it," he said, and the stiff suspicion in his eyes made her wonder if he suspected her of infidelity, and that was something she wanted to dispel quickly.

"It's about Caine."

"Fuck! Did that bastard touch you?" Thrusting her body away from his, he leaped out of bed before she got her hair out of her eyes. "I promise, baby. I'll make the fucker suffer, I should've—"

Leaping to her knees, she clambered over the bed and caught his shoulders before he could walk away from her. "He's not obsessed with you," she said, searching the confusion in Brodie's features. "It's not him who's been stalking you. I mean it is, but…"

His scrunched expression betrayed that he wasn't following her, and she didn't blame him. "You're not making any sense."

"It's Cuckoo, Corvi, Mischa, whatever you want to call her. She's the one… she's been directing him, since the beginning it's been her." He still didn't seem to get it. "She told me, today in Grant's office. She told me how she used Caine to get to you and about how he got his scar after he found you and her in bed together. She told me that after you dumped her and took off with Art, she went to Caine. She makes him report your every move to her. She told him to come to me in Purdy's. She told him to call Grant to insinuate himself into our lives. She's the one who made him bring me to Sutcliffe's compound, everything he's done… he did it for her."

Her chest moved with the heaving weight of every panting breath. Brodie gave nothing away, just stood there absorbing her words for so long that she thought he might burst. For years, he'd accused Caine of being a nuisance and had ignored him because Caine had always been on his tail, even since the early years of their association when Caine idolized him.

"She's in love with you," Zara said, moving her palm to his cheek. "The reason she came to CI was to rekindle your romance. All this time… she's been in love with you and using Caine as a stenographer. He sends her reports, pictures, anything she wants. In return, he gets sex… or at least sexual contact, and a pat on the head. He's not obsessed with you. He's obsessed with her."

This was a lot to take in and she knew that, so she gave him some quiet time. Reading Brodie took work, and she used past experience with him to interpret what he was feeling. But there was no frame of reference this time. No way to judge his reactions to what she was saying because she'd taken what he assumed was a given fact and disproved it in one rush of conversation.

If Art was here, she could've taken the information to him, or they could've delivered it together to give Brodie some kind of support. At the moment, it was just her and she didn't know what he needed.

"I'm sorry, beau," she said, soothing him with a caress. "I'm sorry that I—"

He turned around so fast that she wobbled and fell to sit on her feet to prevent herself from tumbling off the bed. His hand rose to rub the nape of his neck, and she gave him some more time to process. She didn't know what was more shocking to him, that Caine wasn't the enemy they thought he was or that the ex-girlfriend he'd thought was a part of his past had never given up hope of reviving their romance.

When he did speak, his words were quiet but deliberate. "I brought her here because I thought it would force Caine's hand. I thought he'd be angry. Thought he'd come for me and then I'd have the opportunity to end him."

But eliminating Caine wouldn't necessarily change anything. Cuckoo had plenty of friends and could manipulate men with her body, she'd asserted that before. Just one look at her would tell any rational person that Cuckoo had the goods to support her flirtations. Getting Caine out of the way would be getting rid of the devil they knew. Cuckoo's next errand boy may not be as restrained as Caine had been.

"What are you thinking?" Zara asked when silence stood between them for more than a minute.

"That I have to get rid of the disease not the symptom," he said and followed it with an exhale. "Art always told me Cuckoo was crazy." Moving in a half circle as he said the more upbeat words, he fixated on her. "How the hell did you get her to tell you that?"

"I didn't," she said. "I didn't go in with a game plan or anything. She asked me about Game Time. I told her I wouldn't tell her anything and I could see that she was pissed. I guessed that she'd asked you and that you hadn't told her about it either. It got to her that she couldn't manipulate you into giving her what she wanted."

"She's good at that."

"With other guys, sure. But you recognized her tricks, or you weren't interested in taking advantage of her incentive. Whatever it was, it pissed her off, and it only got worse when I called it right. She told me you two were meant to be, that I was temporary and that she'd have you again. Then she went into the whole history lesson. She plans on asking you to kill Caine just as soon as you're back together, by the way."

He took a step toward the bed. "You didn't—"

"Of course I didn't believe her," Zara said and stretched her arms toward him.

He came to her but sat on the bed instead of walking into her arms. Moving upward, he propped himself on the headboard and pulled her over between his thighs to hold her. Brodie wasn't going to go into a speech about how this changed things because she wasn't sure that it did. Caine had still been a bug in his ass for long enough that Brodie probably wanted rid of him even if he was innocent. Except now that they understood the extraneous circumstances, she felt a bit sorry for Caine.

Warmed by the embrace of the man she loved, she was pleased he had accepted the news without flipping out. It was a shock but didn't change their lives. Caine would keep on following them and reporting for as long as Cuckoo needed him or until someone killed him.

Cuckoo was a problem, and Brodie had said he needed to take care of the disease. But the CEO was a woman Brodie had once been fond of. Zara didn't know if sharing a bed with Raven exempted a person from facing Maverick's wrath.

Caine had caused trouble in their lives, and she had no plans to become best friends with him now that she knew he was being manipulated. But Zara did feel awful for him, she pitied him, for being so in love with a crazy bitch who was using him for her own ends. He'd lost years of his life to her cause, and he had to believe there would be some reward for him at the end.

Maybe it was just habit now, he'd been doing it for so long that he didn't know any other way to be. Still, it was sad and spoke volumes about the truth of Cuckoo's character. Art had warned Zara about Cuckoo's psychopathic tendencies, but her pathology ran much deeper than the enjoyment of watching Raven work. Cuckoo could torture a person for years, use and manipulate them, without any remorse. She was a piece of work.

The warmth of her love's flesh was a comfort, and this piece of news made her appreciate the honesty of their relationship even more. "She's been using him for years. She spoke about him like he was nothing, like he was a piece of shit. He has all this love for her, and yet she's plotting to have him killed if her plan comes together."

"She's making him think it's about revenge," he said. Caressing her upper body, he brought his knees up to settle them on her, providing a reassuring cocoon. "That by chasing me around all over and harassing you that they're punishing me for what I did, for ripping their relationship apart."

"What they had wasn't a relationship," she said, tipping her chin up though she couldn't see his face. "A relationship requires respect and compromise. She told me that the reason she hooked up with him in the first place was because she had heard he knew you. Caine probably doesn't even know it."

"He started out crazy," Brodie said, wrapping both of his arms around her shoulders. "He was a regular pro at stalking me even before she came into the equation."

When they were all younger and stupider. Chances were that Caine's obsession with the sniper would've worn off when he found something else to worship. The trouble was, the next obsession in his life was Cuckoo, who commanded him to stalk the man he'd previously revered.

"But that was harmless, he was a pain, but he didn't mean to hurt you. He just wanted to be in the club. She sought him out because he knew how to track you down. She didn't go back to him for love, she went back to manipulate him."

"Everybody has to be good at something."

Slanting her body, she tried to peek up at him. "You better not be making excuses for her."

To pacify, he ran a hand up and down her arm. "Not a chance," he said, kissing her head. "We'll have to take CI out from under her. She's too close now, she could do real damage if—"

"Julian is tracking down Winter Chill." Brodie's breathless silence made her hurry to explain. "He appeared in

Purdy's while I was waiting for Kahlil. He doesn't know he's tracking it down, but he knows Grant's accountant. He'll have the records sent to me later. It might not turn anything up but getting into the personal paperwork might be the way forward. Did you find out anything by following Kahlil?"

She ran her fingernails up and down his forearms that were crossed over her upper chest. "Turns out that beneath that tanned exterior, his blood runs Russian."

"You're kidding," she said, pausing. "He went to meet Sikorski?"

"Yep," Brodie said. "He's a real sick bastard, maybe the worst sadist we've seen. But he doesn't care where results come from. Kahlil probably went looking for him after he got booted by his last employer."

"At least Kahlil hasn't told anyone else about Game Time, Sikorski already knew. How come Kahlil's old bodyguards are running Sikorski's errands?"

"Kahlil probably employed those guys himself the first time, and when he got fired, he had no more need for them."

"And somehow they ended up with Sikorski?"

"Yep," he said. "Vermin like that work for whoever ponies up the green," Brodie said. "We saw something else too."

"Leatt," she said, resting her arms over his. "He came to the meeting in Purdy's."

"We saw. What did he say?"

"That Kahlil recruited him while he worked for Sutcliffe and that they killed Grant because he'd served his purpose. They searched the compound for clues about Game Time 'cause they weren't sure we had it. When they were, they cooked up the latest deal. This is all one big mess. We can't let them have Game Time, but we have to know. How are we going to figure all this out?"

"We always get answers," he said. "Sometimes it takes time, but the truth doesn't want to stay hidden."

As her morning had proven. Brodie slid down the bed, taking her body with his, and she sat up just enough to reach the blanket he was hooking upward with his foot.

Covering them both up, it was time for them to rest. Given all that they'd learned and the prospect of what could happen if they failed, sleep wasn't going to be an easy get.

Caine wasn't what they thought he was, neither was Cuckoo. Sikorski had hidden in the background and had risen up when all parties were at their weakest. Kahlil had a story that she was desperate to know because it would bring peace to the man she loved.

And then there was Winter Chill. They had to track down the Game Time production project or controlling the devices they had would mean nothing.

As she listened to Brodie drift off into slumber, she took stock and realized that she wasn't afraid. She didn't doubt the Kindred's capability. The prospect of pain for Brodie kept her awake. Caine and Cuckoo were coming at him for something that had happened when he was a younger man, a less experienced man. He was still dealing with the loss of Art, and the reminder of the loss of his parents was the last thing he needed while he was finding his feet as the Kindred chief.

Brodie was under a lot of pressure to make the right decisions, to not screw up, and he'd feel the weight of Art's teachings as though his uncle was there over his shoulder watching out for every mistake he might make.

All Zara could do was be here for him as a support, both in their work and in their bed, because saving the world from Game Time meant dealing with emotional issues that he'd sidelined for most of his life. It was all about to come out. It was all about to get real, and there was no assurance that this story would end well for any of them.

SEVENTEEN

SHE WAS COOKING in the kitchen, whipping up something to take over to the hotel when Brodie came in and propped both hands on the lower part of the kitchen island. Glancing over her shoulder, she waited for him to say something, but he didn't.

"What?" she asked, sampling the sauce one more time before she turned off the heat and went to wash her hands.

"Your CI lawyer friend sent you a message," he said.

Snatching the towel, she dried her hands on her journey to his side. "Well?"

"He came through. We'll have to trawl through every transaction. Tuck's gonna come back to start trying to figure it out. Your friend doesn't know what we're looking for, we have to find it ourselves. It might take a while, but we've got the info, that's a great start. Your lawyer buddy saved us some legwork."

Asking Julian had been a spur of the moment decision, one she was glad to have made. "See?" she said. Stretching her smile, she bounced up to sit on the counter. Holding onto his shoulder while Brodie took her hip and slid her to him, he settled between her parted thighs. "I told you it was a good idea."

"I stand by what I said, the dude wants into your pants. He got the job done damn quick for a guy who's just helping out," he said.

"I'm sure a quick blow job will suffice," she said, but when his expression became more deadpan, she shook her head and patted his chest. "I'm kidding."

"Yeah, keep working on that sense of humor, 'cause I think the guy likes his tongue in his head and his balls in his pants, which they won't be if you open your mouth for his dick."

She wasn't the only one whose jokes missed their mark. When Brodie said things like that, she could never be sure if a laugh was the response he was looking for. Levering up to kiss him, she ran her hand over his hair. "You better let this grow again." She missed being able to tangle her fingers in his hair.

"I will," he groaned. "I know you hate it."

"I don't hate it. You look sexy and dangerous."

"Which goes away when it's longer?"

"No," she said, wrapping her legs around his pelvis. "I just like to have something to hold onto when your head's between my thighs."

"Can't say you're not honest," he said and kissed her before unhooking her legs from around him. "I have to get over to the hotel. I'm gonna help Tuck pack up. We don't need to keep watching Kahlil if we know who he's working for and with."

"About that," she said, coiling her leg around his thigh to prevent him from getting too far away.

"What?"

"There's something that didn't come up when we were talking before. This morning, before he left, he spoke into his cellphone like he was recording something. I think he might be a double agent, I don't think Sikorski has him."

"What did he say?" Brodie asked, intrigued enough to return to his previous position.

"The most important thing he said was that he had

poison in his watch."

Why it was there was another question and one that made her think he wasn't being as compliant with Sikorski as they believed. Sikorski would bring money to the table, money that Kahlil probably didn't have. But the Game Time deal he'd offered came with the promise of plenty of green. She couldn't see Kahlil having those kinds of private funds. He dressed well but had maintained a subordinate place in his previous organization. If he'd had the funds to go it alone, she'd guess he'd have tried it by now.

But carrying poison and claiming his aim was to eliminate a target suggested more than it being an undetectable defensive measure.

Possibilities flickered behind his eyes, and she was curious about her love's conclusions. "Why would he say that?" Brodie asked. "Poison for him or someone else?"

"I'm going with someone else because he said if he got close enough, he would eliminate the threat or the target... something like that. I can't remember which word he used."

When his pondering concentration broke, her actions became Brodie's focus. "And you tell me this after having sex with me and sleeping in my bed all day?"

"I'm telling you now," she said. Telling him sooner would have caused him to take action, and he needed his rest. "I tried to call you about the poison as soon as he said it, but you didn't pick up your phone." For this, she gave his chest a shove. "Sometimes I do have important information. I don't just call to ask what you want for dessert."

"I guess that explains why you had a message from Thad about poison. Atta girl."

Anticipating the possible need for an antidote impressed him, so she supposed that she was out of the doghouse for delaying giving him the news. "Just thinking ahead," she said. "Except as it turns out, there isn't one. So we will have to be careful."

He frowned. "Yeah, I read that. He wrote a fucking essay, the toxin comes from fish or something, I don't know."

Zara poked his ribs. "How do you know I have a message from him?" Or from Julian for that matter.

Both men had messaged her private email account when she'd heard from them before finding Brodie in the bedroom. Julian wouldn't even know how to contact a general Kindred address; he didn't know the Kindred existed.

With a knowing look, she dropped the affront to smile. Tuck had said that Kadie acted pissed when he hacked her accounts, but she secretly wanted him to do it. Zara now got what he meant. It was sort of nice that Brodie was interested enough in her life to want to pry into what was going on. And she had nothing to hide from him, so he could read her messages as much as he wanted, just so long as she got to read his in return.

"Just watching your tail, baby," he said, leaning down to kiss her shoulder. "Do you think he wants to take out Sikorski, or is it Leatt he's planning on betraying? We'll have to keep an eye on this one. The shit will hit the fan, someone's getting a dose of that poison, either his partner or his banker."

They would have to watch themselves, too, despite being lucky enough to have others looking out for them. Being part of a group gave them protection that the others wouldn't have. She hadn't seen Sikorski herself today, but she'd met him before. He traveled with others, bodyguards probably paid to take the bullet if one was shot his way. But honor among thieves tended to depend on who could offer the best benefits. Anyone could be working inside. She knew from experience that trusting an outsider with your secrets or your life could be the last mistake a person made.

"What do you think about Leatt?" she asked because she still couldn't understand why he was allied with Kahlil.

"I don't trust him. I never did," he said. That could've had something to do with her sort of faux dating Leatt for a while. "But Leatt's more of a follower than a leader. He didn't come up with the plan, whatever the plan is. That might make him expendable. Psychopaths tend not to carry dead weight, and that's what he'll be to Sikorski. What does he have to offer that Sikorski might need?"

"We'd have said Kahlil was a follower given his history, and it turns out that losing his job is a helluva incentive."

"He's angry," he said. "We can't be sure of how many people he's working with. Recording that message about eliminating the threat, that was for someone."

"Leatt?"

He tilted his head, and his squint made her think he disagreed. "Maybe. But what bonds these guys? It's a good idea to have backup, but far as we can tell there's no blood or sentimental relationship. Kahlil could have a brother or family member in the background. Maybe not. But we've got to be ready for anything. I don't want any surprises this time. Maybe we should keep running the stakeout, see who else shows up." Drawing in a long breath, he ran his hand up to the back of his head and gripped her neck in the other. "Good thing I got some sleep today. It's gonna be another long night."

"I'll pack up some of this food and we can—"

"You're staying here tonight," he said, picking up a tendril of her hair. "I have to focus, and having you there is too much of a temptation."

"You're not going alone," she said, recalling how she'd felt that morning when he'd raced after Kahlil and that was during daylight. "You should always have backup. You just said so right there."

"Tuck's been on watch all day. I'm not asking him to stay there another night. That shitty place hurts a guy's soul, trust me."

"I'm not talking about Tuck, I'm talking about me. If I say no sex then we won't have sex. Taxicab, there you go, now you're not allowed to touch me."

Her smile was meant to portray her confidence, but when he leaned back to eye her chest and opened his hands on her thighs to slide them up under her skirt, her resolve wavered. It grew weaker when his eyes narrowed, and he dipped down to rub the bruise on her neck with his stubble.

He parted his lips and the inhale of breath against her skin made her eyes close. She grew weak when he kissed her once. Tracing his lips higher, he kissed her again on the underside of her jaw and moved over to kiss her chin. With excruciating pace, he let his lips sink onto hers.

She opened her hands on his chest and lessened the

circle of her legs around his hips enough that she could lock her ankles together behind him. Opening her mouth, she expected his tongue, instead he withdrew and brushed his lips over her cheekbone to the shell of her ear.

"I know how to make you beg for me, pretty baby. You blink those big brown eyes and get me hard, rubbing my fucktoy all over me, those hot tits and your smackable ass. You push my property, that body, into mine and you'll make me want you. I can't be close to your tight pussy without wanting it. I don't even have to touch you, I know how to get you so wet you'll be soaking through your panties. You'll be dripping, begging me to fuck you, no safe word can stop you from wanting me. When you want it, pretty baby, you'll get it from me, hard and fast and any other damn way I give it."

Her dry lips came together and she swallowed. He was right, her insides were alive, her blood simmering to a boil. She wanted him. Her man. She wanted him now. Her breasts were so heavy they hurt. The rasp of material on her nipples made them burn, and the zing of torturous want shimmied from her clit to her brain, blanking all thoughts but one.

"I want you now," she gasped and grabbed his belt, but he backed away out of her reach, leaving her panting.

He laughed, a deep, depraved chuckle that tormented her because it punctuated his power over her. "And that's why you're not coming with me," he said, reaching over to skim her chin with a fingertip.

She didn't want him to be right because she didn't want him working alone. With a sigh, she surrendered to his wisdom. Going to their stakeout to back him up would only be useful if they both kept their mind on the job. When there was imminent danger, that was no problem. But alone in a bedroom all night, watching a man who'd probably sleep and only get up to pee, the temptation to take the risk would be too great.

Acknowledging that truth didn't alleviate the weakness in her arms and the giddiness that was making it difficult for her to focus. The tingling need moistened her center in readiness for him, and she couldn't be left hanging all night.

"Okay," she said. "How about a webcam then?"

One corner of his lips curved high. "Nice," he said in approval. "Then I can tease you all night long."

"Without touching me." Which was the point because he needed to keep his wits about him and his attention on Kahlil. Still, that solution didn't scratch the itch of need that dampened her underwear just like he said his seduction would. "Okay… but you have to fuck me now… quick, I swear."

Begging for his acquiesce, she worried he might refuse her. But he came back over and planted a hand on the counter on each side of her, forcing her to lean back. "No time for that," he said. "I won't be able to shower over there if I'm alone, and if I go over there reeking of you and sex… you'll be the distraction I'm trying to fucking avoid. Do you think I don't notice when my body stinks of yours?"

The distraction he didn't want her to be. That could be why he'd showered before Tuck went to bed at the motel and why he'd let Tuck sleep beside her instead of taking the place himself. She knew what it was like to be horny in a room full of Kindred members and unable to satisfy herself. Sleeping beside her love was torture when she wasn't allowed to play with him.

Instead of leaving her hanging as she feared he might, he grabbed her hips, yanked her to the edge of the counter, and winked before he crouched between her parted legs. He sank his mouth against her core. He licked and teased, tasting her drenched threshold with the tip of his tongue then sliding the stiff point up the center of her body's seam to torment her clit.

His mouth was amazing, she'd known he loved to kiss from early in their relationship, and he loved cunnilingus almost as much. His mouth inspired ecstasy. Her legs crossed over each other and rested on his back as her fingers rasped through his hair. His thumbs slid between her folds, and he pinched her clit with a pad on either side, letting him roll and arouse the nub while his mouth went south to tongue her opening.

"God, I want to fuck this sweet cunt so bad," he

breathed the hot mumbled words on her, just a hairs width from her glistening flesh.

"Are you hard?" she whimpered, pushing his head back enough that she could look him in the eye, and the flash of black fire in his gaze made her groan and fall onto her back on the counter. "Oh, God, beau, don't tell me that." With her palms on her forehead, she ran her fingers through her hair.

Wrapping his strong arms around her thighs, he pulled her to his mouth, drawing her clit between his lips. He massaged it with his strong tongue, sucking and pampering it. He spread his hands on her pubis, his thumbs pushing down through her folds to push inside her.

She bucked up at the fiery shot of bliss that forced her to push into his mouth. "Oh, Brodie! Fuck me! Please, baby—"

He closed his teeth and squeezed her clit against her pubis, stimulating it with pressure on both sides. All she could think about was his dick, in his pants, so close to her, yet he was withholding the weapon she coveted. Opening his mouth in a hiss, the pressure of his breath took her to the pinnacle. Screaming out his name again, she arched and panted, trying in vain to take in the oxygen she needed to fuel this high.

Her body was still dragging on the cool counter beneath her with every heaved breath she took. Her legs hung loose over the edge, her hands were covering her eyes with her fingers in her hair, and the arousal still scorched the peaked hairs all over her skin.

When the weight of his hands landed on her knees and pushed up the front of her thighs, she let her hands fall away, and she smiled at him standing there between her legs, stroking her skin. The look of pride in his expression morphed to a concern that hung for a second, and then she saw him change his mind and try to hide the abrupt evolution of emotion his expression had betrayed.

"What?" she asked, sitting up to slip her hands onto his ribs under his arms.

He curved an arm around her to pull her forward so he could kiss her hairline. "Nothing," he said.

Zara caught him with her legs when he tried to

withdraw. "Tell me. Your face just did a weird thing. What freaked you out?"

"Nothing freaked me out, I just had a thought I've never had before," he said and probably thought that this was going to be enough to satisfy her interest. It wasn't. She tilted her head and raised her brows, she wasn't going to let this go. "I love you."

"You've never had that thought before?" she asked because she knew he had thought that before and suspected he was trying to distract her.

He exhaled. "I'm happy. That's what I thought. This. Right now. It's… perfect."

An odd word to choose given all the crap that was going on in every other area of their lives, yet she got what he meant. Smiling again, she stretched her arms and legs all the way around him to clamp her body to his.

"You make me happy," she said. "I couldn't have said it better myself."

His open hands moved up and down her spine while he spoke into the top of her head. "It would be better if we could take that food and go upstairs to spend the rest of the night together." He patted her, but she didn't let go, so he had to seek out her hands to force them from his body. She was disappointed but knew that the mission was more important than their relationship. "Hey," he said, somehow reading her thoughts. He curled his index finger under her chin and with his thumb on the front, he tipped her head back. "This will all be over soon."

Wanting to put him at ease, she smiled, but it felt like she'd heard that a lot. There was always one more bad guy chasing them down or some con where no one knew quite where they stood. "I know," she said, but the words weren't quite as hearty as he needed them to be because he frowned again.

"You want me to stay?" he asked. "If you want to call this whole thing off and split town now we—"

"And what? Leave Cuckoo in charge of the company? It's a race now to see who'll find Winter Chill first. If we win, we control everything. But if she wins…"

He nodded, understanding without her having to finish. "Then I better get going," he said and kissed her before easing away from her.

"Wait," she said, grabbing for him again.

Making love had kept her from getting her own answers. She hadn't been updated with the full details of Brodie's morning with Tuck chasing Kahlil, and they still had to make plans for when to do the Game Time deal.

"What?"

"How long did you tail Kahlil for this morning?" she asked.

"From when we left the hotel right up to your meeting with him. You took a risk."

"I knew you'd be there," she said, the tension seeped out of her body. Being this close to the man she loved did that, it kept her focused.

Running two fingers down from the hair at her temple, he tucked the lock in the scissor of his fingers behind her ear. "I think you should wear an earpiece permanently."

She couldn't tell if he was being serious or teasing her again. "So that when you're stalking me, you can whisper sweet nothings?"

"So I can tell you when it's a stupid decision to go to a meeting with a known criminal without backup."

Sagging forward, she rested both forearms on his chest. "Kahlil called me right before my meeting with Cuckoo—"

"Which was another non-sanctioned decision."

This sounded like he was on the verge of pulling rank. Difficult to believe that just a few minutes ago he'd been eating her out. "It was CI. In the middle of the day. I already asked Tuck to make sure my security credentials were in place. Even if they thought they got rid of me from the system, they wouldn't have. I knew she couldn't trap me. Also, unlike some members of the Kindred, who we won't name now, I have a cellphone with GPS that I answer when it rings. You will always know where I am."

"I will always know where your phone is," he said, stroking the same two fingers through the hair resting on the back of her shoulder. "If some bastard picks you up and abducts you, chances are that your phone is the first thing he's gonna toss."

"Wearing an earpiece all the time won't prevent me from making decisions like I did today. I have to weigh the risks, and today there was virtually none. I know the business district better than Cuckoo and Kahlil. I know the secrets of the CI building better than most of security, and Purdy's is where I killed a man, so I know I can defend myself there if I need to. Besides, I took into consideration that you and Tuck were probably still tailing him, so I guessed you would be close and you've just confirmed I was right."

Her broad smile made him shake his head. "Proud of yourself, aren't you?"

"We have to be clear about something," she said because now wasn't the time to crow. "I don't want to die. I don't want to be stolen by crazy criminals, and I sure as hell don't want to hang out and make friends with your ex-girlfriend. I do the things I do because I'm Kindred and progressing toward our end goal is my job. I don't take unnecessary risks. I do what needs to be done, and if you coddle me and strap me down here at the manor, I'm useless to you."

"And we both know how that turns out for all of us."

"We do," she said, glad that he was understanding her perspective. Feeling useless contributed to depression and feelings of melancholy. She needed to be doing something, staying busy, or her own thoughts drove her crazy. "I told Kahlil that we would exchange Game Time. That we were going to accept his offer."

Any affection in his gaze or touch evaporated, and he stepped away. "What the fuck did you do that for?"

"Because it makes sense," she said, curling her fingers around the edge of the counter to steady herself.

"To give a crazy criminal a dangerous weapon? Explain to me how the fuck that makes sense."

He was getting angry, and she knew him well enough to recognize his fury was nothing to do with Game Time and everything to do with the story that Kahlil was dangling in front of them. "Beau—"

"No!" he said. The bass of that single declaration shook the foundations of the manor, and of her soul too. Stunned static, her bugged eyes spoke for her in the silence because she was unsure of how else to react to that burst of anger. "You don't fucking get it! This is my family! My past! My decision!" His anger reddened his skin and clenched his fists so tight that his muscles bulged.

"I'm sorry, I—"

"No! You don't decide something like that. You don't decide it alone," he said with a sneering scowl that belittled her. "You don't know what you're doing. You're a rookie. You don't hand over dangerous technology to a bastard whose goal is power. You don't do that! You don't decide in the name of the Kindred!"

For all the love they'd shared on this day to this distant, angry stranger before her now was quite a turn around. The shock of his metamorphosis put her in a trance, like she was frozen in time, unable to speak up.

Bending an arm, he pointed at her. "You don't decide. You do what you're told! Don't take initiative! You follow my rules! You've got some fucking nerve." Backing to the door in a final stride, he pulled it open and stormed away. When the door clattered into the frame, she jumped but could still only sit there and stare.

EIGHTEEN

"WE GOT IT!"

For most of the night, she and Tuck had been sitting together going through the accounts that Julian had sent them. She had to trace almost every transaction because even the smallest ones turned out to be relevant. Grant had worked hard to cover his tracks and to be discreet. Tuck took her information and followed the digital trails.

He and Zave had pulled apart one of the Game Time devices a while ago and knew what it took to put the thing together. Armed with that knowledge, he sought every part and tool needed to build Game Time. After matching cash payments to those parts, they built a picture of where Winter Chill was located.

Having traced the last component, all that was left now was for Tuck to go in through the CI system, or Grant's private network, and shut down every level. The information would take time to filter down, but they'd done it, they had made sure no one would be able to put together another Game Time device.

"That's great," she said, moving her hand over the stack of papers in front of her.

"In a day or so I'll go into the individual computers of the engineers and erase any schematics or reports," Tuck said, tapping away on his keyboard.

"You can do that?" she asked because in spite of her mood, she still had to be impressed by his ability.

"It's not that difficult, I'll get a program to do it for me."

It might not sound difficult to him, but not many people would have the skills to do that. Tuck often played down his ability, sometimes he was the Kindred silent partner. His work was integral to their success, but he didn't boast or demand recognition. For fear she might make him self-conscious, she stroked her palm over the texture of the paper beneath it and didn't stress any overt praise. "It's all worth it. The quicker we can wipe Game Time from the face of the earth, the better."

"It helps that almost everyone who knows what Game Time is, is either dead or so far outside the loop they'll never find it."

She nodded. Brodie had been gone for hours. She hadn't heard a peep. They hadn't set up a webcam, he was just out there alone. The Kindred had positioned a camera to watch her apartment, she wished she'd done the same thing at Kahlil's place. She understood the need to be close, to listen in and watch what might happen in real time, and it made sense for them to be close in case he took off again, like he had that morning.

But she couldn't stop thinking about what had happened in the kitchen earlier. She should never have spoken out like she did. Brodie was right that she shouldn't make unilateral decisions for the whole group. Even Brodie rarely did that, he usually took the time to listen to all points of view and reached a consensus. But she hadn't had time to do that.

Kahlil wanted the meeting, and she wasn't in contact with Brodie or Tuck. The alternative was to turn him down flat, but that didn't make sense to her. Then he'd just be a threat and out in the world pissed at them while holding onto a valuable piece of information about Brodie's past.

They had to agree to sell Game Time to Kahlil, doing

that would give them answers about Future's Hope. They might even get the chance to see Sikorski up close. If they did, and they were in a remote enough location, all of their enemies could be taken out in one fail swoop.

"You know I broke up with my girlfriend," Tuck said.

She snapped out of her daze to see him peering over the top of his laptop at her. The glow from the screen lit up his face in this darkened space, and she wondered what time it was. There were no windows in the security room, hence how it stayed so secure and was always so dark. Light from the monitors and a muted blue light above the door were the only sources of illumination. There were florescent overheads, but she'd never seen them on.

"Hmm?" she asked because she hadn't been following. He could have been talking this whole time, and she wouldn't have the first clue what he'd said because she'd been so caught up thinking about Brodie.

"Kadie," he said. "God, even saying her name hurts." He didn't sound hurt, a bit wistful maybe, but she guessed he was trying to make a point from his shrewd look. "I was in love with her. I am in love with her. But I broke up with her because it was best for her. Giving up on what I wanted was the only way to make sure that she could have a happy future. That she could have any future."

Not so long ago, she had told Tuck if he wanted to talk that she would be an available ear for him. They were alone now, in a dark room without any threats around, so she guessed that he was taking advantage of the offer. She'd been slouched down in her chair with her legs stretched out beneath the table. But she sat up straight to show she was interested and listening.

"And now you regret that decision?" she asked. "You know where she is, go and get her. Even if she's dating some other guy, I guarantee he won't be better than you. She'll dump his ass on the side of the road if you come riding up the street beside her on your bike." She shrugged and tried a smile. "If not, there's always Maverick."

He whispered out a sort of laugh and put his elbows on the table. "That wasn't my point. I'm talking about you and

Rave."

"Oh." She hadn't gleaned that. For most of the night, her head had felt like it was filled with water. To understand what she'd been reading, she'd had to read it several times before the information filtered in. Scrunching her brow, she tried her best to focus. "You think I should dump him so he can have a future? Or he should dump me?"

He smiled. "No one should dump anyone. I'm saying, I had to make a choice. And it's not a choice you two have to make. I envy you guys."

They were lucky, and it broke her heart that Tuck had to sacrifice his chance of happiness to stay true to the Kindred. "You could've brought Kadie inside," Zara said. "Brodie would let her stay here with us. You already have your own bedroom, and she'd be safe here."

"I don't think Brodie will let anyone else into the manor," Tuck said, projecting a flavor of amusement. "Sometimes I think he'd kick you and me out if he could."

Except he wouldn't because he'd allowed them both to maintain their role and their clearance for all things manor related when he was languishing in a pit of grievous despair. If they got through that, then they would get through anything. She was about to say that she'd persuade Brodie to let Kadie live at the manor if that was what Tuck wanted. But flashes from their encounter in the kitchen before he left came back to her and dejection swamped her.

"You're right," she said. "We shouldn't make decisions about this house. It's nothing to do with either of us."

"I knew it," he muttered. "I knew there was something wrong. You women, you just get this air about you. I don't know why you can't come out and say it."

"Say what?"

"That something's pissing you off," Tuck said.

"Nothing is pissing me off."

"Sure it is. You've got that same look on your face that you did when I yelled at you in the hotel. Is it Brodie? Did you guys fight?"

There was no point in lying about it because he would

hear what happened eventually, if not from her then from Brodie. She didn't know when or how they did it, but the two men managed to convey vital information to each other, even in times she'd swear they hadn't seen or spoken to each other. Maybe they did it by email… but that would leave a trail both of them were smart enough to avoid.

"I don't even know what happened," she said, cupping her forehead in her hands. "I told Kahlil that we would do the deal, that we would trade Game Time for the money and the story. I know I shouldn't have made the decision just like that, but I thought we were halfway there anyway. Brodie had been so shut off about it, and then we had that party outside and talked about it in here. I thought we were going to do it and I mean, why shouldn't we?" She got up and Tuck didn't even try to respond, just folded his arms and twisted his chair to watch her walk toward the monitor bank and back to him. "Kahlil isn't going to give up easily, and the last thing we need is him going to crazy Cuckoo. If we can get him and his boss out in the open then Raven and Maverick can take care of business, right?"

"It's not quite as easy as that," Tuck said. "If Kahlil's alone, sure, but if he's working for Sikorski, you can't just kill a crazy Russian mob boss and not expect to draw attention to yourself. We don't want his people on our asses, they have a long fucking memory."

That took some of her gusto, she put her hands on her hips. "Did I fuck up? Are we considering *not* using Game Time as a lure?"

"We discussed it. Even if we can't take out Kahlil or his boss, we could put a tracker in the device and let the rats take it back to their maze."

"We talked about that before with Sutcliffe. It's dangerous. To do that, we'd have to risk them arming Game Time and if anything went wrong…"

"You think there would be a problem with my software?"

"No," she said, typical that a man would get defensive about his skills. "I mean, we thought that Sutcliffe would lead us to his den, and then he told me that they were planning an overseas war. You've no idea how scared I was then, he could have taken Game Time to an airfield and put it on a plane… What kind of range does your tech have? And if they have their own tech people who take it apart or look for trackers, we're doomed."

"We can give them a dummy device," he said. Leaning forward to rest his elbows on his knees, he put his plan together. "We take out the guts of the machine. Leave in the tracker and the kill switch. We'll pack in some explosives, a fuse, turn Game Time into a good old-fashioned bomb."

"A bomb?"

"Sure," he said, sitting back again. "It has the added advantage of a built-in gas dispenser. We can increase the intensity of the explosion if we fill the canisters with flammable gas and put the valves on a manual or automatic release. Then when the gas leaks into the air and mixes with the oxygen… All it needs is a spark and boom."

If he wasn't talking about something so devastating, she would probably laugh at how proud he sounded. But his great plan had one major flaw. "That's an excellent idea." Going back to her chair, she slumped down again. "Except Brodie took my head off when I told him I'd agreed to Kahlil's terms."

"It's the story," Tuck said, turning to the table. "You can't take it personal. He's not pissed at you. He's pissed about his parents."

"I know," she said, putting her arms on the tabletop. "I do know that. He's lost Art and Grant, I know he claims not to care about his brother, but it has to hit him somewhere, right? Since Future's Hope exploded, he's suspected there were other forces at play. He never believed it was an accident."

"It's one thing to believe it. It's another to have your suspicions confirmed."

Yeah, but she couldn't give him the time and space he needed to work it out like she'd done after Art's death. They didn't have the same window to let him adjust and to come to terms with this revelation because Kahlil wouldn't wait around forever. "Kahlil is impatient. He wants the deal done. I don't know if it's Sikorski or Leatt or whoever he was recording the message for, but something has him spooked. He told me that he wants to leave town."

"So let him leave."

She took a deep breath. "I'm worried that if we let this slip through our fingers now, we won't get another chance. Kahlil has kept this secret for a long time because of his loyalty to the man he used to work for. If that man hears somehow that he's trying to sell the secret or that he's working for Sikorski to obtain Game Time…"

"The previous employer might stop the leak."

"Permanently," she said. "If we let Kahlil go and something happens to him, there's no one else alive who will tell us the truth."

"But there is a truth and if Raven decides he wants it, then he'll find a way to get it. No matter who he has to put a bullet into."

She shook her head. "Bullets won't work this time," she said. "It was so long ago that the circle of people who know the details is probably getting smaller every day. How long will it take Brodie to decide? Six months? A year? Ten years? This will eat him up inside, and he'll resent himself and probably us for not taking the opportunity when it landed in our lap."

"We have to consider that Kahlil might be bullshitting us."

"How does he know who Raven is if he doesn't know McCormack history? Do you think Grant told him? I doubt it. Grant was in bed with Sutcliffe practically from day one. I think he just strung out the negotiations because he enjoyed toying with the interested parties. It made him feel important that they were clamoring for something only he had."

She hated to talk ill of the dead, but in retrospect and given how Grant was at the end, there was a deeper pathology at work. One that had probably been ignited on the same day Brodie had first seen the darkness—on the day their parents died.

"It's tough. You can't force Brodie to do something that he doesn't want to do."

"No," she said. "I know."

"I can call Zave, see if he has any thoughts on it," Tuck said.

"Thad said that Brodie and Zave were close. Do you think Brodie's opened up to him about it?"

"They were closer back in the day, but yeah," Tuck said. "Zave lost his parents too. He was an adult when they died, but I think talking to Brodie helped him to process. Talking to someone who had been through it gave him some perspective."

"How did his parents die?" she asked and a slow frown began to creep to his face.

"Hold on, his parents are dead too," Tuck said and flew up out of his chair to rush out of the room.

There might be logic in what he was doing, but it offered her no explanation. She didn't want to be left behind. Departing the desk and the room, she rushed to the stairwell door that was still closing. She could hear him running up the stairs and knew she'd never catch up because he was faster and had longer legs. But she did her best and navigated the warren of a house to get to the kitchen where he was sitting at the head of the coffee table opening a laptop when she joined him.

"How many of those things do you have?" she asked, wondering why one laptop wasn't like the next as she dropped onto the couch and lay down to catch her breath. Her cardio workout always got her blood pumping, but she was used to having some kind of a warmup first.

"Zave's parents were killed when he was in his twenties," Tuck murmured and began to type. "Speak to me, pet." Computers were his pets, it seemed to be his universal name for all programs, like he believed the vast interconnected consciousness of the global digital network was a living, breathing creature.

"You're trying to find out specifics?"

"I can't remember the date, but I remember going to the funeral… Well not going, I was on over-watch."

Of course he was. It didn't surprise her that the Kindred—if they even were that back then—were paranoid even on somber occasions. "Over-watch for what?" she asked, but he was still typing.

"I have to call him and find out why—" Something caught his eye and he looked up at the door then sat back. "Your boy's on his way up."

She glanced from him to the door and back again. Art could do that, he could look at the door and tell that Brodie was coming in. She still didn't know how it worked. But then she'd only found out after living in the house for more than three months that there were cameras watching her in her bedroom.

The first time she'd been in this house, she'd been on this couch when Brodie came in and found her with Art. Lying down, she let her hands fall into her hair, considering what Brodie's mood might be when he got here.

"Why did he leave the stakeout?" she asked Tuck.

The hacker was typing. "Don't know," he muttered. His attentiveness level fell to a one as he scowled at his computer screen. "I have to talk to Zave."

He stood up, balancing the laptop on his forearm. "Where are you going?" she asked. A surge of panic made her roll onto her side and stretch her arm to the coffee table, thus blocking his route. "Wait for Brodie."

"You're not scared to talk to your own boyfriend," he said. "He might not come in here; he might go upstairs."

"If he has something to report then he'll be coming to find us."

"Look out the window, Zar, it's dawn. He probably thinks we're asleep."

"He knows we were working," she said and he had, except he hadn't commanded that they stay up all night. Their work could have been finished fast, or they could have abandoned it to refresh themselves with a nap. "I should make coffee."

"I think it's time for us to hit the hay," Tuck said when she stood up in front of him and his laptop.

The door opened and she turned to see Brodie come inside and remain by the door. The tension in his body and the glare on his face made her hold her breath. Tuck was right, she wasn't afraid of Brodie, but she was afraid of him putting up more roadblocks to something which just made sense.

"Tomorrow at noon," Brodie said.

"For what?" she asked. Had he bought plane tickets and made a unilateral decision that they were going to leave the country? He needed to be more specific.

"Our meet with Kahlil. Gives us about thirty hours to make plans."

She hadn't expected him to come in and announce that. "Do you want me to call him and set it up?"

"What happened to the stakeout?" Tuck asked, his voice suggesting he'd deciphered something that she hadn't.

"It's done," Brodie said. "And I already set it up."

Her love was full of surprises this morning. "You spoke to Kahlil?"

"It's what you wanted, isn't it?" Brodie asked.

"I have to talk to Zave, then I'm getting some shut eye," Tuck said, moving her aside to pass the couch and exit.

"I guess we should all get some sleep," she said, but when she walked Tuck's route, Brodie moved into her path to block her way. While he examined her, he said nothing. She gave him the time he needed to find his words.

"I'm an asshole."

An excellent start, in her opinion. "I know," she said, folding her arms.

"You're the first person who's made me feel bad about that… You're doing it right now, and you're not even saying a word."

She didn't want to punish or belittle him. "I'm not here to make you feel bad. I… I push because I love you. I won't let you take the easy path just because it's easier," she said.

"Usually I don't give a fuck about hurting someone's feelings, but what I said to you… I've been thinking about it all night. I couldn't focus."

She couldn't deny that she'd been hurt, and that he'd said such things when she was just getting over her own insecurity about not having a place here was the worst timing ever. "I ended up being the distraction you were aiming to avoid," she said, expanding her lungs and slipping her arms around him. "I didn't mean to step out of line. I'm not trying to—"

He scooped her head into his hands. "I gave you the floor. I put you in charge, and then the first time you did something I didn't like, I threw my weight around. I stand by what I said about the meetings. You should never go into a place that could be unsafe without the rest of us behind you. But you're the most qualified to coordinate us, to make plans and decisions."

She didn't feel like that, these men were trained and experienced, she was still a newbie. "How do you figure that out? I don't know what I'm doing. I have no experience. I'm still learning and I—"

"There is no book on how to handle this shit. We'll have meetings like the one downstairs where people throw ideas into the ring. But one person has to coordinate the effort, ask the questions that will inspire us to think and problem solve."

"Art used to do that," she said, because she'd seen it in the limited time she'd known the man. Art didn't go out into the field, he'd told her that, which was another reason him showing up in the Atlas warehouse had been so unexpected. But she couldn't compare herself to the chief he was, Art was worldly, and she had never left the country. "He had a lifetime of experience."

"I don't know shit about hacking, and Tuck shoots like there's a bug in his ear. Think any of us know how to build the crap Zave comes up with? And Thad, he's an optimistic, upbeat little fucker with zero combat experience. But he's pulled bullets out of all of us. Stitched us up. Given us meds we'd have had to jack if it wasn't for his prescription pad. We can't even say the shit he brings, but he's got a drug for every day of the week."

"You all bring something to the team."

"And so do you," he said and carried on before she could interject. "You ran a goddamn billion-dollar corporation. You sat in on strategy meetings, stood up to arrogant fucking business men who tried to dismiss you. How many fucking staff did you oversee? Five? Ten? Twenty?"

"It varied through the years."

"You know about shit the rest of us have never seen. You can read accounts and legal contracts that are foreign to us. You know where the boss hides the money. You broke into Saint's office, and with one look at a file, you did what it took us six months to achieve. You know how to work people. And fuck, baby, you killed a man for threatening to reduce you to an irrelevant object he could fuck around with."

"Why are you saying all of this?" she asked.

It was nice to know that she was appreciated, but she hadn't voiced any more doubts about her place in the Kindred.

"Because I can't run this shit, you can. Combat decisions will be made as a group, but I need someone to keep this shit together, someone who is used to juggling a whole bunch of balls all at once."

Being a sniper, he was used to having a singular focus with Art telling him what to pin it on. Sometimes he probably didn't know why, he would never question Art's decisions. Just like her. He'd declared himself and his rifle as dedicated to her. Raven had killed on her command before, and now he was handing her his sword.

"You want me to run the Kindred?"

"The logistical stuff, yeah. You've been doing it for months, since we lost Art. He always dealt with supplies, he cooked, looked after us all, called us on our bullshit. You've been doing that."

Running the manor was Art's job before it was hers. She hadn't realized that she'd fallen into the supporting role Art had once occupied. Brodie and the others didn't have the time to deal with bullshit like paying bills or grocery shopping.

Her head fell when his hands dropped. Zara tried to step away, but he caught her waist to haul her back. "I'm not sure how I feel about this," she said. "It's too much responsibility for me to take on."

"You're doing it already, and responsibility is more your thing than mine."

"What if I make the wrong choice?" she asked. "What

if I send you into danger?"

"You won't," he said. "We consult on ops, Art always did. But he had to sign off, if you say yes or no, we'll find a way to make it work."

This wasn't like working under Grant, she wasn't going to be disciplining anyone for acting on impulse. But coordination, she'd done that at CI, delegating tasks that Grant needed done to work efficiently.

"Okay," she said, nodding. "We'll do it together."

"We've already been doing it together," he said, and although there was no lust in his eyes, she smiled. "Not that."

Brodie needed support, and he was calling her his constant. "Art meant the world to you, and I know it's important to you to honor his memory. But I know he took care of things for you so that you would be better in the field, rested. I can't make decisions about missions, but I can make sure that you all have everything you need to complete your work."

"There's one thing that we will have to deal with together today."

"What?"

"Cuckoo."

He hadn't been calling Mischa that when she first came to bail him out at CI. Finding out the truth of what she was up to with Caine and what she'd been responsible for all of these years must have sullied his opinion of her.

"You can deal with her alone," Zara said because she didn't covet standing between the old lovers. "I don't want to be in a room with you and her together. It will be too… weird and difficult."

He frowned. "Why would it be difficult?"

She sighed and balled her fists on his diaphragm. "Because you used to fuck her, beau. I don't want to see you interacting with her. It will just make me think about… the things you did with her and the things you do with me. She'll rub my face in it and…"

"Rub your face in what? You're the one who gets access now, the only one. And what I had with her is nothing like this."

"You didn't love her?"

"I didn't know what love was," he said. "I think I thought I was in love with her… maybe."

"I knew you weren't when Art told me you left her on his recommendation. I knew if you loved her, you wouldn't have given her up easily. But I don't know how long Art spent persuading you."

"He didn't like Cuckoo from the start," Brodie said, and she thought about her conversation with Art in this room when he'd first told her about Cuckoo. "But he didn't put up major objections to me sleeping with her until a month or so after we started."

"Art didn't like me at the start either," she said, though it wasn't that Art didn't like her, he was just wary of what a woman could do to Brodie if she chose to take advantage of his skills.

"Art wanted us to be together," Brodie said. "He didn't say it like that, but I got the gist."

"He said it to me," she said. "He was pretty upfront and forceful about it to be honest."

"He did?" Brodie asked, and instead of getting defensive, she sensed his want to know more. After losing someone, she guessed it was nice to get new information about them, even if it was second hand.

"Yeah," she said, taking his hand to lead him over to the couch, where she sat and pulled him down with her, just where Art had once sat. "We were sitting right here, and he told me that I was good for you. I told him not to push, then you and Tuck walked in."

"I remember that morning, I knew something was going on."

"He wanted what was best for you. He wanted you to be happy. To find your normal."

That was how he'd said it when he was dying and his blood stained all of their hands. Thinking about that day made the memory bittersweet. It was reassuring that she'd gotten Art's seal of approval before he died, for her and for Brodie too. But she couldn't help but wonder how it all might have been different if he'd lived.

"Do you think we'd still be here?" she asked. "If he was still with us?"

"That we would be together?" Brodie asked. "Way you're telling it, the old man was damn sure about forcing us together whether we wanted to be or not."

"You don't feel forced," she said, with a wave of concern that made her recall other things Art had said while he was dying. "He said that you loved me, that I loved you, that's not the reason that… that's not why you picked me or let me hang around while you were grieving."

Cupping her face, he grazed his thumb over her cheek. "Art had a way of knowing what I was thinking before I did. You're sort of the same in that way. He knew that I loved you, I just couldn't say it because… I don't know, because I just couldn't."

"You say it now," she said. Though she could count on one hand the number of times he had said it, she still liked to hear it. "I wonder what Art would think about this, about us finding our way together, about how the Kindred has changed without him."

"We haven't changed that much," Brodie said. "He'd be pissed at me for dropping the ball for so long."

"I don't think so," she said, leaning against the high arm of the couch and lifting her legs over his lap. "He wouldn't want your grief to consume you. But I think he would appreciate you grieving him, it showed how much you cared… it showed me a lot about who you are, and that his death affected you in the way it did was endearing."

He blinked. "Endearing?"

"I was flying in the dark. I could barely find my way to the garage, and it's right at the bottom of the stairs. I didn't have a clue what I was doing or how to run this place."

"I let you down."

"No," she said, sitting up and holding the back of the couch to help her keep her balance while his strong hands rested on her legs to give her an anchor. "I liked looking after you and that you let me… I appreciated it. Seeing you affected like that, it made me hope that you could one day love me… and now you do. Being thrown in at the deep end was the only way I'd have learned. Otherwise, it would've been too easy for me to let you or Art do everything. This place, and you, it's home to me now. I don't feel like just a guest when I'm here. I just wish we didn't have to lose Art for us both to learn our lessons."

When his gaze left hers and he started to caress her legs, she worried that she'd pushed too far. In speaking about Art and that dark time in their lives after losing him, she was reawakening demons that Brodie had barely managed to put back in their box. Sliding a hand to his face, she pulled him closer to kiss his cheek then nuzzled near his ear.

"I love you and I will always be here. I will always be beside you… no matter what we face."

He didn't respond in words. His hands stopped on her flesh and he breathed for a few seconds. Then in a quick action, he scooped his arms beneath her body and stood up, carrying her off.

"Even when I'm being a jerk, I'd never walk away from you," he said, taking her to the door.

It was nice to get that assurance and to know that even if one was out of line, it wouldn't jeopardize their love. "Where are we going?" she asked because with Brodie, she could never be sure what he had planned.

"Time to go to bed, partner."

"Sleep is for the weak," she responded and opened the kitchen door to let them out of the room.

"Who said anything about sleep," he said. She should've realized that he was talking about sex after his reference to spending the night thinking about her.

"Shouldn't we be planning tomorrow's op?"

"You might get to call the shots to ensure a team effort in the field," he said, stopping on the stairs to bend and put her down. With the upper stair digging into her lower back, she was forced to arch against him when he lowered to kiss her, then he murmured his words into her mouth. "But don't forget who's in charge of this body in the bedroom."

"We're not in the bedroom," she teased, opening her arms wide to drape them over his shoulders.

"Wherever the fuck we are, your pussy is mine. If I

want it, you bend over and yield.”

The tickle of her clothes made her wriggle and wish they were in the bedroom. “Tuck is home,” she whispered, tightening her arms to lift herself into another kiss. “We should go to bed… where it’s private.”

“He said he was going to sleep.”

“He also said he was going to talk to Zave, and he could be downstairs doing that.” Meaning he would have to come upstairs to go to bed and finding them in flagrante delicto while he was aching for Kadie would be incredibly insensitive.

“Whatever you want,” Brodie said and scooped her up again. This time they were torso to torso, giving her access to kiss his throat as they ascended. “You said we had to talk to Cuckoo. Don’t you want to get that out of the way instead of taking it to bed with us again?”

Running his hands down her hair that was cascading around her, he didn’t bother holding her tight because she was clinging to him so much that their bodies were glued, just as they loved to be.

“We’re getting some sleep, some food, recharging. Once the sun goes down, we’ll get her at the apartment. While we’re there, Tuck will clear her from the CI systems so she’ll have nothing to go back to.”

Being an ex didn’t warrant her any kind of special respect. Brodie was pissed. In a few short hours, the bane of both their lives would be erased from the picture, and she should take Griffin Caine with her.

NINETEEN

BRODIE WAS RIGHT about one thing. Sleeping through most of the day and then enjoying a meal with Tuck while Zave and Thad were on video chat with them did leave her feeling recharged. Everyone was in lock step, and they were determined to achieve their goal. Brodie chose to fixate on taking down Kahlil and Leatt, and in drawing out Sikorski, so she kept her mouth shut about his parents and the others seemed to be doing the same.

Acting as though receiving that information was just incidental seemed to be Brodie's way of dealing with it. For now, while they were still mission-focused, it would work. After time and distance, Zara would worry about being the girlfriend who had to help her man work through whatever consequences this news would have.

When she got the time to think about it in the shower before they left the manor, she'd prepared herself to go through another mourning period with Brodie. Yes, his parents had been gone for two decades. From how he relayed the story to her in the past, losing them had been the catalyst for his darkness to seep in. Art had pulled him out of that once, and she had done it after Art was lost.

If she had to do it again, then she would. Loving someone wasn't about the good times or the adventurous missions. It meant sticking with them even when they went a bit crazy, as she had done after losing Grant and losing her way. Brodie had been there even when she jetted across the country, no distance was too far for him to travel to get her back.

These wonderful romantic thoughts kept her warm as she climbed off the back of his motorcycle and handed him her helmet. "I'm trying hard to remember how good you are in bed," she said while he hooked the helmets on the handlebars. She took that move as a good indication that they wouldn't be upstairs for long.

This was her apartment building and a place where they'd shared happy memories. Except this wasn't one of those times. Brodie was sure that this confrontation with Cuckoo should happen here and that doing it as a team was best. Zara thought she understood that logic, until the bike stopped in the rear service alley and they got off. Abstract was over, she had to follow through.

He didn't respond to her quip, just unzipped his jacket to reveal the black tee shirt she'd watched him don after creeping into the shower with her and interrupting her thoughts. He was good in bed. He was attentive. He'd kill for her if she asked him to. Listing the reasons she loved and respected him was helping her with the turmoil the anticipation of this meeting was causing.

Brodie took her hand, linking their fingers together while he entered the security code to get into the building through the rear. He knew his way through this building like it was his own, and he should, he'd snuck in here enough times in the dead of night.

"You have the power to talk me into anything," Zara grumbled as she followed him up the stairs, trailing one step behind him. Out-sassing Cuckoo when they were alone was fun. With Brodie in the fray, things could get dirty.

Brodie's hand slipped out of hers. He slowed to skim it up her spine and moved in close enough to speak into her hair. "You had my cock in your throat twenty minutes ago. If things get too tough in there, feel free to call that out."

Turning her glare onto him, she couldn't help but feel he was enjoying this. "Hope that memory is clear in your mind, bucko, 'cause it'll have to last you a long time if things get tough in here. I still don't get why I have to be here."

They kept moving up the stairs, one gradual step at a time, making virtually no sound. "Solidarity. And she's a woman. I can't smack her around if she starts shit."

Zara stopped and with a hand on his chest, she brought him to a halt on the step below hers. "You expect me to smack her around? Throw in some jello and a couple of bikinis and you've got yourself a show." He inhaled to retort, but she lifted a finger. "You make a quip about a threesome, and you'll be in the basement for the next month with only Maverick to keep you warm at night."

Pulling on her neck to bring them together, he burrowed his mouth in her hair and the quick, shallow huffs of humidity in her locks made her think he was amused. "You are the complete package, Swallow."

As much as she appreciated unsolicited compliments, she surrendered her tension to rest her body against his then lifted in a full body nudge. "Get your game face on, Rave. We're here to evict an enemy."

"On it," he said and separated their bodies to continue up the stairs. They were one flight away when he spoke again, and their easy rapport was gone. "Baby, anything she says in there…"

"She could never make me doubt us," Zara said, wanting to reach out and reassure him. Bringing her here, doing this as a couple, was a risk for him. He hadn't said it aloud, but the trust exercise for them would be a harsh slap in the face for Cuckoo, and that was what she needed.

Much as she hated to face it, Zara had to admit that Brodie knew the psycho and knew how to influence her. This unannounced meeting was about more than getting Cuckoo out of CI. This was about Brodie showing his ex that there was no equivocation. He didn't want her, didn't love her. He belonged to another woman, and he wasn't interested in playing Cuckoo's games.

Zara wasn't sure of the etiquette when going to your own apartment to evict an unwanted, unofficial, tenant from the property. That Cuckoo was Brodie's ex was just another factor complicating the situation.

She didn't have to ask questions, her man had a handle on how to deal with this. Zara would take her lead from him. Brodie took a key from his pocket—one she didn't know he had—and put it in the lock. "Is that my key?" she asked because she didn't have her purse with her.

"The spare from the drawer," he said and glanced down at her. "You should keep better track of this shit. Do you know how easy your place is to break into?"

Well, that was a dumb question, one that gave her an opportunity to get her sass on. "Having walked in on a certain unexpected guest more times than I can count," she hissed. "Yes, I do."

He kissed her head. "Hang back a second."

So she'd come all this way just to act as look out. Fine by her. Brodie opened the door just enough for him to go inside, then he stayed put, blocking the gap in the entrance. There were cameras at the manor and while Tuck was working to erase Cuckoo from CI, he was also watching the feed that had been switched over to the security room monitors.

"Showing up unannounced," Cuckoo drawled from somewhere in the apartment. Zara couldn't see where because Brodie was in the way. "Rude, but not unwelcome. You're not a patient man or a considerate one. You take what you want... so take it."

The seductive lilt of the accent as it rolled off her tongue didn't make Zara jealous. In fact, hearing the European list Brodie's apparent attributes amused her. Brodie was patient, when he wanted to be, and he had to be considerate of her now that they were sharing a bedroom. Cuckoo had a point about his sexual proclivities, but Zara was confident he'd been sated at the house, so he wouldn't be taking what Cuckoo was putting on offer.

"I'm not here to play games, Mischa. I'm here to tell you to pack your shit. You're on a plane tonight."

"Your little project pouting, is she?"

Brodie moved forward, and Zara took this as a cue for her to make herself known. Following her love inside, she closed the door with a flat hand. Brodie took a sideways step, which allowed Zara to see her apartment and Cuckoo, who was in the middle of the room wearing a long silk robe.

The alluring pose allowed one leg to peek through the material, but when she registered Brodie wasn't alone, she quickly straightened and pulled the fabric over her knee. "What is this?"

"You've fulfilled your purpose," Zara said, stopping beside Brodie, who draped an arm over her shoulders. "Your services are no longer required. You're fired. Put it anyway you like."

"You have to get out of town," Brodie said.

"You cannot be serious," Cuckoo said, her gaze darting between them before her hands came to rest on her hips. "Is she so insecure that—"

"This isn't her," Brodie said. "It's me. You've had Caine on my tail for years, reporting to you. You can play him like a fiddle. I don't need that shit. You're pathetic."

Zara hadn't expected him to be so direct. Shock made Cuckoo blink a dozen times, expressing that she hadn't expected it either. It was a smart move to use the same words and tone with Cuckoo that she had used to describe Caine, but it had to be ego bruising.

"This is a game," Cuckoo said. "It's all a game."

"And that's why you'll never get the prize," Brodie said.

"Because you're the only one playing," Zara said. They hadn't rehearsed this but being here to witness the wrath of Cuckoo build behind that flawless face made her anxiety worth it. Now Zara understood her true purpose for being here. Brodie wanted to shatter any and all hope Cuckoo might have of winning his affection.

"You can't give me what I want," Brodie said. "I thought you were a smart woman, but all this time you've been chasing after me like a lost little pup. I need my woman to be stronger than that. Need my woman to be able to handle herself."

"I can handle myself," Cuckoo asserted, as though the suggestion that she couldn't was offensive. "I have run companies, I have—"

"Always had guys give you what you want," Brodie said. "You're no match to my girl. You can't live up to her. She can't be replaced and sure not with the likes of you."

Zara was learning new things about herself, Cuckoo was getting her just desserts, and Zara enjoyed watching it. "The likes of…" Cuckoo stuttered. "I am a hundred times the woman she is!"

Brodie's arm slid farther around her shoulders, pulling her into him. "She got to the top by working hard and proving herself, all you're good for is a suck and fuck. Any board in the world you haven't whored yourself for? That doesn't make you worthy, it makes you sad."

"Pitiful," Zara said. Another word Cuckoo had used to describe Caine.

The confused dismay on Cuckoo's face grew until suddenly it vanished and she smiled. "You're saying these things because she is here," Cuckoo said, pinning her disgust on Zara. "You don't know who he is. You don't know what he needs."

"There's only one thing I need," Brodie said. "The woman at my side now."

"No!" Cuckoo asserted, curling her manicure into her palms. "You love me! You only left because of that sick, stupid old man—"

"If that was true, why didn't Raven come back to you as soon as he was free of that man?" Zara asked. Referencing Art was rocky territory, and Zara still felt protective of Brodie's feelings for his uncle. "I understand your pain. I can't imagine what it would be like to love Raven and not have him reciprocate. But you lost any sympathy that we might have had for you when you told me what you did to Caine… You don't love Caine, you played him. Stalking Raven was never going to make him fall in love with you because this isn't about love, it's about control. You wanted Raven because he was the one man who walked away from you before you were done with him."

"You know nothing," Cuckoo said, lowering her voice to a growl. "He called me here, gave me his company because he—"

"Cormack Industries is no longer under your control," Zara said. "Your credentials have been revoked, and an announcement will be made tomorrow that you are no longer with the firm. It will also be announced that CI is merging with Knight Corp, and talks will begin next week to arrange the terms of that union."

Zara didn't care that the woman was angry, she didn't care that Cuckoo felt belittled and victimized. This situation only occurred because of the way Cuckoo handled herself. Dragooning a man into a life of servitude, forcing him to stalk and harass the apparent object of her love, showed Zara Cuckoo's level of compassion, and it was the level she'd get in return.

"Pack your shit," Brodie said. "You're done."

"A taxi will be here for you in ten minutes," Zara said.

Cuckoo squeezed her lips together and held her breath. Zara wondered if she was going to have a full-on toddler tantrum. Releasing the steam of fury in one long inhale, Cuckoo spun around and marched into the bedroom, slamming the door behind herself.

"Should we go after her?"

"Why?" Brodie asked. "If she climbs out the window, we get what we want. There's nothing in there she can steal. I had all the furniture moved out of here and put into storage. Nothing in here is our responsibility 'cause everything you see was rented in Cuckoo's name."

Circumstance had prevented her from voicing her gratitude. "Except your chair," she said, recalling it in their manor bedroom.

"That's right," he said and squeezed her close.

"She could call up reinforcements," Zara said.

Pushing her forward, Brodie moved her to the black leather couch that faced toward the windows and sat down. Zara stayed upright, looking around at the familiar space that was now alien to her. She had been full of ideals when she bought this apartment, few of which had come to fruition.

Zara couldn't deny that the space was beautiful with its hard wood floors and grand columns, but it wasn't her home anymore. It wasn't her sanctuary. Though she couldn't pinpoint if that was because she considered the manor her home now or if because Cuckoo had sullied this space so it no longer felt clean or safe.

"The sole reinforcement she has is Caine," Brodie said, scooting back on the couch to lean forward. "And we can take him if he shows up."

If Cuckoo had an army of men at her disposal, she wouldn't need Caine as badly as she did. Zara dropped to the couch. Sitting on the edge, she turned herself toward Brodie and rested the sides of both her clenched fists on his knee. "I'm ready."

"For what?" Brodie asked, insinuating an arm around her hip so he could pat her ass.

"To sell this place. It's time to move on."

"It's about fucking time," he said.

Shifting to sit back, she brought her feet up and curled against his side. Brodie had been trying to coerce her into giving up this apartment since Art died. Something had held her back. She wanted to be independent, to have her own safety net to fall into if things went south. None of that mattered anymore, her connection to this abode, where she'd felt so safe, was no longer driving her.

She and Brodie had proved that they were capable of working through issues and wouldn't push each other away. It would be sad to no longer have access to this beautiful space, but the manor was filled with its own treasures. There was plenty of room there that she could get away from the others if she needed to.

Once it was on the market, it wouldn't take long to sell, and then she could move on with her life with Brodie, fully committed to their future together.

***

IN THE END, Cuckoo went quietly. Zara had expected a dramatic showdown, but the European didn't gather enough steam for that. It was sort of anticlimactic to see Cuckoo just slide into the cab and peel away from the curb. They watched her go and then that was it, one thing on their to-do list was checked off.

Returning to the manor, they stayed up late preparing for the meeting with Kahlil. Brodie and Tuck left base to scout the location and discovered there were no windows or overlooking areas of the empty, dilapidated office block that Kahlil had selected. Brodie was disappointed that they wouldn't be able to have over-watch observation points. On the flip side, neither could Kahlil. They would have to play this one straight.

Zave and Thad were flying over to act as backup because she, Raven, and Tuck were all going into the meet. Kahlil had specified that he wanted her and Raven, taking a third person just made sense. Kahlil was expecting two but would be received by three, and he'd just have to live with that. Zave and Thad weren't here yet. Their flight was due to land in the morning, and she just prayed they would get here in time without any hitches.

All three of them worked out in the gym then had a late dinner. It was the early hours when they retired to their bedrooms. Although they weren't particularly tired, it was important that they were well-rested and alert when meeting with Kahlil.

Sitting in the middle of their bed, Zara watched Brodie come out of the walk-in closet and strip off. "How are you doing?" she asked because he was scowling again and she'd noticed that expression several times tonight. It wasn't unusual for Brodie to be glaring at something, but she wanted to know how much time he'd spent worrying about what would be revealed.

"Pumped and ready to get this over with," he said.

When he came over to the bed, she lifted the blanket for him to slide beneath it to lie out on his back. He pulled her into his side, pressing her chest to his ribs to tuck her under his arm, which curled so he could toy with her hair.

What they learned tomorrow could change everything Brodie thought about his childhood. "No matter what Kahlil tells us tomorrow, it won't change how much your parents loved you."

"I know. I'm not thinking about that."

Twisting to her front, she laid her crooked arm on his chest and flattened her palm on it to prop her chin on her knuckles. "So what are you thinking about? I know you're nervous."

"I'm not nervous. I don't get nervous before ops. We've talked about it. We know what we have to do."

"This isn't like ops you've done before. This one is personal."

That got him to focus on her. "You don't think the last couple have been personal? We lost the chief and Saint. Every time you got yourself in trouble, it's been personal."

"You know what I mean," she said. "You might find out something that you don't like, and you'll have to deal with someone talking about your business. Most of what I know about your past comes from what other people have told me because you hate talking about your past that much. Are you worried that you won't be able to control yourself?"

His shrug moved both of them, and he scooped a hand behind his head. "Sure, if he pisses me off, he'll get a bullet between his eyes. But that's likely to happen anyway. Once we know what he knows, we can erase him."

Zara was worried that Brodie would struggle to restrain himself. He could be volatile if someone overstepped the mark, and by his measure that was guaranteed tomorrow. They were going there specifically with the goal of finding out a truth Brodie had coveted for so long.

"If it gets too difficult, if you need to walk away, then walk away," she said. Another reason for taking Tuck was to take the pressure off Brodie, who might not be thinking clearly. If Brodie freaked out and wailed on someone or threatened to murder them or just flat out left the building, she and Tuck would be able to hold the meeting together and get what they came for.

"I would never leave you unprotected," he said, pushing her head onto his shoulder, probably because looking at her while he was contemplating the possibilities was too revelatory. She was getting good at reading him and watching the nuance of his expression would tell her how he was handling the prospect of tomorrow.

"I won't be unprotected, Tuck will be with me," she said, tracing her fingertip down his abdomen, into and out of his belly button, then down the line of hair that led to his groin. The blanket was draped over his hips, limiting her access to her toy. "We're there to support you with whatever you need tomorrow, and when it's done and we're back here… we'll deal with whatever you need together."

"I'm not worried about hearing his story," Brodie said. "It's not gonna be nice, but whatever, I'll deal with it. I've heard criminals spout all sorts of shit."

She didn't doubt that, she'd been a part of the Kindred world for a short time in comparison to Brodie, and she'd already heard some whoppers of ego spin their yarns. "By not volunteering anything, I have to guess," she said. "I know something's on your mind."

"I'm thinking about what comes next," he said. "If we get the names of the people responsible for sabotaging Future's Hope."

"Then you'll want to go after them," she said. "That makes sense and that's what we're all planning to do. You don't have to worry about another mission, we're prepared."

"I promised to take you away. Maybe it's not worth chasing the past when for the first time, I have a future to think about."

Brodie didn't think about the future, and when they first met, he'd told her that he didn't make plans beyond tomorrow because life was dangerous and no one could be sure they had a future. Art had taught him that every person was on a path to the one day in their life when they wouldn't come back. Art had reached his one day in the Atlas warehouse, and on that day he had told Brodie to embrace a normal life because he had a woman to love.

Since she was thinking of the chief, it stood to reason that Brodie was too. "Are you thinking about Art?" she asked, and Brodie's hand stilled in her hair.

"How did you know that?"

"Because Art was the one who told you that you had a future. He told you to embrace what we have… Are you finally thinking that marriage and kids and normal could be a part of your life?"

"Is that what you want?" he asked. "Marriage, kids, normal."

Brodie had turned her traditional thoughts of the future on their head until she wasn't sure what might crop up further down the line. "I want whatever will make us both happy," she said, sensing how carefully she had to tiptoe through this minefield of a subject. "If you want to get married and have kids, we'll do that. But you're the one who told me you had mortal enemies. I think it makes sense to eliminate as many threats in our lives as we can before we can think about settling down into the bliss of normalcy."

"That means taking out Caine and Sikorski. We'd have to get rid of Kahlil and whoever else he might point his finger at."

"I know," she said. "We have plenty of time to think about normal. Let's just focus on where we are now and the task that needs to be done."

This was like a role reversal conversation. Brodie was usually the one reining in her talk of superfluous things. She didn't begrudge Brodie his hesitancy, and it was flattering that he was so concerned for her future and her safety.

Tomorrow, Brodie would get the last piece of the puzzle about his past, and the news would send them on a new journey. Zara just hoped he wouldn't self-destruct while listening to the distressing story about the loss of his parents on the day that had haunted him for more than half his life.

TWENTY

ZAVE AND THAD'S plane was delayed. Typical that both men should have the ability to fly aircraft themselves, yet they were stranded at an airport. The mission carried on. Kahlil wouldn't care about their cohorts being held up. Their reduced numbers were a bonus for him. Brodie didn't want to give Kahlil extra time to prepare or call reinforcements. They had to go ahead.

In a rare occurrence, after the van was stocked, the main gate was opened, and Zara was the one allowed to drive through it. Brodie and Tuck were on their motorcycles to give them the option of a quick escape should the need arise. There wasn't anything in the van that couldn't be left behind as a last resort, and she knew how to stay low and loose if she had to ride bitch with Brodie to make a break for freedom.

The men on their bikes flanked her front and back, making her feel like the President being escorted by two trained lethal weapons who were on the lookout for any threat who may try to get to her. Having Brodie in her line of sight through the windshield and Tuck in her side mirror was reassuring. Each of them wore earpieces that allowed them to communicate, and she was wearing her pendant that transmitted a picture to the manor.

Stopped at a light, she began to murmur the words of a song that had been stuck in her head. She couldn't have the radio on to distract her, as it might interfere with the signal they were transmitting to each other.

"Don't be nervous," Brodie said, and the sound of his voice in her ear startled her.

Talking to herself was a habit she was accustomed to, though other drivers might be surprised to see her lips moving in conversation. "I'm not nervous," she said.

"You're singing," Brodie said. "That's oral fidgeting."

If he wanted to dish out orders, she'd give him a distraction of his own to help relax him. "You've never had a problem with anything else oral I do," she purred.

"I rule that mouth, pretty baby, and right now you keep it shut."

Opening it, she drew in a breath because now wasn't the time to tease and torment him, at least not too much. She wanted him to be focused, given that it was likely they'd need him to bail them out today. The Kindred would be looking to Brodie to lead, and he was in that mindset. But there was no telling how what Kahlil had to say about Future's Hope would affect Brodie's focus.

They drove the final few miles together in the same formation. The streets they passed through grew more dilapidated and desolate the farther they got from the shore. The gray building that was their destination was soon upon them, and she knew to follow Brodie's bike into the adjacent alley because Brodie had broken down the itinerary for them. They were a great team.

"Everybody check in," Brodie said in her ear as they stopped their vehicles. On one side was a solid boundary wall that linked to nothing. On the other side was the door they'd use to enter the meeting.

She couldn't blame Kahlil for choosing this old office block on the outskirts of town. The area used to be bustling when the factories were still in production. These days, it was mostly occupied by hobos and criminals. The Kindred belonged to the latter group, so they were right at home.

The windows were boarded up, and the rear exit was blocked by a steel screen, bolted into the wall to secure the now condemned building. They had to go in the side, through the only accessible entrance, which could lead to them arriving in an ambush. But the choice made sense. Although there were buildings around, there was no line of sight. Kahlil knew what Raven was capable of and had chosen a location accordingly. If they'd objected, it would suggest to Kahlil that they planned to hurt him.

She waited in the van while the other two dismounted their bikes and removed their helmets. Following his instructions, Zara stayed put until Brodie came over and opened her door with Tuck at his back. The van key was left in the ignition as he'd coached her to do on their dry run. Brodie had every detail covered.

"You ready?" Brodie asked her. Typical that he should concentrate his concern on her when they all knew this meeting was going to be stressful for him. Focusing on her kept him distracted. Lifting her palm to his face, he caught her wrist to pull it down. "We don't know who's in there. Until we do—"

"We're colleagues," she said, shirking her familiarity. "Got it."

Kahlil had to know that they were romantically involved and would tell any cohorts about it. That didn't mean they should flaunt their relationship, as it could tempt observers to use it against them.

Brodie went first and Tuck gestured for her to follow. So in the same formation in which they'd ridden over, they went toward the side door.

Tuck took hold of her shoulders to guide her aside when Brodie sidestepped in the other direction. She knew by now not to make a target of herself, so she waited being as still as she could be. After Brodie had checked out the inside, he gestured them in, and they followed.

The room they entered was stripped of everything. Mold grew on the walls, the floorboards were stained, and a wooden staircase to the left was rotting away and crumbling.

Kahlil was already here, against the far wall with a

black suitcase behind him and no weapon in sight. Good thing she'd warned the others about the poison in his watch.

"No weapons? Show me your belt, empty your pockets." When everyone did that, Kahlil seemed satisfied. "I want you over here," Kahlil said, and he seemed more agitated than usual. They all began to move, but he jumped forward. "She stays there. You two come here."

She didn't want to be separated, but brief eye contact with Brodie gave her his command to stay. If anything happened, he'd probably tell her to run. But with a tense and edgy opponent in the room, she thought it best not to cause trouble. All she could do was stay near the door and watch as the three men moved past each other in a wide arc, keeping distance between them and eyes on at the same time.

"Where's Leatt?" Brodie asked. An unaccounted for party posed too many questions. Whatever Leatt was up to, they had to assume it was sinister.

"Close by," Kahlil said. "He won't be joining us."

Interesting. What was the point of having a partner if he wasn't around to watch your back? "Ben won't hurt me," she said to soothe Brodie whose mind was working fast, she could see it behind his frown.

Kahlil wasn't bothered about easing their worries. "She's going to take me outside and show me the device is here," Kahlil said, snatching her wrist.

Her love's scowl sharpened. "She'll walk nice and calm with you if you take your hands off her," Brodie said. "Touch her again and I'll be waiting inside that door to break your neck."

And he would do it too. The intensity of his eyes and the growl in his voice made Kahlil let her go and hold up his hands in surrender. No need to aggravate an already tense situation. Glancing at Brodie, she got the nod and went outside to wait for Kahlil, who walked out backwards, still holding up his hands.

Something silver was hooked over his thumb. "What's that?" she asked, leading him to the van. "The shiny thing in your hand."

"The key for the suitcase we left in there with your

friends," he said, his attention darting from the van to the building entrance.

Something else was going on here. Unless she had underestimated how intimidated Kahlil was by Brodie. "Why are you so nervous?" she asked, opening the rear doors of the van. "Shooting you gets us nothing. We're here for the story."

His attention piqued and he relaxed for the first time. "The story? You will exchange the device for the story alone?"

Before he could look too closely at the Game Time device, she slammed the doors. "Why?" she asked, turning expectation onto him. "Is there a problem with our money? What's in the case inside? You have to show it to us."

Brodie had chastised her for fidgeting, yet it was clear to her that Kahlil was the one on edge. Grabbing her arm, he hauled her toward the entrance, ignoring her question. "Move," he insisted, and she was dragged along at his side.

"You'll want to let me go before Raven sees you."

Kahlil didn't argue, just appreciated the reminder, and let her go. Kahlil was usually cool, confident to the point of cocky, but he wasn't as assured today.

"We agreed no weapons," Kahlil hissed, pushing open the door that had swung shut behind them.

"He is a weapon," she mumbled before stepping inside behind him.

Brodie and Tuck were still there against the far wall, except now there was distance between the two Kindred members. The suitcase hadn't moved, but that didn't surprise her. They didn't care about the money.

"I'm satisfied," Kahlil said.

She wasn't sure if she should join her faction or stay with Kahlil. Weighing the advantage, she concluded that she would rather be near the door to ensure escape for her side if the need arose. Instead of backing toward the door, she took a few steps forward, deciding that she wasn't going to give Kahlil the chance to grab her again.

So far, no one had pulled a weapon or gotten too aggressive. This was a business transaction, though not like any she'd been party to at CI. It didn't seem to matter how often she reminded herself that these men were professionals.

The image of losing Art and losing Grant kept replaying. They couldn't afford to lose anyone else. It would devastate the team and would be the end of the Kindred. She didn't know how they could possibly rebound from another tragedy.

"Tell us what we want to know," she said because she wouldn't make Brodie ask.

Kahlil took another look at each of them and began to move backwards toward the door. She feared that he planned to take off, but instead of going out, he planted his back on the wall near the doorframe.

"Your father was a stubborn man," Kahlil said. "I was still a kid, running errands for the boss, desperate for his praise. I was working low-level security. I was a nobody. But I kept my mouth shut. I was there in the room, but not in the room. I was invisible to anyone who mattered. The boss was angry, he wanted the device, and your father said he was shutting down the project."

"The project," Zara said and didn't mind turning her back on her cohorts to examine Kahlil. "You mean Game Time."

Kahlil nodded. "Threatened the family and everything, nothing worked. Your old man was happy to let his family die, let you and your brother die, before he would let go of the device."

If Kahlil wanted to piss Brodie off, he had to have a death wish. Brodie and Grant had a bust up over their father, and it ended their fraternal relationship. At that point, Brodie had chosen to let Grant live, but that was his brother, he wouldn't be so kind to a non-relative.

"Watch yourself," Zara warned, though she imagined Brodie's expression was doing the same thing. "You're outnumbered."

Assessing the scene, she began to think, and Brodie must have noticed her frown when she twisted enough that he could see her profile. When Kahlil spoke, he was quickly interrupted. "I—"

"What?" Brodie asked. "Baby, what is it?"

So much for being colleagues. "He's alone, and I think the suitcase is empty," she said. This was wrong, Leatt wasn't supporting him, and Kahlil wanted them to deliver Game Time for the story alone. Something smelled off.

"It is not!"

Kahlil was adamant, but when her eyes met Brodie's, she knew who he trusted. "You lost your banker," Brodie said, coming to the same conclusion she had. Her love became rigid in the way that always made him look like a man out of patience. "You fucking with us?"

"I'm not!" Kahlil insisted and threw a glare at her. "I wouldn't be telling you the story if the deal was off."

"So far I haven't heard shit," Brodie said. "We knew my father shut down the project and ordered everything shredded."

"But it was Frank Mitchell!" Kahlil said, maybe as a distraction technique. "He agreed terms, he said if we got rid of your father then he would control the company."

Shit, that was a shock that would increase Brodie's volatility. "No," she said, thinking about what Grant had told her about Frank's reaction to the loss of his best friend. "Frank Mitchell was against selling Game Time in any form."

"Not always," Kahlil said. "He was the one who opened negotiations, and he did it in secret for months. He was convinced that he would be able to talk his friend into selling. I think that Frank's continued pressure was what caused McCormack to snap and order all evidence of the device destroyed. That was when my boss and Frank Mitchell panicked. McCormack was putting the order through, and if the schematics were destroyed, we would have had no way to develop the device. Mitchell grabbed what he could, put a physical file together and everything digital was destroyed."

Which explained why Tuck found nothing on the CI system when he went looking. The computer files were already obsolete, but they'd been erased several times through the years. It also explained where Grant had gotten the Game Time file from. He inherited all of Frank's personal belongings after his death, which would've included the physical file.

That betrayal would've cut Grant deeper than it would Brodie. But it wasn't pleasant to know one friend had betrayed another. The Kindred valued loyalty. "So, they killed

McCormack Senior and his wife because… they wanted to do the deal with Frank?" she asked.

"Frank was the one who gave my people access to the boat," Kahlil said. "He was the one who encouraged McCormack Senior to go out on the water that day. He wasn't supposed to take his wife, Melinda, but her presence didn't stop them from following through."

How horrific to know that McCormack Senior's best friend and confidante had been the one to set him up. Game Time poisoned every person and relationship it touched. Brodie was fixated on Kahlil, and his set expression told its own story. This wasn't easy for him to hear, but these answers were going to give him closure.

Their relationship had withstood the Game Time curse, at least it had until now. With the revelations of today, they would face their biggest test yet. She had been the one to encourage him to listen to Kahlil, and depending on how he absorbed this news, they could face turbulent times ahead.

Zara maintained her lead on the interrogation. "If he wanted the couple out of the way so he could sell Game Time himself, why didn't he?"

Kahlil sucked in an expressive breath. "Murder isn't for everyone," Kahlil said. "I saw him once after the accident—"

"It wasn't an accident," she said. Her defensive anger almost overwhelmed her, and she could only imagine how Brodie was feeling. "They were murdered."

"I saw him once," Kahlil said, not acknowledging her statement. "He was a mess. It could've been guilt about orphaning his best friend's kids. But I don't think anyone anticipated the reaction to the loss. McCormack had a lot of friends, there were tributes and an outcry to find out what happened. The heat was immense. It got to my boss too. Everyone agreed to lay low for a while."

"Frank could've just sold the files with the schematic."

Though there was heat from law enforcement, Frank wouldn't want to make any deals that were too lucrative, especially for him personally because that would thrust him into the field of suspicion.

"For a fraction of what he'd get for the device," Kahlil said. "This was twenty years ago, the technology sucked. CI would've had to put all their resources into it, and my boss didn't have the kind of resources needed to do that. Frank had to get his people to develop it, but like I said, he couldn't push too hard on that button because the world looked to the kid."

Grant McCormack Junior. "Grant was in charge at CI," she whispered.

He'd been hands-on from a young age, almost immediately after losing his parents. She guessed it helped him cope with his grief.

Kahlil's brow lowered. "He was a dumb teenager, well, not so dumb… his father had taught him so much about running the company, more than even Frank realized. If Melinda hadn't been on that boat, she would've let Frank run things at CI, and she'd have protected her boys from having to take on responsibility too young."

But with her dead and ownership switching to the boys, Frank didn't have the leeway he was counting on. The situation would have worsened for him when Brodie and Grant went their separate ways. Frank had to take guardianship of Grant to ensure he kept his position of power at the firm. Getting Brodie out of the way would've been a bonus, except the separation of the boys drove them to the extremes of their choices and entrenched Grant further into CI.

Frank didn't have the influence he needed to divert all of CI's resources to the development of Game Time. He couldn't let on to Grant that it existed, or the kid might ask questions about his father's choices and his father's death. Grant also had the power to order all remaining information about Game Time destroyed, and Frank had been through that already with Grant Senior.

Killing off a kid was a different ballgame, and if Frank learned he didn't have the stomach for murder after his complicity in the death of his best friend, he wouldn't want to repeat that experience with a minor.

Kahlil continued. "Frank saw what my people were capable of when Future's Hope went up in smoke. He worried for his own safety. If he handed over this device, there was no assurance that he wouldn't be a victim of it."

Brodie had explained to her how wireless technology sucked in the days of the original negotiations. A failsafe kill switch would be a pipe dream, as would GPS in the terms they knew it today. Frank was afraid of the people he'd jumped into bed with and racked with guilt over the loss of Brodie's parents. Then he had a kid looking over his shoulder, breathing down his neck, questioning his every decision. It was no surprise that the deal had fallen apart at that stage, especially with society and the media scrutinizing their every move.

Brodie still hadn't said anything. She wanted to go over there and hug him, to soothe and stroke him while he told her how this tale altered his mood and his perception of the people in his past. But it wasn't the time to coddle him, they had to get their money and get out of here.

They had to express interest and give importance to the cash so as not to raise suspicions. What they wanted was for Kahlil to take Game Time to his nest. They would track it there and—a noise startled them all from their reverie.

"What is that?" she asked but knew what it sounded like: an engine.

"It's the van," Brodie said.

The sound of the engine made them all start moving, but they quickly came to a halt when Caine entered aiming a gun at them. "Everybody stay still," Caine said.

His familiar arrogance grated, and his sinister smile spoke of his delight at outmaneuvering them. He didn't even know that he was being played. It was sad that he thought he was a partner instead of being just a pawn.

"What's happening?" she asked.

"We're just taking what belongs to us," Caine said, choosing to move closer to her, although she backed off. "Mischa wants what's hers."

"None of this is hers," Zara said.

Cuckoo was scorned and Game Time was her way of

getting revenge. But the couple wasn't stealing from just them, they were stealing from Kahlil, and it was him that lunged at Caine and tried to grab for the gun. "Get out of here," Brodie called out to her and began to rush forward.

But Caine and Kahlil were locked together, both hands on the gun, right in front of the door. One shot went off and she leaped away. "His watch," she cried. "There's poison in the watch!"

Why she warned Caine of that, she didn't know. It seemed unfair that Cuckoo would get the prize and Caine would receive all the pain. But she wasn't being selfless, they had to find Game Time and Caine was the only person who could tell them where Cuckoo was and what she was planning.

The gun went off again, and she tried to run forward to get to the door, though she didn't know where she was planning to go because the van was gone so she had no transportation.

Caine went down, and Kahlil leaped over him to snatch a handful of her hair. Yanking her back, the pain in her head made her scream and grasp for his clenched fist. But he hauled her in front of him, and the barrel of the gun he'd taken from Caine pushed into the back of her skull.

"Get it!" Kahlil hollered, his breathing labored. "You go and get that damned device, or your lady friend gets a bullet."

Hissing through her teeth at the pain of his fingers tugging on her locks, she watched Brodie's dark determination taint his features. "You're a dead man," Brodie growled.

"We need the device," she said, still holding onto Kahlil's hand on top of her head. "You need to get it back from that bitch. We can't trust her with it."

"Swift," Brodie said over his shoulder, but Tuck was already moving forward.

Tuck pulled his phone from his pocket. Caine began to laugh. Kahlil's grip was so tight that she couldn't lower her head to see Caine, but the sound came from the floor and with pain in his tone, he sucked in a breath.

Caine's proud satisfaction made her sick. "You won't find her with that damn thing," he said. "You think we didn't know that you'd use a tracker? Used one of your own devices I stole from you, that thing with the button that sends out a pulse."

"The EM pulse," Tuck murmured. "Damn, it will have fried all the circuits."

Screwing them over pleased Caine. "Swiped it from you a while ago, knew it would come in handy."

"They'll have to rebuild the chips before they can use it," Tuck said, though the Kindred knew the device was lacking key components and carrying a few additions. "I can go back to base, hack her cellphone, we can trace her signal—"

"She'll be long gone by then," Caine said, still pleased with himself, which showed a new level of arrogance after he'd just been shot by his own gun.

"Tick, tock," Kahlil said. "Both of you go, find that woman, bring me my product."

"Go," Zara said. "He can't hurt me or he'll lose his leverage."

"I'll snap his neck now," Brodie said, and the precision of his focus rivaled Maverick's sight.

"I'll shoot her and when she hits the deck, I'll kill you," Kahlil said. "Maybe your other lady friend wants to do business."

Cuckoo wanted to do business that would suit her and *only* her. Knowing that Kahlil would be unsuccessful in coercing Cuckoo was little consolation to Zara because he'd only find that out after killing all the present Kindred members.

"Go," Zara said. "Find her. Bring her ass here."

Kahlil backed away from the door until they were at the bottom of the stairs. "You've got one hour. If I don't hear from you, this woman dies."

TWENTY-ONE

TUCK WENT OUT the door so fast, onlookers may have believed the building was on fire. Brodie was slower, much slower, and seemed pained to take his eyes from her. But they couldn't say goodbye or reassure each other, Zara just had to hope that they would succeed.

Tuck's bike started as Brodie crossed the threshold and entered the alley. No one inside said anything else until both bikes sped away.

"You can let me go now," Zara said to Kahlil. "Caine doesn't have a weapon, and he wouldn't risk his life for me."

Kahlil's grip did loosen and after a few more seconds of considering it, he shoved her at the bottom stair and marched to the door. "You stay there," he said to her and took up position against the doorframe.

Caine was lying on the floor in front of the door. It was his body that prevented it from closing. The dark stain on his thigh wasn't huge, so she guessed Kahlil had missed hitting anything important, but the trickling stain did indicate that the wound was still open.

"You're some kind of idiot, Caine, you know," Zara said, rubbing the back of her head and trying to finger comb her matted locks.

"You shut your mouth," Caine said, pressing a hand to his leg while he tried to better his position by shuffling on the floor.

Zara wasn't going to let it go. Cutting in on a deal going down was one thing, doing it for a woman who ridiculed you was another. "She's using you. You think that you're some kind of team? She took what she wanted and left you here to get shot. What does that say about how much she cares about you?"

The squint of pain he wore didn't lessen, and he pressed harder on his wound. "She cares. If she knew—"

"What?" Zara asked, pulling her legs up and wrapping her arms around them. "She would come back for you? She would care for you? No, she wouldn't. She wants what you can give her, she thinks you're an idiot. She thinks you're pathetic."

Pissing him off and telling him the truth were favors. Caine should be more grateful. "No, she—"

"Don't believe me?" Zara asked. "She told me everything, about how you and she were a thing, but she dumped you for Raven. She told me how you got your scar and how she didn't care about you until Raven left her. She's using you to monitor him, and she laughs about your dedication to her."

His focus rose from his wound, and the squint became a scowl. "No, you're wrong," Caine said.

"Am I?" Zara asked, turning her wrist toward him to display her watch. "If you don't believe me, you can believe her."

Pressing play on her watch, she let Cuckoo's words fill the room. "And he's pathetic, serious self-esteem issues. He believes that I think more of him for being so ridiculous. He honestly thinks we have some kind of relationship, that I value him."

Zara's response was on the audio too. "But you don't. He's worthless to you."

"His worth is what he tells me about Raven's life…" Zara pressed stop and waited for Caine's reaction. Some of his arrogance receded, and his frown grew deeper.

"Let me see that," he said, holding out a hand.

They were half a room apart and Kahlil had told her not to move, so after she unfastened the watch, she held it toward him. "It doesn't serve my purpose to run your errands," Kahlil said, the gun loose in his hand at his side as he peeked out the door.

"Yes, it does," Zara said. "If we can make Caine see that the woman who stole your product is not the woman he believes she is, he'll be more inclined to be helpful. He knows where Cuckoo is going."

"Why do you call her Cuckoo?" Kahlil asked, and he must have seen her point of view because he came to her and took the proffered timepiece.

"Because she's insane," Zara said, moving down from the stair to sit on the dirty floor with her spine against the wall and her legs stretched out in front of her pointing at Kahlil and Caine. "And because she tries to steal the nests of others." She might not have tried that when she was given the name, but she had McCormack Manor in her sights these days, and that was Zara's nest, not hers.

Kahlil bent to give Caine her watch. The stalker reached up, but instead of grabbing the watch, he grabbed Kahlil's gun hand and drove something into Kahlil's leg that made him scream and release the weapon. Kahlil staggered back and holding one ankle, he hopped then fell to his ass.

"What did you…?" she exclaimed. Caine's smug smile was back, and he held up two watches, hers and Kahlil's. She gasped. "You stole his watch."

"You saved my life. I let him get the gun so I could get the watch," Caine said and turned Kahlil's watch to show that the crown was missing. "You were right, there was a needle in there."

A needle loaded with poison that was now coursing through Kahlil. Panic and desperation flitted over Kahlil, but there was nothing any of them could do. She had a cellphone and could call a hospital, but she would have to make a break for it first. Surging onto her feet, she was planning to make a run for it when Caine pulled himself up to sit against the door, with the gun pointed at her.

She stopped. Kahlil didn't care about the gun now that he knew he was dying. "We've been here before," she said, familiar with being at this end of Caine's barrel. "You're not going to shoot me."

The pain must have numbed because Caine's smile reached pleased. "You're my hostage now."

"But you want Cuckoo to get away, you don't need me. If I go, Raven's not coming back here. You can get yourself help, go to a hospital. There's no reason for you to keep me—"

"I have to keep you. But you have a reason to stay," Caine said.

At first, she was unsure what he meant, and then he threw Kahlil's watch to the other side of the room away from them all and turned his attention to hers. If he played that recording and believed Zara's version, then he might be willing to help her track down Cuckoo. She did have to stay.

As he rewound and began to listen, she observed anger and frustration and shame as they crossed his face. He had to already have suspicions about Cuckoo's motives for maintaining her relationship with him to be this open about the chance he'd betray her. That Zara had warned him about the poison was another bonus.

Kahlil tried to get up, fumbled, then fell, rolling onto his stomach. He wretched but used his elbows to drag himself forward and out the door. Caine didn't even look up, but Kahlil didn't matter to him. Caine had wanted his gun back, and now that he had it, Kahlil was no threat.

Zara knew how protective a man could be of his weapon, and Caine was no exception. He listened to the recording all the way to the end. When it was finished, he just sat there staring down at it.

Seeing him broken didn't make her feel good. Her sorrow over his heartache was limited. Zara was more interested in where Cuckoo was and how she could intercept her. While he sat there holding her watch, staring at the concrete, she crept over and he didn't lift the gun to threaten her. Crouching at his side, she used what strength she had to rip the shoulder seam of his long-sleeved tee shirt. Looping it around his thigh, above the wound, she tied it as tight as she could then sat back.

"I'm sorry," Zara said, because it seemed like an appropriate response. "She's a bitch."

"Yeah, but she's good," he muttered. "I've been working for her for so long, I thought we had something. But this time, being with her again, in the same room, I knew something wasn't right."

Just as she'd suspected, Caine was questioning his partner and the job they were doing. "She left you here, I would guess that's proof enough that she doesn't care in the way you thought she did."

Zara couldn't be outright cruel, mocking him would piss him off. Not only was he holding a gun, but she was trying to win his favor. "Yeah," he mumbled.

Testing the chance of his betrayal, she softened her voice. "Was there a plan beyond her taking what she wanted and abandoning you here?"

"Yeah, she's got a contact coming with a boat to pick up the product from the docks. She told me to watch you, to make sure you didn't get away."

That wasn't what Zara would classify as a plan. That was Cuckoo getting away without a scratch and Caine staying here to carry on reporting like a good errand boy. "Which docks?" Zara asked, treading carefully, she kept her tone gentle. "If you tell me I can—"

"She's not carrying her cellphone, not the one you people have the number for. That one was scrambled to send you on a wild goose chase if anything went wrong. It will take you guys all day to track her, and your boys are probably miles off course."

These words were no longer cocky, but that was understandable given that he'd just been told what he thought was fact was fiction. Cuckoo had used him and made a fool of him for years, and he was being confronted by this fact while in an enemy camp.

Resting a hand on his arm, she made the connection before she pushed. "Tell me where she is, Caine, show her that you're not her bitch anymore."

"You won't be able to stop her alone," he said. Being shot meant he wouldn't be going anywhere with her.

That would be the next concern, getting the location was number one. "Tell me where."

Drawing in a breath, he lifted his chin and although he wasn't smug, he was certainly sure of betraying the woman that had led him on. "Atlas."

"I'll call an ambulance," she said as she strode toward him. "They'll take care of you and Kahlil."

Caine wasn't bothered. "If he's not already dead, I'll deal with him. We've got a car in the street, blue sedan, take it, the keys are in it," Caine said. "I'll look after myself, you just stop that bitch from winning."

Caine's venom had a new target, and Zara knew he held a grudge. There was no time to tend to anyone, but he was right about Kahlil, it seemed, because when she dashed out into the alley, there he was lying on his face, unmoving.

Running to the end of the alley, she sought out the car and jumped in to get moving. It was fitting that they were going back to where they started, and that could be why Cuckoo chose this spot. She'd hated Art and what he'd done to her relationship with Brodie.

Triumphing on the site of Art's demise would please Cuckoo. It was also a functional space, abandoned, far from anything, and with direct access to the water. If she had someone picking up her and the product, they could do it there and have no interference.

Calling Brodie got her diverted to voicemail, as he was probably driving, or in a battle with Cuckoo already. Zara left a message to tell him what had happened and where she was going. She couldn't waste time by waiting, so she left Tuck a similar message and just hoped that the guys picked up their messages before they went to whatever bogus site Cuckoo's scrambled phone sent them to.

One positive thing about Cuckoo picking this spot was that she knew it and the others would too. Because there was nothing else around, the sound of a car would announce her arrival, so Zara parked on the docks, away from the warehouse and made her way to Atlas on foot, doing her best to stay out of the way.

Atlas was there, just as it had been before, with its large, faded and peeling sign above the door. If she hadn't known it was here, it would have taken her a long time to pinpoint this warehouse as Cuckoo's location.

But Cuckoo was here. Zara pressed herself into the wall outside the warehouse and glanced inside. The van was parked in the middle of the space. Cuckoo was at the rear of the vehicle and was oblivious to Zara. As she twisted herself to face away again, she caught sight of the stain on the concrete floor, the stain Art had left there, the site of his demise.

She had to get inside, to get to the van and either steal it or disable the device. Game Time wasn't small enough that it could be carried by a single person. Unless Zara could drive the whole lot away, the other option was to take advantage of the destructive force Tuck had built into it.

As soon as she saw that Cuckoo's back was turned, Zara had to take her chance to make a move. There was no room for hesitation. She had to be decisive. Creeping into the warehouse, she did her best not to make any sound that might draw attention to her.

Cuckoo was on the phone, sauntering away from the vehicle that was parked almost in the same spot she and Grant had parked their van in. It was just farther from the wall it faced this time. Funny how things came full circle, but she couldn't be distracted by irony.

Cuckoo was ranting about her success to whoever was on the other end of the phone. Zara knew this shipment would never reach its destination. She wouldn't let it happen. The rear doors of the van were wide open and closing them would draw attention to her presence. But she couldn't risk the cargo tumbling out if she did manage to start the vehicle and drive out.

Her speculation turned out to be moot because when she got to the cab and boosted onto her tiptoes, she saw that the ignition was empty. Tiptoeing to the back of the van, she paused to examine Cuckoo, who had stopped walking, but was still talking. The woman had the keys, looped around her middle finger on the hand she was holding the phone with. No chance Zara was going to snatch and run with those.

Glancing into the cargo-hold of the van, she saw it. Game Time was here. While Cuckoo carried on her conversation with her back to the van, Zara crept inside to see if she could disable the device. The electronic kill switch would fry the circuits, and the explosives the Kindred had added would make sure that this device was nothing but smithereens of scrap metal after it was triggered.

Except the side panel of the device was open, and wires were pulled out. Caine had admitted to frying the circuits. Zara located the small black box that she knew was connected to the kill switch, but the red wire that gave it power was pulled out and she had no tools to open the panel. She was no electronics whizz either, so even if she did get it open, she was as likely to blast herself to high heaven as she was to achieve her goal.

The remote kill switch was dead. But she couldn't just give up and go home, she could be the last line of defense, the last person to lay eyes on this machine before it was put to purpose. Exploring further, she found frayed wires and dead circuits. Cuckoo didn't seem to have located the explosives. From what Tuck had said, they were built into the frame with a fuse connected to… hope. The gas canisters in the machine had been loaded with flammable gas, and there was a traditional fuse deliberately built in as their backup. But she'd still need a spark.

Considering how to achieve ignition, Zara slid up the panel that hid the gas bottles, and when it was off, inspiration struck her. Pulling her cellphone from her pocket, she squashed it between the two canisters then gripped the closest. Clenching her teeth, she turned the manual valve to release the gas into the air. There was no needle for her to watch to check it was working; the machine was built to be covert.

A gunshot blasted just a second before she heard the ting of metal on metal. Spinning around, she leaped out of the van to see Cuckoo slinking toward her with a gun in her hand. The first shot hadn't hit her, so it was a warning, or the woman was a bad aim.

Turning to grab each door, Zara slammed the van doors knowing that she was concentrating the gas. She didn't have a lot of time and needed to know that when she ordered the spark, it would be enough to combust the gas, which should ignite the explosives.

Backing away from the van, Zara's awareness wasn't on Cuckoo or getting shot, it was on getting away from the unstable device. With every backwards step, every second, that van was becoming a more powerful, more destructive, more lethal bomb.

Eyeing the van meant Zara wasn't giving Cuckoo the attention she craved, but she got it when the next shot sounded, and the force of an impact threw Zara backwards onto the floor. It was pressure not pain that made her fall, but Cuckoo's perverse laugh helped Zara understand what had happened.

The van was rigged, she had to get out of here, but pain burst through her body, and her hand moved to the source. When she looked down at her reddened hand and the expanding stain on her top, she began to panic. Blood. She was bleeding. She was shot.

Panting through the pain that grew with every drop of blood that dripped from the gunshot beneath her ribs, Zara rolled onto her front and crawled the last of the distance to the wall. Using a pipe that ran upwards, she pulled herself onto her feet.

"You just won't quit," Cuckoo said, leveling her gun at Zara again.

Zara wasn't ready to concede. "It's like you said about American women," Zara said and coughed as her chest tightened. "We're peppy."

"And not too smart." Cuckoo said, taking one stride toward her, which brought her nearer to the van. "Do you want to die? It's such a shame he's not here to see it."

"Kill me," Zara said, taking her weight away from the wall and squaring the pendant to make sure the camera was lined up. If she was going to die here, she wanted to make sure the Kindred knew who to make pay for her murder.

"Any final words?" Cuckoo said, pulling back the hammer of her gun.

It didn't take too much thought for her to come up with a reply. "Two," Zara said and raised her voice to call out as loud as she could in this echoing space. "Treason terminate!"

Cuckoo frowned at her seeming insanity, and Zara took the chance to dash the remaining few feet to the door, where she slipped around to the other side of the concrete wall. Less than a second later, the deafening blast of an explosion burst in her ears. She fell forward, despite being protected from the blast, the wound in her torso was sapping her energy.

Rolling to her back, she took her hand from the bloody mass of her shirt. The manor was so close, but there was no way she was going to make it there on foot, and she had no vehicle nearby. If Cuckoo was still alive, she was injured, so neither of them would be in a fit state to initiate another battle.

Still, Zara tried to stand and got up into a kind of staggering crouch to hurry as fast as she could to hide behind a stack of crates at the corner of the building. They might not be up for another battle, but Cuckoo had been armed, and she wouldn't be pleased now that her product had been destroyed.

The building was burning in a brilliant fire, and as she collapsed, Zara saw smoke darken the sky. It was fitting, she thought as she closed her eyes. Game Time cursed them all and in succeeding to destroy the device that had stolen so many lives, it had claimed one last victim.

Her eyes were heavy and her body ached. There was no getting out of this one. She would die here alone, and all she could think about was Brodie. Would he go into mourning again? She couldn't allow it. But she'd made no plans for her own demise, hadn't added her final instructions to the script with the others.

Closing her eyes, the smell of burning debris and heavy smoke polluted the air. But she'd completed her mission, she wasn't a failure, and she'd made a difference in the world.

***

SHE COULD HAVE been lying on the dirty ground for a minute or a month. Her concept of time was lost with her consciousness. Sure that the sensation of his fingertips on her cheekbone was an illusion, she turned toward the touch, appreciating the dream while it lasted.

"Come on, baby, let me see those beautiful browns, open up."

Swallowing the bitter taste from her mouth, Zara did her best to part her eyelids, and that was when she realized she wasn't lying on the cold ground anymore. Her body was up, not all the way because her feet were still touching asphalt, but her upper body was on something warm, something solid, something familiar.

"Brodie," she said, immediately recognizing her mistake. "Uh… Raven. I—"

"Open your eyes for me, baby," he said, and she didn't like the concern in his voice. He must have reached the same conclusion she had about her prognosis. "Atta girl."

Sorrow welled up when she blinked and read the fear in his gaze. "I'm sorry, beau," she whispered because suddenly she was, sorry for all the things they hadn't done. Sorry that she'd come here alone. Sorry that she hadn't agreed to his suggestion that they say to hell with everything and leave town.

"What were you thinking?" he demanded, and for some reason, his anger was easier for her to absorb than confronting their pain.

Hot tears leaked from her eyes and ran quickly to her ears with others following in their tracks. "I love you. Please don't close yourself off again," she said. If she was on a clock, she didn't want to waste time on an argument. Being practical, taking action, was something she did well, and she'd rather focus on that than saying goodbye. "I didn't make plans. Put me beside Art. You won't be able to explain this to the cops and—"

"Hush," he said, stroking her hair away from her face

with a flat palm. "You're not going anywhere."

His other arm was around her, but it was only when he pushed harder that she felt the crushing weight of pressure he was applying to her wound to try and stem the bleeding. "I feel numb."

"You're in shock," he said. "You've lost a lot of blood."

"I love you."

"You've said that already," he said, and she took her hand to his face when he looked away. He seemed impatient, like he was waiting for something, and it wasn't for her death. Her vision was too blurred to focus on specifics, she felt his mood in her heart, and the grief made her whimper.

He'd thought Art was going to be okay, and his uncle was dead a minute later. Brodie wasn't great at accepting being out of control. But she didn't have the wherewithal to decipher what was going on in his mind. Her body was getting heavier, and it was harder to keep her eyes open.

She heard a car before she loosened. Brodie stood, taking her dead weight with him in his arms. There was movement and sound, but she lost track of it all. When she next heard his voice, they were in a vehicle, in the back seat with her head in his lap and his heavy hand pushing on her injury.

"Wake up, Swallow! I didn't tell you to sleep. Keep those big browns on me."

But every time she opened her eyes, they closed again. "Where are…" she whispered. "Where are we going?"

"Base," Brodie said, resting a hand on her forehead. "Thad's there waiting to patch you up."

"No," she mumbled, shaking her head. "Can't… can't open the gate. Art will—"

"Hush."

"Art will be mad. You **can't open the gates… Art will…**"

"We make exceptions when our hottest member is bleeding out."

Her mouth was dry, but she couldn't feel her body, just intense heat at the top of her head that seemed to be mangling her thoughts. "Tuck… Tuck's hot."

"She's delirious."

"She better be." She wasn't sure who was talking or what they were talking about. Invasive white noise faded in and out, making her ears buzz.

"Brodie," she muttered, hoping her love was nearby. "Brodie."

"Stay with me, pretty baby. Keep those eyes open, keep talking."

Her eyes were glued shut. Tears still managed to escape though. Brodie had been right. She hadn't realized it because with him she'd felt invincible, and she'd let him down. "One day," she murmured. Her body rocked with the motion of the car, and she was glad to be here, in his arms, with the chance to say what she needed to. "I let you down, baby."

"Yeah, you did," he said, his voice was harsh, stern, like her chief giving her orders. "You're not gonna do it again! Open your fucking eyes, Swallow."

"Fuck, man, she's blue," Tuck said.

"Just shut the fuck up and drive," Brodie demanded. Their voices were fading, and she wanted to sleep, just for a little while before the end, before she said goodbye. Something bit into her body, and she was shaken so hard, her head snapped back. "Open your fucking eyes, Zar, stay with me!"

"Got to go," she whispered, words were getting more difficult as moisture left her mouth. "Too tired. One day… you were right, beau… one day."

"No! You fucking listen to me, you're not going anywhere. You stay with me, Zara! I can't do this alone! Open your fucking eyes."

But she couldn't, couldn't open her eyes, couldn't feel her body, couldn't breathe. "Have to…" she whispered, parting her lips to pull in one last heavy breath. "Close the door."

Her thoughts faded to black. The last thing she remembered was craving Brodie's kiss one last time.

TWENTY-TWO

"I GUESS I WAS WRONG."

Opening her eyes, Zara blinked to see Art standing over her in a brilliant white suit. "You… what?"

Sitting up, she looked left and right. This was the manor kitchen, except it wasn't, everything was the same, but not quite right. The windows were whited out, and the place was immaculately clean and everything was brand new. Everything except the couch she was lying on, it was the same one she'd sat on while talking to Art on her first trip to the manor, old, worn, and comfortable.

Art sat down next to her extended legs. "I told you to look after him," Art said.

"You're… how are you here?" she asked, launching herself forward to wrap both arms around his neck.

"Oh," he chuckled and returned her hug for a few seconds. Patting her back, he took her shoulders to ease her away. "You are the one who shouldn't be here."

That didn't make sense. Nothing made sense. Shaking her head, she pulled up her knees to bring both of her legs around Art. Twisting, she leaped to her feet to rush for the door. "Where's Brodie? He'll want to—"

Yanking open the door, she was met with brilliant white light and nothing beyond. Slamming the door, she squeezed the handle as tight as her closed eyelids.

Game Time. Cuckoo. One day. The end.

"I told you to look after him."

Spinning around, she backed up to the door. "I'm dead. This is…" She'd never believed in an afterlife; she'd never given it much thought. But it was the only conclusion that made sense. Why they were in this familiar place that wasn't the manor. Why she was looking at a dead man.

Glancing down, she saw a loose silk white dress hanging on spaghetti straps to the floor. Curling her toes, she knew her feet were bare, but when she touched her hair, it was fashioned into some fancy up-do.

"I didn't say goodbye to him," she said. "He needs us, he'll never make it through this. He has no one left."

"Should've thought of that," Art said, rising to his feet and sliding his hands into his pockets. "You let us all down. You were supposed to be his normal."

"You think I wanted this?" she demanded, shoving away from the door. Moisture stung the corners of her eyes. "I didn't want to leave him. I love him."

He grew stony, and an icy breeze swept around her calves. "Not enough," Art said. "I sacrificed my life for you to have each other, and this is how you repay that?"

"You're mad at me?" she asked, edging over to him. "I did everything I could, everything I could for him."

"I told you to be normal. I told you to give up all the macho bullshit."

"We had to find out, had to know what Kahlil knew about Future's Hope—"

"You think that matters?" Art asked. No longer cool or accepting, this man was angry and his scowl hurt her heart… if she still had one. "You think one incident twenty years ago was enough to lose your life for? He's all alone, Zara. You left him alone!"

"No!" she said, slamming her hands onto the back of the couch. "I supported him! The Kindred is his life! He needed me!"

"He still does!" Art said, rounding the couch. "You think he'll survive alone? He lost his parents! He lost me! You're all he has left!"

She knew that, and the skidding tears wouldn't slow. Falling against Art, he took her into his arms and soothed her by stroking her hair. "It's okay," he said, soft again, more like the Art she needed. "I told you he needed you. I told you to be with him. That you weren't like her."

"Cuckoo," she said, pushing away. "Is she here?"

If the Atlas warehouse had claimed Mischa's life, Zara could face her murderer. "I haven't checked the newest residents," he smiled, touching her cheek bone, stroking her as Brodie would.

Getting the chance to talk to Art again made this transition easier. "Are you happy?" she asked. "Is this a good place? You get to be with your sister, your brother-in-law. You know the truth. You know every truth."

His smile grew warm. "I do." He nodded and turned her to lift her onto the back of the couch where she'd once sat. "I know he will make it if you are with him. I know he needs you. I know I left him in your care."

Trembling, she sucked her lips around her teeth to chew on the lower one for a second. "What if I'm not enough? What if I can't get him through?"

His confidence didn't waver. "You can get him through anything," Art said. "But you can't do it from here. You need to go back to him. You need to make him see that his priority one is you."

Heavy sorrow made her crave her love. "He's lost everything. I thought I would lose him, too, when he grieved you. I worried that Grant's death would push him over the edge, that I might lose him for good."

Art cupped her chin and tipped her head up to look her in the eye. "You're doing just fine. That door needs to stay open. Without you, he's lost."

Her head began to spin, and she closed her eyes to try to regain her focus. Her ears were pounding. "Tell Grant I'm sorry."

Art frowned. "Grant?"

Zara opened her mouth to ask questions, but a heavy black cloak fell over her consciousness again, and her mind was erased.

TWENTY-THREE

IT WAS WARM. Whatever was over her body was clamping her down tight, and she didn't appreciate being restricted. Picking up one leg, she attempted to kick but found herself sluggish and slow.

"Art," she croaked, trying to seek the answers the celestial ambassador had. "Art…"

"She's awake."

The words were filled with anticipation and hope, and as she forced her eyes open, she was met with a flurry of movement, though it took her a few seconds to realize the formless shapes encroaching on her were bodies and none of them were Art.

After a few more blinks, she saw Thad nearest, Brodie behind him, and Tuck at his back. "Where's Art?" she asked, and the men shared a frown. "He was just here."

Thad tipped his head toward Brodie to explain in an aside. "Hallucinations are common in near-death experiences. People often see dead relatives, bright lights, sometimes it's a familiar place. Typically, patients mention a feeling of euphoria or despair."

Hallucinations. Was Art just a delusion created by her

dying mind? Standing at the end of the bed, Zave drew her eye, his brow was furrowed in what had to be concern.

That made her attempt a smile. "Xavier," she whispered. "Were you worried about me?" She got a kick out of that because he rarely looked at her and spoke to her even less.

"I'm not usually present when the women wake up," he said.

She had no idea what that meant or if she was even supposed to know. Given what she'd just been through and this family's penchant for cryptic, she didn't waste time sweating it at this moment.

Taking in her environment, she recognized the ceiling and the bed, but couldn't figure out when their bedroom had become a common room.

"Beau, why are there so many people here?"

Tuck answered. "We had a pool going about whether Thad was shitting us about his day job. But he came through and patched you up good."

"I feel heavy," she said when she tried to push up and failed to sit.

Brodie pushed Thad out of his way with a forearm and sat on the bed beside her. "You're gonna stay right there."

"You're doped up," Tuck said. "You're probably feeling pretty high."

"This close to my beau, I always do," she said, turning her smile to Brodie, who leaned over her to squeeze her shoulders. "Why am I doped up?"

"The bullet sliced through the periphery of your liver and lodged in a rib. It will need a few weeks to heal. But you'll be good as new," Thad said.

"The bullet." Events were still jumbled. It took her some time to put the disparate pieces together. "You saved my life," she said, flashes of what had happened in the warehouse crossed her mind's-eye. She'd believed that she was going to die. She'd said goodbye to Brodie and everything, which might explain the grimace on his face and the negativity radiating from him now.

"You bastards clear out of here," Brodie said,

smoothing his rough fingers along her cheekbone.

The others left them alone in the bedroom, except when the door closed, Brodie still didn't speak. She wanted to know why he was brooding but was so tired that she doubted her ability to probe him.

"You saved my life too," she said, her eyes closing again. "If you hadn't found me when you did—"

"I don't know if I'll be able to get the image out of my head," he said, flattening his palm on her cheek. "The explosion, the fire, all that smoke… we were still half a mile away, but…"

"You knew it was Atlas. Going back there must have been difficult."

"We got your message… I didn't give a fuck where it was, I gave a fuck that you were alone. What the fuck were you thinking—"

"Caine told me that she was there and that she had someone meeting her, someone with a boat," she said. Digging her nails into his arm, she pulled and forced him to help her into a seated position.

If she remained lying down, she would fall asleep again. The exertion of sitting up was enough to make her rest on the pillow Brodie adjusted behind her. If her rib was damaged, she was pleased Thad had loaded her up with painkillers, otherwise getting into this position may have hurt a lot more than the dull throb she felt around her diaphragm.

Brodie wasn't finished chastising her. "You should've waited."

"It all worked out." Maybe it hadn't ended without a hitch, but it had ended. "Have you seen her, I mean… did she… make it?"

Zara had taken life before. Though killing Elvis was self-defense, she could probably argue the same about Cuckoo. But it had to be a head fuck for Brodie that his current girlfriend had killed his ex.

"Tuck did a drive-by, there's nothing of the device left, and we already made sure that the van wasn't traceable. Kraft says there's nothing in the police system. They're not gonna waste their time tracking down something that far away from anything worth protecting. I don't think anyone even saw or reported the fire."

That worked out in their favor because if Art's blood was still there, then the blood of the goons Brodie had killed would be too. They didn't need anyone sniffing around. It paid to have a cop keeping an eye on things for them.

Cuckoo would most probably have been taken out by the blast, but even if she made it out alive, she wouldn't last long without medical attention. The remaining Game Time devices were under lock and key in the manor weapons room, and the viruses untouched in cold storage. The world would carry on oblivious to how close they'd come to annihilation, yet again.

"Is Kahlil dead?" she asked, rubbing her hand down Brodie's forearm then locking their fingers together as he nodded. "Caine?"

He shrugged. "He'll live to fight another day... we think."

That kind of ambiguous answer made her nervous. "You think?"

"Thad says it doesn't look like there was enough blood loss to suggest Caine had died."

She'd tied off his leg, and he'd said he would take care of himself. "No body?" she asked.

"No sign of him," Brodie said.

Caine wasn't the most imposing threat. "Sikorski will want to know where his device is."

"He can want all he likes," Brodie said. "You were right about the suitcase. It was empty... We think Sikorski pulled out of the deal, leaving Kahlil high and dry. He was the banker, wasn't he? Don't know what happened to Leatt, probably scurried away when Sikorski pulled the money."

"Man, you're thorough," she said. "How long was I out?" That they had time to return to the scene, check everything out, and clean up suggested they hadn't been pacing by her bedside.

"A day. Thad kept you under because we knew you'd be a terrible patient."

A terrible patient, but she was a better one than he

would be. She sighed, instead of picking a fight. "This isn't over?"

"It is for you," he said.

She didn't expect him to say that and certainly not in such a decisive tone. He pulled the blankets from her body, kicked off his shoes, and slid in beside her. "You're taking me off the board? I proved myself, didn't I? I can be a valuable member—"

"Our most valuable members are alive ones," he said, taking her hips to slide her downward. He coiled an arm around her head, giving her cheek something to rest on as he gazed down at her. "You're gonna get better, and when you're up to it, I'm taking you away. Out of the country, just like I promised."

She didn't know what had brought this on now, but she didn't like it. "You can't. There are too many variables. We have to find out what Sikorski is up to. Caine is still out there. Leatt too. There are people who want to take us down and—"

"Enough," he said, stern and impatient. "Let it fucking go, Zar. You almost died. Do you get that? If we hadn't found you or that bullet had been an inch any other way…"

"I risked my life because it's right. I risk my life to do what has to be done. I risk my life to make you proud."

His expression changed. Anger morphed to intrigue, but he was still frowning. "You think that's what you have to do to make me proud? I'm proud when you come home without extra holes in your body. I'm proud when you're smart, level-headed, and have plenty of backup."

"I couldn't let her go," Zara said. It would've been too much of a risk to just walk away or wait while Cuckoo's cohorts got closer with every passing second. "Someone needed to take responsibility and… you loved her once, in your own way. I wouldn't put you in the position of having to take her down."

"You didn't think I'd do it."

When he left the bed, she lost his support so flopped down. Her vision was lost in the mound of pillows she fell into and the hair that fell over her face. Brushing them aside, she turned her head to see him standing near the end of the bed with his back to her.

"You would do whatever needed to be done, I know that," she said, sorry that he thought she'd doubted him when that wasn't the case. "But I love you, and it's my responsibility to protect you from pain, and not just physical pain. Killing her yourself, after all you'd been through with her, the guilt could've eaten you alive."

Spinning around, he wasn't consoled by what she'd said if his expression was anything to go by. "Do you know how many people I've killed? How many men, full of potential, with their lives in front of them that I've taken away from their families and kids? You think I couldn't put a bullet in one dumb bitch who—"

"Your dumb bitch," Zara said. "She wasn't a stranger. She belonged to you once. She loved you."

"I don't give a fuck," he said, moving in her direction. "To protect you, I wouldn't blink. I'd put a bullet between my own damn eyes if it made you happy and kept you safe."

"A man will do almost anything if you threaten the thing he loves," she muttered his words to herself, and the possibility that she could be used to hurt Brodie terrified her. "I want you to live forever, that will make me happy."

"I'll get our team working on that," he said, sinking onto the bed again. "I would've done it." He took a section of her hair and let it float through his fingers. "I'd have killed her and I'd have been proud of doing it if it kept you safe."

He wasn't the only one who felt that way. "That same drive that you have in you, it burns in me. As much as you want to protect me, I want to protect you. It's not a weakness, it's a byproduct of real love."

"Real love," he said.

She smiled. "That's what we have, baby," she said. He left the bed and went into the walk-in, so she guessed that part of the conversation was over, and he wasn't in the mood for mushy. "There's still one thing you haven't told me." Since he was out of the room, she raised her voice, but she had to get an answer to her burning question. Something she had to know before her next near-death experience. But Brodie didn't respond, so she just called out, hoping he'd find it harder to avoid answering while he wasn't distracted by physical contact. "What did you and my dad talk about when you went inside with him?"

Brodie didn't reply. She guessed he was ignoring her and probably hoping she'd pass out again. Except when he came out of the walk-in and started toward the bed, she recognized his determination, he was intent on something.

"I haven't looked at this for twenty years," he said, focused on his closed fist that had something inside.

She felt like an idiot for not checking how he was doing after learning what had caused his parents accident. "Oh, God, beau, I'm sorry."

She tried to sit up again but couldn't. He didn't help her up when he came to kneel at the side of the bed. Leaning against the bed, he rested his upper arms on the mattress. With both hands clasped around something, he put his closed fists on her abdomen.

"What is it, baby?" she asked, running her hand over the top of his head. "Is it about your parents?"

"Yeah, I guess," he said, focused on his hands. "And yours."

Opening his hands gradually, he kept them hovering over the item he had left sitting on her stomach for half a second before pulling both hands away. Resting on top of her was a small, red leather box.

"What is that?" she asked, but she knew what the cube shape looked like.

"It was my mother's," he said. "And I went in to talk to your father to tell him I intended on giving it to you. Open it."

Her hands were shaking, but it was contrary to her nature to refuse his orders. So with the bottom in one hand, she pulled until the hinge gave, and she was looking at the most beautiful vintage ring of diamonds set in platinum with a single princess cut diamond in prominence at the front, held in place by four corner prongs.

"This is a… it's a…"

One corner of his lips rose a fraction. "Bet you never thought I'd ask you to make it official."

She hadn't, but she tore her eyes away from the ring to fix on him. "Official means paperwork."

"The world already knows Brodie McCormack isn't dead. He just inherited the family firm, remember?" He reached over to stroke her face. "Signing my name next to yours isn't something I'd be ashamed of doing. You are the one who brought me back to life."

Curling her lips around her teeth, she didn't want to get emotional because she knew it hurt him to see her upset, but tears escaped anyway. "Beau," she whispered. He slunk up onto the bed and lay on his side, propping his head on a hand.

"Yeah," he said, still wearing a typical scowl. "I'm asking. You gonna make a big deal about this?"

Brodie didn't like big shows of emotion, so he wouldn't appreciate her gushing. But being proposed to by the man she loved was a massive deal, in any woman's book.

Clutching the ring box in her cleavage, her smile split her face. "Zara McCormack," she said. "I think I like that."

Taking the ring box from her hand, Brodie opened it to remove the ring. He tossed the box aside and took her hand to put the ring on her finger. "Sounds sexy as fuck to me," he said. Sandwiching her hair against her cheeks, he pulled their mouths together, as eager to take control as she was to relinquish it to him.

No amount of danger could extinguish their love. No secret, no person, no aspect of their past could change the love that had grown between them. Brodie wasn't a typical prince. But these days, when Zara pictured her future, the only thing she was certain of was him. This heirloom was his promise that nothing would shatter their bond.

TO BE CONTINUED...

Thank you for reading this tale!
If you can, please take the time to review.

~

Ask your local library for more Scarlett Finn novels!

~

For all things Scarlett Finn check out:

www.scarlettfinn.com

BOOK FOUR

It's not over... until it's over.

SWIFT

Kindred Book Four

SCARLETT FINN

OUT NOW!